WAITING ON *You*

USA TODAY BESTSELLING AUTHOR

NIKKI ASH

The magic is in the people we
share the moments with.

WAITING ON YOU PLAYLIST

Sparks Fly (Taylor's Version)—Taylor Swift

There's Nothing Holdin' Me Back—Shawn Mendes

Down (feat. Lil Wayne)—Jay Sean

On Purpose—Bellah Mae

Try Sleeping With a Broken Heart—Alicia Keys

There's No Way—Lauv

I Can Feel It—Kane Brown

Message In A Bottle (Taylor's Version)—Taylor Swift

As Long As You Love Me—Justin Bieber

You Are In Love (Taylor's Version)—Taylor Swift

To Ashley and Arianna, for the friendship and laughs and
girl trips that lead to luggage getting stuck in cobblestone and
book babies being born.

PROLOGUE

Paige

Fourteen Years Old

"YOU CAN'T GIVE UP," DAD YELLS ON THE OTHER SIDE OF their bedroom door.

It's closed, so they don't know I'm here. I wasn't supposed to be home for another two hours, but Mrs. Simmons got food poisoning and had to cancel math club.

"What the hell am I supposed to do without you?" he asks.

"I've tried," my mom cries, her voice raspy and weak. "But I can't do it anymore. I need you to not fight me on this. My time is limited, and I want to spend it with you and Paige."

"You're asking me to sit back and just let you die!" Dad argues. "You can't ask me to do that! That's not fair."

Ever since Mom found out that she has cancer, Dad has been extra nice to her. He's even stopped moving us all over, choosing to stay in London because Mom said this city makes her happy.

She's been fighting the cancer for a long time now, but from what they're saying, it sounds like it isn't getting any better and Mom is going to stop her treatments. I don't know a lot about cancer, but I know that the treatments make her sick and miserable, but without them, she'll die, which is apparently what she wants to do.

"No," Mom says. "I'm asking you to understand that I'm choosing to enjoy the time I have left with the people I love."

"Paige is going to be devastated," Dad says, his tone filled with emotion. "She needs you."

He's not lying. My mom is my best friend, and I can't imagine my life without her. She gets along with my friends and boyfriend, and everyone loves her. She's the person I go to when I'm having a bad day. She listens and never goes all *mom* on me the way a lot of my friends' moms do.

Every weekend, holiday break, and even many afternoons after school, we explore together. I hate moving, but she's always made it a fun adventure, and because of her, I have already experienced so much that the world has to offer. She can take the simplest of things and turn it into something magical.

"She'll be okay," Mom chokes out. "She has you. And when I'm gone, you will have each other."

No, I won't be okay, I think, but don't voice out loud. *I need you to fight. I need you to want to live for me. Don't you want to keep making new memories with me? Our latest scrapbook isn't finished yet. There are so many pages that need to be filled. I need you, Mom!*

"Damn it, Finley!" Dad barks, making me jump. I've never heard him raise his voice to my mom, let alone yell at her like that. "This isn't what I wanted! What the hell am I supposed to do with a teenage girl? You need to fight!" he says, as if plucking the words straight from my head. "She needs *you!*"

"She will have *you!*" Mom sobs.

"I didn't ask for this," Dad hisses, and even though I should be focused on my mom choosing to die, his confession has me taking in his words.

"*You* wanted this," he continues. "The family, the *baby*. I told you that I was scared that I wasn't cut out for that type of life, but you told me you would be by my side. That we would do this together. You wanted *her*. And now, you're going to abandon her instead of fighting for your life…*for her*. You're going to leave me, and I'll have to raise her on my own. That's not what was supposed to happen!"

"That's not fair," Mom cries, her sobs getting louder as my heart cracks in my chest. "I can't fight anymore. I'm too tired and weak, and I don't want to spend what's left of my life fighting. I just want to be happy for the little bit of time I have left."

Oh my God…

My mom is going to leave me.

My dad never wanted me.

Where does that leave me?

I've always been closer with my mom, but I thought it was because my dad works long hours. He's a pilot, and he's gone a lot while my mom doesn't work and has always been home with me, so it makes sense that Mom and I are closer. But I never knew that my dad didn't want me. He's older than my mom by twelve years. She always jokes that he's an old man, and he always says she has a thing for older men.

He was between flights when they met at a bar, and they hit it off. Within a few weeks, they were married, and soon after, I came along. I once asked Mom why I didn't have any siblings, and she said I was so perfect that they didn't want any more kids. But now, it sounds like it's because my dad gave in to her wanting me despite him not wanting to have a family.

I think back to all our memories, the birthdays, the family trips.

My dad has told me more times than I can count that he loves me and is proud of me.

Was it all a lie?

When I get back to my room, I close my door softly so they don't know I'm home, and I bury my face into my pillow as I cry.

My mom, my best friend, is giving up and letting the cancer win. She's going to leave me, and when she does, I'll be left alone because the only other person in my life never wanted me to begin with.

Later that night, Mom finds me in my room, but I pretend I'm asleep and stay there until the next morning, wanting to prolong the devastating news I know is coming.

She has chosen to stop the treatments.

She has six months, if she's lucky, to live.

I want to ask her why I'm not enough for her to want to fight for her life, but instead, I tell her I love her and that everything will be okay, knowing that it won't be.

We spend the next several months making the most of our time together. Dad takes shorter flights, and we spend time together as a family. We visit all the best spots in London, and Mom makes each new place feel magical. We fill up the rest of the scrapbook and start a new one …one that will never get finished because we don't have enough time.

I never tell her what I overheard, but deep down, I'm selfishly dreading the day she leaves me. I'm praying the cancer will somehow leave her body, and with the way she laughs and smiles, I sometimes wonder if maybe the doctors were wrong and my mom is healthy.

But then, one morning, everything takes a turn for the worse. Mom is hospitalized due to an infection, and it all spirals from there. She has a stroke and sinks into a coma, and a few days later, with Dad and me by her side, her heart stops beating.

Dad and I cry, begging her to come back.

But she's gone.

And it feels like she took the magic with her.

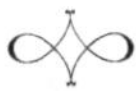

The day of Mom's funeral, Dad hands me a light-pink envelope with my name scrawled across it in Mom's handwriting.

He's been distant since she passed away. At first, I tried to be there for him, but the more he pushes me away, the more I realize that what I overheard that day in their room must be true. Dad hadn't wanted me, but now, he's stuck with me.

I go to my room and open the envelope, both nervous and excited to read my mom's words. I don't know when she wrote the letter, so I don't know what I'll get.

My dearest Paige,

From the moment I found out I was pregnant with you, my world changed for the better. You are not only my daughter, but you are also my best friend. You are the light in the dark and the magic in an otherwise ordinary world.

If you are reading this, I am gone. I hate that I won't be on this earth to watch you grow up and be the extraordinary woman that I know you'll be. But please know that if there's a heaven—and I believe there is—I'll be watching you from above.

There are a few things I want you to remember as you go on your journey in life. First, the magic doesn't lie. I felt the magic the day I met your father and again when you were born. And I feel it every day that I spend with you guys here in London. When we go on our adventures and make our scrapbooks, the magic is there. Never lose sight of the magic, my sweet girl.

The next thing I want you to remember is to always believe in yourself. Follow your instincts, your gut, and most of all, your heart. It will never steer you wrong.

Find your passion. When I met your father, I was lost. I had so many jobs that I didn't love, but then I became a wife and a mom, and I learned that my passion was my family. I don't care what your passion is, but make sure you find it and never settle for anything else.

Please continue our scrapbooks. I loved creating them with you, and I hope, one day, you'll continue them with whoever you find the magic with. Whether it's a significant other or your child, I hope you will continue our tradition of going on adventures and documenting them because that's what life is about.

I'm so proud of you, Paige, and I feel so blessed that I got to spend so many years with you. I want you to laugh and smile and love hard. Be careful who you give your heart to because you, my girl, deserve all the magic in the world and I don't want you to settle for anything less.

I love you, and I'm always here.

Love,
Mom

CHAPTER ONE

Present Day

"I UNDERSTAND IT'S A GOOD OPPORTUNITY, BUT YOU SAID THIS is where we would settle down. You knew when I agreed to move here that I didn't want to move again. I want to get married and start a family. And I thought that's what you wanted too."

I will my tears not to come as I stare at the man who was supposed to be my *forever*. We met three years ago, and he told me on our first date that he knew I was the one for him. On our fourth date, he told me he loved me. And within six months of being together, he asked me to move in with him.

A year ago, he came home and said he was offered a promotion, but it meant moving to Houston, Texas. He asked me to join him, and even though I loved my job at Benson Liquor, loved being in the city my mom had adored, I agreed because I loved John as well.

I still love him, but right now, I don't like him very much.

He promised Houston would become our home, and since that was all I wanted—to settle down and create a life with the person I loved—I agreed.

I took a job I enjoy with my best friend, Anastasia, at Kingston Limited, and John and I started to make roots. At least, I thought we had.

"You can't expect me to give up this once-in-a-lifetime opportunity," John says with a huff. "It can mean doors opening for me. If it works out, this will be our last move."

"That's what you said last time."

Literally. I'm pretty sure those were his exact words. I should've known he was lying when I suggested we buy a home and he insisted we rent instead. But love makes people blind, deaf, and dumb, so I went along with it anyway.

Looking back with new eyes, I can finally see how selfish John has been since the beginning. I moved into his place because he had more stuff and it was closer to the tube. He didn't care that I loved my flat, that it overlooked my mom's favorite part of London.

And when we moved here, it was because he was chasing his promotion. He didn't consider my job or what I would lose by leaving. It was all about him.

"I bet Benson would give you your job back," he points out.

"I don't want my job back!" I say, emotion clogging my throat. "I want to stay in Houston."

The fact is, I didn't even want to live in Houston. My job is in Rosemary—a good thirty minutes away. My best friend lives in Rosemary. But John wanted to live in Houston, so we moved to Houston. Now, I'm going to be stuck here while John is back in London. Because John put his wants and needs first and I allowed my own to be put on the back burner.

"You said we would make a home here," I add, losing the fight to not cry as tears spill over my lids and track down my cheeks. "Why can't what we have here be enough?" *Why can't I be enough?* "I know the promotion means more money, but we have plenty of money. We both make a good living. Please," I beg, "stay here with me."

"Paige!" John snaps. "Stop acting like a brat and be an adult about this."

His words shoot me straight back to my past, to a time I try not to think about.

"Please," I beg my dad. "I don't want to leave. This is our home. This is her home."

Dad's gaze flits to mine for only a second before he looks away. Ever since Mom took her last breath, Dad has barely looked at or spoken to me. I get that he never wanted me, but shouldn't the fact that Mom loved me be enough for him to at least care about me?

"I've made my decision," Dad mutters. "We're moving."

Mom has only been gone for two weeks. Fourteen days. And my dad has decided to take a job in Rome. He doesn't care that this is the home we've lived in for the past several years, the last place I felt the magic.

Mom's gone, and if my dad has it his way, so will every memory we created here. The trips to the Tower Bridge to look at London from the top. It was so magical. The walks to Kensington Gardens. It was her favorite place. We would sit on the bench and talk while we people-watched. Our favorite bookshop was nearby, so she'd buy us each a new book, and then we'd have tea while we read. When she was doing well, we'd take the tube to Chinatown and eat at our favorite Chinese restaurant.

I already lost her. I don't want to lose this city as well.

"You promised Mom this would be the last time we moved," I remind him, hoping mentioning her will thaw his icy heart. "This is where she wanted to make a home. I have school and friends and a boyfriend!"

And a dad who never wanted me, *I think to myself.*

If he moves me from here, away from the city my mom loved, away from the friends I've made, away from the only place that actually feels like home, what will I have left? A man who can hardly stand to look at me?

"Well, your mom isn't here!" Dad barks. "Stop acting like a brat. You're not a baby anymore. It's time to start acting like an adult. We're moving, and that's the end of it. You'll make new friends, and there will be plenty more boys."

We moved the next day and spent the next year in Rome. Dad was gone so often that it felt like I was living on my own. The home he rented was beautiful, but it was filled with silence…emptiness. The magic was gone.

Then, he moved us again to the States my junior year. My senior year, he met a woman closer to my age than his. They started a new family and had a baby the same month I graduated.

All this time, I'd thought when he told Mom he didn't want to be a dad, he meant in general, but it turned out, it was just *me* he didn't want. *Me* he couldn't love.

I left for college a few months later, and Dad settled down. He stopped moving, he took less flights, and stayed local, proving once again that I wasn't enough to stick around for, but Debbie and their daughter, Kristin, were.

I came home for Thanksgiving and again during winter break, but it was hard to watch. To wonder why *I* wasn't enough. Why he couldn't love me, didn't want to be home with me, but he wanted and loved the new baby.

And then they had another baby. Another girl. Ashleigh. And I stopped going home. I made excuse after excuse until Dad stopped asking.

I rented a small apartment off campus so I could stay year-round. And after I graduated, I moved back to London, hoping it would make me feel closer to my mom since it was the last place where she had been alive. Unfortunately, I didn't feel the magic there. I just felt…alone.

With a degree and MBA in marketing, I took a job at Benson Liquor and hoped, one day, I would find myself a home. A place where I felt loved and wanted and cherished. I craved the magic I had felt when my mom was alive.

Before she gave up and left me…

I thought maybe I could have that with John, but I'm starting to realize that, once again, I was wrong. Because right now, as John sighs in frustration, I feel anything but loved or wanted or cherished. Once again, it feels like I'm not enough. And there definitely isn't any magic.

"Look," John says, cradling my face. "Let's just give it some time. We're both busy with work, trying to make a future for ourselves. I can fly in for Thanksgiving, and you can visit for Christmas. We'll talk and video-chat. We'll figure it out. Who knows? Maybe you'll realize you miss London and want to move back."

His lips quirk in a boyish grin, and I sigh in defeat, not verbalizing what I'm thinking: *I wish you would choose me…choose us. Put us first. Think about my wants and needs and not just your own.*

Instead, because there's nothing I can say to change his mind, I nod in agreement and say, "I guess we'll see how things go."

CHAPTER TWO

Paige

Five Months Later

"I'VE ARRIVED. I'M WAITING FOR MY LUGGAGE, AND THEN I'M going to catch a cab to John's flat."

"How was the flight?" my best friend, Ana, asks over the phone.

Since I'm surprising John and no one else knows I'm here, she made me promise to call her when my plane landed so she'd know I was okay.

"Long, but I got a lot of work done."

"You're on vacation," she chides. "No working until you get back."

"Yes, boss," I say in a mocking tone.

Ana is the co-chief executive officer of Kingston Limited, the liquor company I work for. Her husband, Julian, is the other CEO.

When John insisted that we move to Houston, they were looking for a chief marketing officer since theirs had been promoted to chief operating officer, and they offered me the position. I love my job, and the fact that I get to work with my best friend again—we worked together at Benson Liquor—only makes it that much better.

"Text me when you get to John's place so I know you've arrived safely."

"Will do."

While I wait for my luggage, I pull up John's address so I have it on hand to give to the driver. It's been a long five months, and despite our best efforts, John and I haven't been able to see each other. He was busy during Thanksgiving, still getting used to his new position, so he didn't come home, and then when I mentioned Christmas, he told me he would be too busy to give me the attention I deserved and insisted I stay home.

If I'm being honest, things between us are more than strained. He wants me to move back to London, and I want to stay in Rosemary. When the rent went up, I made the decision to move to Rosemary since it was closer to work and would save me on gas. I found a beautiful three-bedroom, two-bathroom home not too far from Ana and work and bought it.

John wasn't thrilled that I had done that, but I told him it was a good investment. The owners had been desperate to sell, and I'd gotten it at over thirty percent below market value.

I've moved too many times over the years without having a say, and then I moved to Houston for John. For the first time, I put my foot down, choosing to live where I want to live—choosing to put myself first since, apparently, no one else is going to—but I have a feeling it's going to be one of the many reasons our relationship ends.

We used to talk every day, but then it turned into a few times a week, and now, it's dwindled down to maybe once a week. I'm hoping this trip will help us figure out where we go from here because we can't keep going the way we are—nor do I want to.

The truth is, we probably should've broken up a long time ago, and if it wasn't for our friends Marina and Paul getting married this weekend—with both John and me in the wedding—we probably would've.

But there's a small part of me—the romantic who loves to read romance and see women much like myself get their happily ever afters—that's not willing to throw away a yearslong relationship without at least trying one more time.

Since today is Valentine's Day, I booked my flight early so I could surprise John and we could spend the next few days together—and hopefully either rekindle our romance or agree to go our separate ways.

The cab driver takes me to John's flat, and since I'm trying to surprise him, rather than call for him to let me in, I follow another resident in and up the lift. It's still early, only eight in the morning, so I know he hasn't left for work yet. My hope is that he'll call out to spend the day with me, but if he needs to go, we can, at the very least, enjoy the evening together.

He's on the second floor, and when I get to his flat number, I try the doorknob to see if, by chance, it's unlocked. It is. So, instead of knocking, I swing the door open, and I'm about to yell, *Surprise*, when my eyes land on John standing in the kitchen.

Only instead of cooking, like one would do in the kitchen, he's got a woman bent over the counter, and he's thrusting into her from behind. They're both naked, their clothes strewn all over the floor, and she's screaming out his name like you hear in those pornos where you can't help but roll your eyes because there's no way that guy is fucking her so good that she needs to scream that loud.

Since the kitchen is near the foyer, he must hear the door creak open because his gaze lands on me, and his thrusts come to a standstill, his eyes opening comically wide.

"Well," I say, trying not to let my emotions show through, "I hope once you're done, you plan to wipe down the kitchen. It's not very sanitary to fuck where you eat."

The woman's face whips around, and that's when I notice she's not just any woman…

"Phoebe," I gasp, my gaze locking with my old roommate.

When I moved to London, I wanted to live near where my mom had loved to go for walks, but the only available flat had two bedrooms, and since I only needed one, I rented it out. Phoebe answered the ad and moved in, and we became roommates—and eventually best friends—living together until I moved in with John.

"Paige." She stands and scrambles to get her clothes on.

When we spoke last week, she told me that she and her boyfriend had broken up and she was seeing someone else.

"Please," I tell them both curtly, "don't get dressed on my account." I force a smile onto my face. "But tell me this." I look at Phoebe. "Is this the new man you're seeing?"

"We wanted to tell you," she cries.

"Let me guess," I say dryly. "You didn't mean for it to happen, but John was missing me and lonely, and you were heartbroken and in need of comforting, and one thing led to another."

I cackle humorlessly, fully aware that I'm ten seconds from losing my shit. To think I flew in early to try and salvage our relationship. What a joke. "Well, you can have him. Because if he can cheat on me, who's to say he won't do it to you? And as far as our friendship goes, it's over."

"Paige, please," Phoebe whines.

"Please, what?" I snap. "Please forgive you?"

I glance back and forth between her and John. While their betrayal hurts, for some reason, I also feel a huge sense of relief. Like the stress of our unsteady relationship no longer weighs on me. I wanted to marry this man, create a life with him, and thankfully, he showed me who he really is—a cheater and a liar—before I could do anything I would regret.

He's never once put me first, and even at the end of our relationship, instead of breaking up with me before moving on, he put himself first. And the same goes for Phoebe. She didn't once think about how this would hurt me. How it would affect our friendship. They both only cared about themselves—and I guess each other. But neither one of them cared about me.

I open my mouth to say something, but I close it because there's nothing to be said. I knew John and I were on shaky ground, but I would have never thought in a million years he would hook up with one of my friends. We went on double dates. John played poker with her boyfriend on Wednesday nights. But what's done is done, and now, it's time to move forward …*alone*.

As I turn to leave, John calls out my name and rushes over to me. "Wait, please," he says, grabbing ahold of my wrist. "I'm sorry. You know I love you."

"You're sorry? What are you sorry for? Cheating on me with one of my good friends or for getting caught?" I pull my wrist out of his grasp. "Your sorry means nothing, and the fact that you can tell me you love me after fucking another woman speaks volumes about your character."

I don't know why, but in this moment, the words my mom wrote to me before she passed away come back to me: *The magic doesn't lie. I felt the magic the day I met your father and again when you were born. And I feel it every day that I spend with you both.*

"What you and I had wasn't magical," I tell John, the truth of my words hitting me in the gut. "It was nothing more than an illusion."

I glance at Phoebe, who's standing there with her arms around her and tears sliding down her face.

"Good luck," is all I say before I drag my luggage out the door and slam it closed behind me, ready to move forward with my life.

I snag a cab and take it to the hotel where the wedding is taking place since I have nowhere else to go. And it's not until I'm standing at the check-in counter and being told they're booked solid so I can't check in until my scheduled check-in date that I finally lose it.

I have nowhere to go.

John cheated on me with my friend because I wasn't enough for him to be faithful. Did I not love him enough? Give him enough attention? Was it because I refused to move to London?

I just wanted to make roots. He knew how many times we'd moved over the years, and I told him I wanted a place to call home.

My thoughts go back to my mom giving up, to my dad not wanting me. He moved on, found someone to replace my mom and me as if we were completely disposable.

The same way John so easily replaced me.

Am I ever going to be enough to be considered irreplaceable? For someone to put first?

And what about the magic? I haven't felt it since my mom died. Maybe it's only just an illusion and I'm looking for something that doesn't exist.

No, I tell myself, refusing to believe that. The magic is real. I just need to find it.

But what if I don't? What if the magic died with my mom and I never feel it again?

My phone dings, and when I pull it out, I find a text from Marina, asking me to call her.

John or Phoebe must've told her what happened.

Or maybe she already knew, and she's concerned about her wedding. I'm a bridesmaid, and John is a groomsman. Maybe she wants me to hand over my dress to Phoebe so she can walk down the aisle with John.

My thoughts go back to Phoebe bent over the counter. Her breasts are smaller than mine. And where I'm five foot eight without heels, she's petite, probably a good six inches shorter. She'd never fit into my dress, which means Marina will need me to walk down the aisle with John with a smile plastered on my face.

Great. Just what I need. To attend a wedding right after ending a relationship.

"Ma'am, is there anything else I can help you with?" the woman at the desk asks in her smooth British accent, reminding me that I'm standing in the hotel lobby, in London, the city where I found out my dad never wanted me, where my mom took her last breath, and now, where the man I once thought was my forever cheated on me with a woman who I thought was my friend.

Mom always made it seem like London was this magical place. But now …

Tears prick my eyes, and I grab my luggage, rolling it behind me toward the exit, suddenly feeling claustrophobic, like I'm being suffocated by so many different emotions.

When I step outside, the cool air hits my face and freezes my tears to my cheeks. I have no idea where I'm going, other than needing to get away.

So, I'm not paying attention when the front of my shoe gets stuck on an uneven piece of the cobblestone, and I stumble forward into the middle of the road. I try to stop, but the velocity propelling me forward is too strong, and my hands and knees hit the ground just as a car is driving in.

I close my eyes, knowing there's no way I'll make it out of their way in time, and pray I don't get run over.

I'm still praying when strong hands lift me off the ground and into their arms.

My eyes pop open, and I'm met with reddish-brown eyes that remind me of Kingston's bourbon whiskey. It has notes of vanilla and caramel to give it the perfect amount of sweetness, and I briefly wonder if this man would taste as sweet.

Jesus, did I hit my head on the cobblestone?

"Are you okay?" a smooth, masculine voice asks, breaking me from my thoughts. "You took quite a fall."

His words lack the British accent, telling me he's not from here.

"I'm going to set you down," he says once we're back inside the hotel lobby.

There's a couch in the corner, and he gently sets me on it, then kneels so he's at my level.

"Does it hurt anywhere?" he asks, his whiskey-colored eyes peering into mine.

I wiggle my toes and fingers and then glance down at my body, mentally checking to see if anything hurts.

"Other than my pride, no," I mutter.

The gentleman surprises me when he barks out a laugh, and I can't help but notice the way his Adam's apple rolls down his throat. His hair is styled neatly to the side, and he's sporting a few-days-old stubble. He's wearing a gray suit, but even with his body covered, I can make out his muscular form underneath.

"Thank you," I murmur. "Today has sucked, and being hit by a car would've made it suck worse."

His lips quirk, as if he's trying to tamp down a grin.

"It's only"—he flicks his wrist and glances down at his watch—"nine in the morning. Surely, there's still time to turn it around." Then, he reaches out and brushes his thumb along my cheek, reminding me that I was crying.

"Unless you have a magical wand that can turn back time so I don't show up at my ex's flat and walk in on him screwing my friend in his kitchen, I don't think so."

I roll my eyes, hating that John made our relationship into a damn cliché. I mean, seriously, would it have been too much for him to break up with me before he dipped his cock into her vagina?

"Jesus, I'm sorry," the gentleman says.

The sincerity in his apology has me choking up again.

"It's okay." I shrug, trying to act like my heart and ego aren't bruised.

"Are you staying here?" he asks.

At his words, I remember my current predicament.

Oh shit! "My luggage!"

"Right here," he says, pointing to my still-intact luggage. "Are you staying here?" he repeats.

"I am, but not until Friday. I'm here for a wedding. Like an idiot, I showed up at John's flat early, thinking I would surprise him for Valentine's Day." I laugh humorlessly as the image of Phoebe bent over his kitchen counter pops back into my head. An image that I wish I could scrub from my brain. "I came here, hoping I could check in early, but it's completely booked. So, I need to find somewhere to stay for the next couple of nights."

I'm about to stand and thank him—and I should probably also apologize for spilling all my drama into his lap—when he gently places his hand on my knee.

"What's your name?"

"Paige."

"Paige ..."

"Abrams."

"Wait here and let me see what I can do," he says with a wink that has no business being as sexy as it is.

He stands, and I can't help but watch as he heads across the lobby with a purposeful stride that screams confidence with just a hint of arrogance. Like he knows his place in this world.

While I wait for him to speak to the front desk—knowing there's nothing he can do, but thinking it's sweet this stranger would try for me—I unbutton my jacket since it's warm in the lobby and pull out my phone that's been buzzing like crazy, remembering that I never responded to Marina's text.

There are several other texts from John and Phoebe that I immediately delete because there's nothing they can say that will make what they did okay.

I stop at the one from Ana.

> **Ana**: Hey! I got worried when you didn't call or text to confirm you'd made it to John's place, so I called John, and he told me what happened. THAT FUCKING ASSHOLE!!! Call me, please! I'm worried about you.

I glance up and see the gentleman—whose name I never got—walking back toward me, so I send a quick text to let her know I'm okay and I'll call her in a few minutes, and then I pocket my phone.

"Good news," the gentleman says. "They had a room available after all."

He hands me a mini envelope with a key card sticking out of it.

"What? Seriously?" I gasp. "Thank you!"

Without thinking about what I'm doing—just so thankful that I don't have to try to find somewhere to stay on Valentine's Day—I throw my arms around the man's neck.

"You're welcome." He chuckles when we separate. "I hope your day gets better, Paige."

The kindness from this stranger causes my eyes to prick with unshed tears. Why is it that a stranger can be so sweet and genuine while a man who swore he loved me could treat me so badly?

"Hey," the gentleman says softly, wiping a tear that I didn't realize had fallen. "That guy doesn't deserve you. I know it hurts now, but one day, you'll meet a man who treats you how you deserve to be treated, and that asshole will be nothing but a lesson learned."

His words slide in through the fissures in my heart and soothe it like a balm. The truth is, I'm more upset about wasting my time with someone like John than the act of him cheating. Yes, the betrayal hurts, but more than that, I feel like I've been let down. I gave our relationship all of me, and I'm left with nothing.

The gentleman clears his throat, and I push my thoughts to the side. Once I'm in my room, I'll let myself wallow, and then tomorrow, I'll wake up and start from square one once again. Only this time, I'll think twice before I give myself to a man who doesn't deserve it.

"What's your name?" I ask, needing to put a name to the face of the kind man.

"Nate."

"Thank you for everything, Nate." I stand, and he backs up to give me some space. "I don't know how to repay you for your kindness, but thank you."

"It was my pleasure," he says with a small nod. "Enjoy your stay at the Bradford Hotel."

CHAPTER THREE

Paige

"THIS CAN'T BE RIGHT."

I glance down at the envelope that specifies my room number and compare it to the door number I'm standing in front of. They match, but something must be wrong because this is the penthouse suite, and I know I didn't book this room. I make a good living as the CMO at Kingston, but not *that* good of a living.

Pulling the key card out, I place it against the door, and the green light instantly appears, the door clicking open. I push it all the way open and step inside, letting the door close on its own while I take in my surroundings.

This isn't a room. It's a goddamn apartment. The living room is almost the same size as mine at home, and the kitchen is sleek with state-of-the-art appliances.

I leave my luggage in the foyer and go on a quick tour, finding there are two gorgeous, massive bedrooms and two full-size bathrooms—one of them complete with a Jacuzzi tub that could fit five people.

When I pull the curtain open in what appears to be the master bedroom, I'm hit with the most stunning view of London, making my heart swell. It's been over a year since I've been here, and I didn't realize how much I needed to see this to remind myself that despite the bad that's happened here, it's still the place my mom loved. The last place I felt like was home. And I'm not going to let shitty situations, like my dad moving us away or John screwing my ex-friend, ruin the magic my mom felt here.

I unlock the French doors and step outside, inhaling the crisp, fresh air. It's almost ten, so the sun is shining, helping to warm the chill in the air.

"I miss you, Mom," I murmur, hoping she can hear me.

I stand on the terrace for several minutes, taking in the city, and decide that I'm going to make the most out of this trip. It might be the end of a chapter in my life, but it's also the start of a new one.

But first, I need to get the room mix-up handled. I find the phone and dial the front desk, hoping they can find me a different room. While I appreciate what Nate did, I can't afford to stay here for five nights.

"Good morning, Miss Abrams. My name is Jennifer at the front desk. What can I help you with?"

"Hello," I say, already missing the room before I've even lost it. I mean, can you blame me?

After what I witnessed this morning, the perfect way to start my next chapter would be in style. Hell, if John's card was the one on file, I might've considered keeping it…

I know. I know. That's immature and petty, and I need to be the bigger person. *Sigh.*

"I think there's been a mix-up," I begrudgingly tell the woman.

"I'm in room 1901, but it's the penthouse, and I booked a standard room with a king."

"According to the notes, you've been upgraded," Jennifer says sweetly.

"Yes, I can see that. However, I can't *afford* the upgrade. So, I need to be moved into a standard room, please."

Please let there be a standard room available, I plead silently.

"Hmm, can you please give me one moment while I look into this?"

"Of course."

The music starts up, and I wait patiently. I probably should've gone down there since I'm going to have to anyway to get my correct key card—unless this is the only room available, which is how Nate got me a room after I was told they were completely booked.

Damn it, that's probably what happened.

I'm about to hang up and go down to the lobby when Jennifer comes back on the line.

"Miss Abrams?"

"Yes, I'm here."

"Great. So, I have good news. The price of the penthouse was overridden, and you will only be charged the price you were given for a standard room. Is there anything else I can help you with?"

"Umm, no," I say in shock, having no clue how this happened. "Are you sure?" I ask because if this is a mix-up and I'm charged for this suite, it's going to get declined because there's no way my credit card limit is enough to cover the bill.

"Yes, ma'am. If you check your email, we've sent you an updated invoice with the free upgrade."

"Okay, thank you."

I hang up and check my email, and sure enough, it's there, in black and white.

"Well then," I say to myself, looking around at my room with new eyes. "Should I take a bath or visit my favorite parts of London first?"

I glance outside. "London first, relax after."

After changing into fresh clothes, hanging the rest of my wardrobe in the closet, and calling Ana to update her on everything, I head down to the lobby so I can start exploring. I have two days before I have to deal with the wedding, and I'm going to enjoy them.

Besides, it's Valentine's Day! And there are very few places more romantic than London. Who knows? Maybe I'll meet a gorgeous Brit I can get under to help me get over my cheating ex.

I'm stepping out of the elevator when I spot the gentleman from earlier. Wanting to thank him again, I call out his name, and he turns his head, his masculine features morphing into the most devastatingly beautiful smile.

"Did you get settled in?" he asks.

"I did. And get this. Somehow, there was a mix-up, and I was upgraded to the penthouse suite…at no charge."

Nate's smile widens. "That's a damn good mix-up."

"Right? And I even called to make sure I wouldn't be charged the difference, but they insisted I wouldn't be." I shrug. "Maybe it's a sign. I was starting to wonder if it's possible that the magic I used to feel in London when my mom was alive was made up, but then you were able to get me a room early, and the view…it reminded me of the magic."

I take a breath from my long-winded monologue and internally cringe. "Sorry. I'm sure you have better things to do than listen to a crazy woman go on about magic."

"Actually," he says, "it's one of the most refreshing things I've heard in a while."

He glances over at the coffee shop that's attached to the hotel and then back at me.

"Would you like to grab a cup of coffee with me? I'd love to hear more about this magical London." A genuine smile spreads across his face, telling me that he's not making fun of me.

"Sure." It's not like I have any concrete plans, and it's been a while since I've spoken about my mom.

Since there's no line, we both order, and Nate insists on paying. We find a small table in the corner, and after our drinks are ready, we grab them and have a seat.

"Now, tell me about the magic," Nate says, taking a sip of his drink.

"It's hard to explain," I admit. "It's more like something I feel. When my mom was alive, we traveled a lot because my dad was a pilot. Well, he still is…" I groan, wishing I hadn't mentioned him at all. "Sorry, he's, umm…a sore spot."

I sigh and shake my head, refusing to let my dad's choices affect me. I accepted a long time ago that when I lost my mom, I lost him too. Sure, he calls me every month to ask how I'm doing, but our conversations are awkward, and I don't know why he even bothers. John once told me I should tell him to stop calling, but I can't bring myself to do it. He's the only family I have left, and I think a small part of me hopes that maybe he's calling because he does love me despite what he told my mom.

"Anyway," I continue, "my dad was offered a job based out of London, so he took us to visit, and my mom fell in love with the city. She insisted we stay, and it was the first and only time we stayed somewhere long enough for it to feel like home. "Every day, we would explore the city in some way, and I fell in love with it right alongside her…"

"Why do I feel like there's a but coming?"

"Because there always is." I laugh through the tears I'm holding back. "She died from cancer, and then my dad moved us to Rome and then to the States.

"When I graduated from college, I came back here, wanting to be close to my mom…to the magic I'd felt when she was alive. But it wasn't the same," I admit. "I love this city, but I don't know if it's because she's not here or because, without her, I feel so alone, but it feels like the magic is gone. Or maybe it was all in my head and the magic never existed."

The thought that the magic never existed hurts my heart worse than catching John and Phoebe together. The memories of living in this city with my mom are how I want to remember her. When I moved back here and didn't feel the magic, I chalked it up to being so busy with work that I didn't have time to truly enjoy the city the way she and I had. But now, I'm here, and if I explore the city and find out the magic really is gone, I'm afraid it's going to feel like I've lost my mom all over again. Only this time, it will be worse because without the memories of the magical city, I'll have nothing left of her.

"Show me," Nate says, snapping me from my thoughts.

"What?"

"Show me," he repeats. "You said your asshole ex cheated, so you have a few days before the wedding, right?"

"Yeah…"

"Well, I have a few days as well, so how about you show me London through your eyes, through your *mom's* eyes? And I'll let you know if it's magical or if it's all in your head."

"Seriously?" I choke out, wondering why the hell this guy would want to spend his time exploring the city with a stranger.

"Yeah." He places his hand on mine, and a warmth I've never felt before seeps into my skin and heats up my body. "Show me the magic."

When his bright brown eyes meet mine, I pull my hand back, overwhelmed by the intense connection I feel with him.

Maybe it's because I'm filled with a myriad of emotions—between my life feeling up in the air and being in the city my mom once loved—but I feel exposed, and as much as I want to let this man in, I can't risk being hurt again. We're both nothing more than two strangers who happen to be in the same place at the same time, and once we check out of this hotel, we'll go back to our lives and never see each other again.

And then it hits me...

"Are you in a relationship?" I ask, needing to know.

Before John cheated, I wouldn't have even thought to ask. But now, I feel like I can't assume anything. My trust has recently been destroyed, the wounds still fresh, and while I shouldn't take it out on Nate, I can't help how I feel.

"What?" He looks at me like he's been slapped.

"Are you dating anyone? Engaged? Married?"

"No," he bites out. "If I were, I sure as hell wouldn't be sitting here with you, hoping you'll spend the next few days with me."

"Sorry, I had to ask."

"I get it," he says. "Unfortunately, I experienced almost exactly what you went through."

"You did?"

"Yeah." He sighs. "I dated this girl throughout college, and when we graduated, I went to work for my family's business. Some personal stuff was going on, so I was working a lot of hours, and I thought she understood. Until I came home early one night to surprise her and take her to dinner and found her in bed with my best friend."

"How did you get past it?"

"With time," he says with a shrug. "But also, I was glad I found out then, before we got married and had kids."

"Yeah," I agree, having thought the same thing earlier. "The last thing I'd want is to put my kids through a divorce. I know divorce rates are high, but my hope is that I'll find someone who will want me forever. Before my mom got sick, I felt what it was like to have a family. Even though I hated moving around, no matter where we moved, I had my parents. Now"—I exhale a harsh breath—"I feel like I have no one."

"It'll take time," Nate says, giving my hand a squeeze. "But one day, when you've met the man you'll spend your life with, you'll look back and be grateful that asshole showed his true colors so you could move forward."

"You haven't moved forward," I point out since he said he's not in a relationship.

"No." He smiles sadly. "I'd like to. I'd love to meet someone I can share my life with. My parents have been married for over thirty years and are still madly in love."

"But…"

"But sometimes, I think maybe I'm destined to be married to my job."

"Or maybe you just haven't met the right woman yet."

"Maybe."

His eyes lock with mine, and butterflies, which have no business being anywhere near me, attack my chest.

"So, what do you say?" he asks. "You going to show me the magic of London?"

I open my mouth to say yes, but stop myself because maybe I'm thinking too much into this, but I can't risk it. It's easy to get swept up in a city like London, and right now, I feel extremely vulnerable.

"I live in Houston, Texas," I tell him, not bothering to mention Rosemary since it's too small of a town for anybody to know. "Do you live anywhere near there?"

The chances of him living near me are slim, and since I've already experienced the heartbreak of being in a long-distance relationship, I'm not doing that again. Which means, if I'm going to spend time with his gorgeous man, I need to make sure the line is clearly drawn so there's no risk of it blurring.

He quirks a questioning brow, but then says, "I live in—"

I shake my head. "Don't tell me. Just answer my question. Do you live near Houston? Close enough that if there were an emergency, like, say, if a huge spider appeared in my shower and I needed you to come save me, you could be there before the spider killed me?"

He snorts out a laugh. "What the hell kind of spiders do you have in Houston?"

"The kind that nightmares are made of," I deadpan, making him laugh again.

"No," he says with a sigh. "I don't live close enough to save you from the deadly spider, but—"

"No buts," I say, refusing to let him come up with an argument. "I did the long-distance thing and have the heartbreak to show for it. I'm not saying this thing between us could be headed in that direction. And I don't want it to sound like I'm being presumptuous. But I need to protect myself, just in case.

"So, if I agree to show you London over the next few days, you have to agree not to share anything about yourself. What happens in London stays in London."

"Okay," he easily agrees. "What happens in London stays in London."

CHAPTER FOUR

Nate

"THE TOWER BRIDGE, HUH?"

"Not just the Tower Bridge." Paige scoffs. "The top of the Tower Bridge."

She steps up to the counter and orders our tickets, and before she can even think about paying, I tap my phone against the card reader, so it charges me and not her.

I came to London on a business trip and was heading into a meeting at the Bradford Hotel when I saw a beautiful but distraught woman trip over the cobblestone and land in the road. If I hadn't witnessed it myself, I would swear that shit only happened in those sappy romance movies my mom and sisters-in-law watched.

I yelled to my driver to stop and then flew out of the car, picking her up and bringing her inside before she got ran over, while my driver grabbed her luggage and left it with us.

Paige was a mess, her eyes filled with tears, her face splotchy from crying, but she was still the most stunning woman I'd ever laid eyes on, and all I could think about was how I wanted to fix what was wrong.

I couldn't fix the fact that her ex had cheated, but I could help her get a room. And since my family owns the hotel, I had her upgraded at no charge. It took everything in me to walk away, but I had a meeting I couldn't cancel, and I knew she wasn't in any place to have some random guy flirting with her or asking her out. That would've been both rude and insensitive.

But then, as if fate had stepped in, I ran into her again in the lobby. And this time, she was more put together. She had stopped crying, and her face was no longer splotchy. She smiled at me, and her beauty tripled.

I've dated my fair share of women, but I can't remember ever feeling the instantaneous connection I felt with Paige. As I listened to her talk about her mom and the magic of London, I was enraptured by her presence, her words, her passion.

I wasn't sure if she felt the connection, until I asked her to show me around London, wanting to spend more time with her—and the truth is, every time I'm here, I'm so busy with business that I've never actually explored London—and she made me promise not to share anything about myself, telling me that she's worried she'll get attached and want more.

I get it. We don't live near each other, and she just got out of a long-distance relationship that ended with him cheating. Hell, my life is so busy, I barely have enough time to date someone who lives in the same city as me, let alone try to get to know someone who lives hours away. Logically, her keeping me at a distance makes sense. But that doesn't stop me from wanting to spend the time I have with Paige.

I was supposed to be in meetings all week, and I've never canceled one in my life—I thrive on being responsible—so I shocked even myself when I emailed my assistant, Nolan, and told him he'd be handling the meetings today so I could go sightseeing with a woman I barely knew. The whole thing sounds crazy, and if my dad knew what I was doing, he would ask if I should be mentally evaluated because it's so out of character for me. But I can't help it. There's just something about her that I'm drawn to.

"Here you go," the woman behind the window says, handing us our tickets.

We get in line for the lift, and since it's not busy, it goes quickly. It takes us straight to the top, and once we get out, we walk toward the center. The ground is see-through glass, allowing us to get a cool view of the cars driving underneath.

"Look over here," Paige says, taking my hand in hers and guiding me over to the edge of the bridge so we can look out at the city.

The sky is bright blue today with only a few clouds, which is rare. Boats are making their way down the river, and people, who look like little Lego people from this high up, are walking up and down the sidewalk.

Out of the corner of my eye, I see Paige's face split into a beautiful, serene smile. She inhales deeply and then releases it, and I imagine she's letting all the bad out and replacing it with the magic she spoke about.

"Tell me about it," I say, wanting to hear what's got her smiling.

"See that area right over there?" She points, and I follow, my gaze landing on an area of shops across the way. "That was my mom's favorite breakfast place." She smiles softly. "We would walk along the bridge and stop there for breakfast. She'd order the same thing every time—avocado toast and an espresso."

"And what would you order?" I ask, wanting to soak in whatever she'll give me of herself.

"Waffles," she says with a light laugh. "I love waffles."

As she continues, telling me how she and her mom would spend their day, her eyes lighting up at her favorite memories, her gaze remains on the outside while mine stays on her. Because the truth is, the magic isn't in the city. It's in the people we share the moments with. That's why she hasn't been able to feel the magic without her mom. Because it was their relationship, their bond, that made her feel the way she did.

Which is why I understand Paige wanting to draw the line between us from the get-go. She felt what I felt—the instantaneous connection between us. But she's not in a place to put her heart back on the line. And I get it because I experienced it firsthand—getting your heart stomped on and having to pick up the pieces so you can attempt to move forward.

And the worst part is that even though we're long-distance, it's only a few hours. If I lived just a little south, this would be an entirely different story with a completely different ending. But that's not how life works.

Despite all that, standing inside the Tower Bridge with Paige, experiencing the magic through her eyes…it feels like there's nowhere else I should be but right here with her. Even if it means that after our time together is done, I'll walk away with nothing more than the memories I made with this beautiful woman.

"So, what do you think?" she asks, pulling her eyes from the view outside and meeting mine.

"I think you were right. It's magical."

She nods in agreement. "I never should've let the bad overtake the good."

"Sometimes, we have to see it and feel it in order to remember it."

Her eyes well up with tears, and she closes them.

"Yeah," she chokes out as her fingers, which are still intertwined with mine, tighten their hold. "It's been a long time since I felt it."

Someone walks by and bumps into Paige, so I step behind her and encircle my arms around her to protect her from the outside world.

With our bodies so close, I can smell her sweet, feminine scent. I try not to get too close, but when she leans back and relaxes into me, I allow myself to relax as well.

After several minutes of us both taking in the view in front of us, I lean in and murmur into her ear, "Thank you for sharing the magic with me," wanting her to know how much it means to me. It's not easy to let someone in when you're feeling vulnerable.

Paige audibly sniffles and then nods, and after a few long beats of her remaining silent, I assume that's the only response I'll get from her.

But then she whispers, "Thank you for helping me to remember the magic."

And for the first time, I wish my life were different. That I were just an average guy who worked a regular job so I could stop everything and see where things could go with the mesmerizing woman I met in London.

But that's not who I am. I have a family and obligations back home. People who depend on me. And because of that, I know all I can give Paige is London. Thinking I could give her anything more would be unfair to both of us.

CHAPTER FIVE

"**S**O, WHAT'S NEXT?"

I try to focus on Nate's question, but it's hard when all I can think about is the way he wrapped his arms around me while we were in the Tower Bridge and made me feel safer than I'd felt in a long time.

Safe to remember the magic. To feel it the way I'd felt it when my mom was alive.

I knew deep down that John and I were over before I even stepped off the plane, but after spending a short amount of time with another man, I know it's for the best.

Is Nate the man of my dreams? No. We don't live anywhere near each other. But he's woken up my heart and reminded me what it's like to feel.

"Paige," Nate says with a smirk, "you look like you're off somewhere far away."

I laugh. "I'm here. I was thinking we could go to Chinatown. It's a bit of a ride, but they have delicious food. I don't know how much time you have though or if you have somewhere you need to be."

"I have all the time in the world and no place to be but right here with you. And I'm starved. So, point the way."

The ride to Chinatown doesn't take too long, and we spend it getting to know each other on a surface level. Nate's favorite color is black even though I insist black is not a color. He went to college and majored in business. He has two younger brothers, who are both married, one with kids, so he feels like the odd one out.

I tell him I can empathize since my two closest friends, Ana and Kira, are both in relationships and have adorable children.

Nate reads fiction when he has time to read, so I tell him about the book club Ana started and that he should check out some romance books since they're the best escape.

Surprisingly, instead of him scoffing or making a comment about him being a man, he pulls out his phone and asks for my top recommendations.

"If you could travel anywhere in the world, where would you go?" Nate asks as we walk down the street toward the Chinese restaurant I haven't been to in over a year.

"I don't know," I say with a laugh. "We lived in Finland, Japan, Ireland, the UK, Rome, Türkiye, Germany, and too many states to name. My mom made it a point to explore everywhere we lived. I was young, but our trips were still memorable, and we would make a scrapbook for everywhere we went, a new page for every adventure. I guess maybe I'd want to go snowboarding. My mom hated the snow, so we never went."

"Really? Well, it might be fate because I have a place in Aspen," Nate says, waggling his brows.

"Too bad, after today, I'll never see you again," I say, bumping his shoulder playfully and making him chuckle.

"You know"—Nate slides his arm across my shoulders and pulls me into his side—"I have been told that I'm extremely irresistible. Maybe after spending time with me, you'll have fallen so hard that you'll be begging me for my number."

I snort out a laugh and glance up at him. "Who told you that? Your mom? She lied to make you feel good about yourself."

Nate barks out a laugh. "We'll see."

"Mmhmm." I roll my eyes, playing it off, while, deep down, I have no doubt that Nate is telling the truth.

I've only spent a short time with him, and I can already tell it would be way too easy to fall for him. Which is why I'm keeping my guard up. It's nice, spending time with someone in London as opposed to being alone to wallow in my self-pity, but after today, we're going our separate ways, no matter how irresistible he thinks he is.

We enjoy our lunch, ordering a little bit of everything, and Nate admits it's the best Chinese he's ever eaten. Once we're done, we check out Big Ben and Westminster Abbey—the royal church where Prince William and his wife were married. On the way back, we stop at several bookstores, and Nate even buys a romance novel. By the time we get back to the hotel, it's late, and we're both exhausted and starved—again.

"We could order room service," he offers.

"You and me in a hotel room?" I shake my head. "Not happening."

"Okay." He chuckles, lifting his hands in a placating manner. "How about we eat at the bar?"

"That's definitely the safer option."

Since it's after dinner hours, the bar isn't too packed, and we're able to find two seats at the end.

"Good evening," the bartender says. "What can I get you to drink?"

"I'll have a Maker's Mark old-fashioned," Nate says.

The bartender nods and then glances at me. "And for you, ma'am?"

"Hmm." I glance up at the bottles along the shelves, and after a few seconds, I spot the one I'm looking for. "I'll have the same, but with Kingston's Yellow Label and extra bitter, please."

The bartender grins. "You got it."

"You know your liquor," Nate notes once the bartender goes to the other end to make our drinks.

"I work for Kingston, so naturally, I'm loyal."

It's a response I've given a million times without thought, but one I shouldn't have given to Nate since it was my idea not to scratch below the surface, and where we work is definitely deeper than surface level.

My hope of him not catching what I said flies out the window when he says, "And what is it you do for Kingston…since you brought it up?" He smirks, knowing he's got me.

"I work in marketing, but that's all you're getting out of me. And before you try to reciprocate with where you work, don't even think about it. My response was an accident."

"Fine," Nate says as the bartender sets our drinks on the bar top in front of us. "I won't tell you that I work—"

Before he can finish his sentence, I reach over and cover his mouth with my hand. "Don't even think about it."

I'm so focused on making sure he doesn't give any clues that will allow me to chase after him once our little…*whatever the hell this is*…is over that I don't realize my hand is pressed against his lips. I feel his smirk beneath my hand, but before I can put two and two together, his tongue darts out and licks up the center of my palm, making me jump back.

"Seriously?"

Nate laughs. "Next time, I'll bite your hand." He playfully snaps his teeth together as if taking a bite out of the air, and I can't help but laugh as well.

I take a sip of my drink, and it's perfect.

"Taste it and tell me Kingston's isn't more flavorful than the crap you're drinking," I say, sliding my drink toward Nate so he can try it.

Nate glances from the drink to my mouth and then leans in. "Okay, but only if I can taste it off your lips."

Wait, what?

"You want to…" I breathe, the air in the room suddenly thick with sexual tension.

"Taste you," he finishes, his mouth only a whisper away from mine. "Say yes," he murmurs.

And because there's no other answer I want to give, I do just that.

I haven't even finished saying the three-letter word before Nate's fingers are wrapping around the back of my neck and he's pulling my face toward his to do exactly what he said—taste me.

His tongue traces the seam of my lips, and when I exhale, it slips into my mouth, stroking, teasing, caressing.

"Mmm," he murmurs against my mouth. "Delicious."

And then he breaks the kiss, leaving me wanting more.

"You're right," he says, sucking his bottom lip into his mouth. "Your liquor tastes way better. It's almost…addictive."

Holy shit. This man is sex personified.

I lift my glass and down my drink in one go, welcoming the warmth from the whiskey. Then, I stand, needing to escape before I do something I might regret.

"What about dinner?" Nate asks, standing as well.

"I'm exhausted," I tell him since it's not a lie. "It's been a long day and…" I glance from his eyes to his mouth, remembering the way his lips felt against mine—soft yet strong. "I can't believe I only just arrived in London this morning. It feels like I've been here for a week."

Nate chuckles and nods in understanding.

"So, tomorrow…" he says, trailing his words and leaving the ball in my court to either pick them up or leave them hanging.

When we were on our way back to the hotel, I mentioned there was still so much to see, and he offered to join me tomorrow. The smart choice would be to walk away now, but the thought of never seeing him again has me thinking like an idiot.

"How about we meet down here at nine o'clock?" I suggest.

"Sounds good."

Nate insists on paying for the drinks, and once he's signed the check, we head over to the elevators. He presses the button for the one I'm getting on since different elevators are for different floors, and once it arrives, he says, "If you need anything, my number is—"

I'm shaking my head before he can finish, but then he clarifies, "My *room number* is 1714," and I release a breath of relief.

"I mean it, Paige, if you need anything"—he steps closer and lifts my chin so our eyes meet—"call me."

Then, he leans in and presses a soft kiss on my forehead, and those damn butterflies make another appearance.

"Good night," he murmurs. "Sweet dreams."

With his words lingering, I step onto the elevator and press my floor number while wondering how the hell I'm going to get any sleep after that damn kiss that still has my body vibrating.

When I get to my room, I spot the large Jacuzzi tub I forgot about, and an idea forms. Nothing helps a woman fall asleep quicker than an orgasm. Nate might be physically off-limits for my own well-being, but that doesn't mean I can't think about him.

And, holy shit, do I think about him…twice.

CHAPTER SIX

"WHY DID NOLAN TELL ME YOU SKIPPED OUT ON ALL your meetings yesterday and you're planning to do the same today?"

I curse my assistant, who's supposed to have my back and not spill shit to my dad, while I try to think of a valid excuse as to why I flew all the way to London to attend meetings about the hotel expansion, only to bail on them all.

When I can't come up with a believable excuse, I go with the truth. "I met a woman."

Stunned by my response, he doesn't say anything for several moments. And when he finally speaks, he's no longer in CEO mode, but instead talking to me as my father.

"What's her name?"

"Paige Abrams. She tripped over some cobblestone, and I saved her from getting run over in the valet line."

Dad chuckles. "Well, that saved the company a lot of insurance paperwork."

"She's only here until Monday."

I know that from seeing her reservation and looking up the wedding that's being held here. Friday is the rehearsal and dinner, Saturday is the wedding, and she's checking out on Monday morning, which leaves me today and Sunday to convince her to give me her number. I already tried to get it from the hotel, but the number on file is local, so it's probably her ex's.

"Okay," Dad concedes. "Go have your fun, but make sure you're still handling things."

"Of course," I say because business has always come first.

I've been working for Bradford Hotels since I was old enough to have a job, and before that, I spent every chance I could learning from my dad because when he's ready to retire, I'll be the one to step into his shoes. And from what he's told me, it'll be sooner rather than later—by the end of this year if Mom has it her way.

My brothers, Dustin and Carmine, also work for our family's company. Dustin is the head of accounting. He's always been a whiz with numbers, so it suits him. He loves his position as CFO and has no desire to change it. Carmine is the head of marketing and does a damn good job. I'd bet he and Paige would get along. When she spoke about working for Kingston Liquor, I could see the same kind of passion in her eyes that Carmine gets when he's discussing his latest marketing idea.

Our father never pushed anything on us, but we're a close-knit family, and working for Bradford Hotels was always what we wanted to do.

Dad and I hang up, and I shoot Nolan a text, letting him know I'm aware that he ratted me out to my dad. Then, I scan the room in search of Paige, hoping she isn't going to stand me up, when I spot her staring down at her phone with a frown marring her beautiful face.

She shakes her head and sighs and then pockets it. Her eyes meet mine, and she smiles, but because I've seen what her genuine smile looks like, I know this one is forced.

"Everything okay?" I ask once I'm standing in front of her.

"Yeah," she chokes out.

"Let's try that again." I palm her cheek. "What's wrong?"

She releases a harsh breath, and her eyes ascend as she tries not to let her tears fall.

"Hey," I murmur, pulling her to the side so we're not standing in the middle of the lobby. "Talk to me."

"Apparently, my friends have chosen sides, and it's not mine." She shrugs like it doesn't bother her, but we both know otherwise. "It was bad enough John cheated on me with my friend, but now, the couple who's getting married, who were my friends first, have welcomed them to attend the wedding together."

"Ouch. That doesn't sound like any of these people are your friends."

"I worked with Marina, and Phoebe was my roommate. By default, their boyfriends and mine became friends. Phoebe and Steve broke up a couple of months ago, and he moved, so nobody had to choose, but now, she's dating John, and that makes things awkward since I'm friends with Marina, but I'm also the only one who lives in a different country."

She sniffles back her cry, trying to be strong. "Marina said she didn't know, but she can't let this ruin her wedding, and since they were both invited, John asked if we could trade seats. Since Phoebe and Steve only recently broke up, Steve is still on the guest list, so I'll be sitting next to an open seat so Phoebe and John can sit together."

"Why even go?" I ask, hating to see her upset and wondering what kind of friends would put someone who's just been betrayed in that position.

"Because I'm in the wedding and it will look petty if I don't show up. Technically, Marina didn't do anything wrong. She's switching me and Phoebe so there aren't any issues, and honestly, I'd rather sit next to an empty seat than with John, but…" She huffs. "I guess I was hoping Phoebe would do the right thing and not go. John and I are both in the wedding, but she's not."

"You already know they're both shitty people," I point out. "Neither of them thought about your feelings while they were together behind your back, so why would they consider your feelings now?"

"I know," she says. "I just wish, for once, someone would put me first."

Her words come out as a whisper, but they hit my heart like a bullet. If Paige were mine, I would put her first every goddamn day for the rest of our lives. She deserves for someone to think about her, to be there for her, to love her, but that can't be me. I hate that our time is limited and that we can never be anything more than a London memory.

"It'll happen," I tell her, tipping her chin up and pressing a soft kiss to the tip of her nose. "Now, what's on the agenda for today? You have over thirty hours before you need to think about that wedding, so put it out of your head, and let's enjoy London."

"I actually had an idea, but I'm not sure you'd want—"

"Tell me. I'm down for anything."

"I was thinking we could go to Bath."

"The city? Isn't it, like…"

"Two and a half hours by train. We could visit the Roman

Baths, and they have the best tea and scones, and there's this cute coffee shop—"

"Hey," I say, holding her chin so she'll look at me. "If you want to get out of here, that's all you have to say."

"Thank you." She releases a sigh of relief. "Phoebe's checking in today, which means…"

"Which means we're going to Bath. Give me ten minutes to pack an overnight bag, and I'll meet you back down here."

"Wait, an overnight bag?"

"If we're doing Bath, then we gotta do it right. And that can't be done in a day trip. Don't worry. We'll be back in time for your rehearsal and dinner tomorrow night."

I shoot her a playful wink, and she smiles—a real fucking smile. And I vow to do everything in my power to make sure that's the only smile she sports while we hang out.

"Okay," she says with a glimmer of happiness in her eyes. "I'll meet you back down here."

After I pack a bag, I text my assistant to let him know I'm leaving and ask him to book us a room in the best part of Bath with two bedrooms and bathrooms. He also books us tickets to see the Roman Baths and makes a reservation for us at the best teahouse since Paige mentioned having tea.

Since I have no desire to ride on a train, I also have him charter us a private plane. It'll only take about twenty-five minutes to get there.

"Umm, where are we going?" Paige asks when we step outside since we're getting in my car instead of heading to the train station.

A burst of cold air hits us, and her hair whips around her face. She tightens her hold around her coat, and I open the door to the car I requested to take us to the airport.

"Bath."

She glances at me suspiciously, but doesn't comment on anything else.

The ride to the private airport is quick, and when Paige realizes where we are, she shoots me a quizzical look.

"Mr. B—" the pilot greeting us at the plane begins, but before he can say my last name, I cut him off.

"Please call me Nate. And this is Paige."

"Welcome aboard. I'm Ron Poole, your pilot today. It will be a quick twenty-four-minute flight to Bath."

"We're flying to Bath?" Paige gasps.

"Quicker than the two-hour-plus train ride."

"And a helluva lot more expensive."

"Don't worry about that," I tell her as we climb the steps onto the plane.

It's on the smaller side, so there are only four passenger seats. We have a seat across from each other, and the flight attendant comes over and asks if we'd like a drink.

"Can I have a hot coffee, please?" Paige asks.

"Of course," the flight attendant says. "And you, sir?"

"I'll have the same."

The flight is, as the pilot said, quick, and once we arrive in Bath, we get into the car I have waiting for us. So that we don't have to bring our luggage with us, Nolan was able to get us an early check-in. The hotel is in the center of Bath in a small courtyard area, surrounded by a quaint bookstore, a tea shop, and a few other shops.

When the car stops, Paige gets out and glances around, and then her eyes meet mine. "We're staying here?" she asks, pointing to the building behind her.

I nod, and she throws her arms around my neck.

"Thank you, Nate. I know you couldn't have possibly known,

but this is the same area where my mom and I used to stay when we came here."

"I'm glad you like it," I murmur, kissing the crown of her head.

My time with Paige might be limited, but I'll do whatever I can to make sure it's memorable.

CHAPTER SEVEN

Paige

WHEN I MENTIONED WANTING TO FLEE TO BATH, I WAS shocked when Nate not only agreed, but somehow, during the ten minutes it took him to pack a bag, he also made travel plans—including chartering a private plane!—booked an adorable hotel in the heart of Bath, got us tickets to see the Roman Baths, and made reservations to the best scone and teahouse in the area.

I don't know what Nate does for a living, but I have no doubt that this is why he's successful. When he sets out to do something, he doesn't do it half-assed.

While Nate checks us in, I text Marina back to let her know that it's fine and I can sit wherever she'd like. She's been looking forward to this day for the past year, and I'm not going to be the reason she has unnecessary stress. But I've already decided that once I leave London, I'm cutting all ties with them. It's time I put myself and my feelings first.

"So, we have a little problem," Nate says, giving me a sheepish look that's so unlike him. "When my assistant booked the room, it was supposed to have two bedrooms, but the hotel is overbooked, and they only have a room left with one bedroom."

"Okay…"

"Which means one bed."

"Oh."

My mind immediately goes to Nate and me sharing a bed. *Does he wear pajamas or only boxers to bed? Maybe he sleeps in the nude.* The thought of him sleeping naked causes a whole new set of questions to enter my brain. *Is he—*

"Boxers," Nate says, snapping me from my thoughts.

"What?" I squeak out.

"You asked if I wore pajamas or boxers to bed," he says with a playful smirk. "I wear boxers. Well, boxer briefs to be exact. But if you want me to sleep in the nude…"

"Oh my God," I gasp. I must've spoken my thoughts out loud. *Please, ground, swallow me up now.*

"Paige," Nate says, stepping closer to me, "are you okay with sharing a bed? If not, I can find another—"

"I'm okay with it," I rush out, not wanting him to have to find another hotel.

He's already done so much, and what's one night in the same bed as Nate? We're both adults.

After getting the key from the woman handling our check-in, we walk outside and over to the building next door. We haul our luggage up to the second floor and into the cutest room.

"Apparently, they consider that a couch bed," Nate says dryly, pointing to the seat that runs along the window.

It looks comfy enough to sit on and read a book while having the gorgeous view of the outside, but it's not something I'd want to sleep on, and seeing as Nate is a good six inches taller than me, I don't think he'd even fit on it.

The bedroom has a large king-size bed with a dresser and a fireplace against the wall. To the left of the bed is a window that overlooks the cute courtyard outside.

I leave my bag on one side of the bed and then check out the adorable bathroom, complete with a vintage claw-foot bathtub. The entire place can't be more than a few hundred square feet, but what it lacks in size, it makes up for in character.

"This place is perfect," I tell him because it is, and I'm so happy to be here, experiencing one of the places my mom loved with him.

"All right, good," he says, hitting me with a boyish grin.

"Thank you for this." I take a step toward him. "You've gone above and beyond."

I wave my hand around the room to make my point, and Nate catches it, threading his fingers through mine and tugging me the rest of the way so our bodies are almost flush against one another.

"You don't have to thank me," he says, his eyes locking with mine.

"What you're doing for me…" I shake my head because it's so hard to put into words how I feel right now.

It's been a long time since someone thought about me and put my needs first. Since the moment we met, he's done nothing but focus on me. Even when I hear his phone vibrating, if we're in the middle of something, he won't check it. When I'm speaking, he listens, and I didn't realize how much I needed that.

For so long, I've felt like my needs come after everyone else's— my dad's job, my mom's illness, John's career. But when I'm with Nate, I feel like I matter. Like I'm worth thinking about.

"I'm quickly learning that there isn't much I wouldn't do for you," he murmurs, his lips less than an inch away from mine.

While I'm trying to figure out how to respond to what he just said, he whispers, "Tell me I can kiss you," his warm breath wrapping around me like a blanket on a cold day.

And because, once again, the only answer my brain will let me give is yes, I say just that.

With my permission verbalized, Nate closes the gap between us and brushes his lips against mine, first the bottom lip and then the top, and then he deepens the kiss, taking my breath away.

"Fuck," he mutters against my mouth. "I was hoping it was the liquor that had you tasting so delicious last night, but it wasn't. It's all fucking you."

He backs up and, keeping our fingers entwined, guides me to the door. "Let's get out of here before I say *fuck exploring Bath* and spend the day exploring every inch of you instead."

I nod in agreement, but as he closes the door, I glance at the bed, wondering if maybe staying in the room so Nate could explore me wouldn't be the better option—especially if it meant I got to explore him too.

CHAPTER EIGHT

Nate and I spend the day exploring Bath. We visit the Roman Baths, which I haven't been to since I was a teenager. We have lunch at a delicious Moroccan restaurant, and then we have afternoon tea at the place he reserved.

Everywhere we go, I recall and share small tidbits about my mom, and Nate listens, asking questions and sounding like he genuinely cares. The day is wonderful, and it's not until we're back at the room that I realize I haven't thought about my disaster of a love life once. When I'm with Nate, I'm so focused on him that it's like the rest of the world disappears.

Nate showers first while I call Ana and fill her in on my time here. She begs for details on Nate, but I insist we talk once I'm home, not wanting to risk him overhearing.

When he comes out, wearing a white T-shirt and basketball shorts, with his hair wet and messy, it hits me that this is the first time I've seen him this casual. Yesterday, he was in a designer suit that fit him like it had been made just for him, and today, he was sporting khaki dress pants with a powder-blue button-down shirt, the sleeves rolled up to his forearms.

Dressed up, businessman Nate is sexy and powerful, but right now, he's downright delicious. His shirt is taut across his chest, and…

"Are those tattoos?" I ask, cutting across the room.

"Paige?" Ana's voice reminds me we're still on the phone.

"I'll call you back," I say and then hang up, needing to check out the tattoos that are peeking out of the sleeve on his left arm.

He glances down at his toned forearm and then lifts his sleeve, exposing the gorgeous ink on his arm. At first glance, it looks like a beautiful forest with the sun peering through. There's a body of water with a reflection of the trees on the surface. But when I look closer, I see three hands, all joined together, hidden in the water.

"My brothers and I got these when we were younger. Dustin had just turned twenty-one, so Carmine and I were taking him out to celebrate with a bunch of our friends. Because we're close in age—me being the eldest, Carmine barely a year younger, and Dustin less than a year younger than Carmine—we hung out with the same group of people."

"Wow, your mom must've been brave to have three boys, all less than a year apart," I note.

"Yeah." He chuckles. "Carmine and I were in the same grade, and Dustin was one grade behind. Mom is tough, doesn't put up with our shit, but she loves us hard."

"She sounds like a good mom."

Nate nods in agreement. "The best."

"Sorry, I got us sidetracked. So, Dustin's birthday celebration?" I prompt for him to continue.

"That night, I was driving," Nate says, his tone solemn. "A drunk driver flew through a red light and hit us, and we were all rushed to the hospital. Carmine had nothing more than a few bruises since he was on the passenger side. But Dustin and I required surgery. My blood type is rare, so my dad and Carmine had to donate, and then Dustin had to have a kidney transplant because he had already lost one when he was younger. Carmine was a match, so he ended up donating it to him, which saved his life."

"Oh my God," I breathe. "Your parents must've been a wreck. All three of their babies in an accident."

"Yeah, my mom swears it took ten years off her life." Nate chuckles softly. "Afterward, we went and got these tattoos to symbolize our bond. My brothers are my best friends. We made sure they were where they couldn't be seen unless we wanted them to be. I also have one on my chest."

He lifts his shirt without warning, and I damn near hyperventilate when his abs are exposed, one by one, until all six of them are on display, along with his chiseled chest.

Strength is what we gain from the pain we survive.

The words over his heart are simple, a contradiction to the deep meaning.

"After the accident, Dustin couldn't work because he had some issues with the transplant."

"Is he okay now?"

"Yeah, he's perfectly healthy, driving his wife, Valerie, insane." The way Nate smiles tells me just how fond he is of his family.

"But at the time, it was touch and go, so I took on his job on top of mine." He drops his shirt and scrubs his hand over his face. "I felt guilty because I had been driving even though it wasn't technically my fault. At one point, I was working eighty-hour weeks."

"And that's when you caught your girlfriend cheating," I say, remembering what he told me about his ex and how she slept with his best friend when he was working long hours.

"Yeah," he confirms. "She said I didn't give her enough attention."

"I'm sorry," I say, placing my hand over his heart.

"Part of me blames myself because I did what she accused me of. I neglected her. But she never once mentioned it. If she had told me…"

"I get it," I tell him. "I knew John moving here without me wasn't a good idea, but I let him go."

Nate nods in understanding. "After I caught her cheating, I lost myself for a while. I was drinking and partying. I hit rock bottom, but my family was there to pick me up. They're my strength. I don't know what I would do without them."

"I love that," I say, swallowing down the ball of emotion lodged in my throat. "That's what I want. A family. A home. I felt it when my mom was alive, but when she died, it's like she took the magic with her. Now, I have no one but me."

"You could have me," Nate says softly, framing the sides of my face.

"Only temporarily," I murmur, torn between wishing I'd never met Nate and wanting to simply enjoy every moment I have with him.

He releases a harsh breath and nods.

"But we have London," I point out, forcing a smile to lighten the mood.

"And Bath," he adds, his eyes filled with want as he looks down at me.

"And Bath," I agree, my stomach knotting at the thought of never seeing Nate again. Of my getting on the plane and him turning into nothing more than a memory.

Our eyes lock for several seconds, and a silent agreement is made between us.

Tonight is all we can have.

Tonight, we can be selfish and take what we want.

But tomorrow, we'll have to part ways.

And then our mouths collide in a needy and desperate kiss, our tongues caressing one another. Nate tastes like lust mixed with heartbreak, and I vow to stay in the moment. Tomorrow, when I'm alone once again, I'll allow myself to grieve him, to miss him, but for tonight, I'm going to enjoy him.

His taste.

His touch.

The way he makes me *feel*.

Nate lifts me into his arms and carries me over to the bed. He lays me gently on my back and then breaks the kiss so he can remove my clothes. First, my shirt comes off and then my bra.

When my breasts are exposed, he takes a moment to give them attention. He licks one nipple, eliciting a moan out of me, while he rolls the other between his thumb and forefinger, pinching it with the perfect amount of pressure to send waves of pleasure straight to my core.

He takes my pants and underwear off next, leaving me completely naked under him. I'm about to tell him to take his clothes off, but before I can get the words out, he sits up and drags his shirt over his head, giving me a spectacular view of his body.

"You make me want to work out," I murmur, reaching up and gliding my fingers down the ridges that make up his six-pack.

"You're perfect just the way you are," he says as he pushes his shorts and boxers down his legs and tosses them to the side.

His cock springs free, bobbing against his stomach, and my mouth waters at the sight in front of me. I haven't had sex in five months, and I'm desperate for some dick.

Nate spreads my thighs farther apart and then drops his hands to either side of my head, his body lowering to mine. He holds himself up enough not to crush me, but with his body flush against mine, I can feel his hard length pressed against my belly.

"Are you sure about this?" he asks, his eyes meeting mine. "I don't want to ruin the mood, but you just got out of a relationship…"

"That was over before I even got on the plane," I admit out loud. "I appreciate your concern, and I'd be lying if I said I was one hundred percent over him because feelings can't get shut off like a light switch. But I want this…" I reach between us and wrap my fingers around his shaft, stroking it from root to tip to make my point. "I want you."

I must convince him because without another word, his mouth presses against mine for a quick toe-curling kiss.

When he pulls back, I whimper, not wanting him to stop.

But then he peppers kisses along my jawline and then whispers, "I'm just getting started," into my ear, and his words, mixed with his warm breath, send a bolt of electricity through my body, hitting me straight between my legs.

I tighten my thighs around his hips, craving the friction. It's been too damn long since I've gotten off by anything other than my toys and fingers.

He brushes his lips down my neck, stopping to suck on the sensitive areas of my flesh while I run my fingers through his hair, wanting to touch him anywhere I can.

When he doesn't stop at my breasts and he keeps descending, kissing my belly and then my hip bones, I'm confused—until he gives the hood of my pussy a kiss and then pushes my thighs apart, exposing me.

"Nate," I breathe, tugging on his hair. "What are you doing?"

"I'm about to eat this pussy," he says, his gaze trained on said pussy.

I pop up onto my elbows just in time to see him lean in and

inhale my scent. His eyes close as a moan rumbles through him, and, holy shit, I've never been so turned on.

He parts my lips and dips his face, blocking my view, and then his warm, wet tongue slides up my center, making me drop onto my back with a groan.

Every guy I've been with treated going down on a woman like it was a chore. They wanted their dicks sucked, so they put up with eating a woman out.

But as Nate devours—yes, devours—my pussy, it's clear that this isn't just a chore to him. Moans, which he doesn't attempt to hide, come from him as he licks and sucks on every part of me.

"Fuck, you taste so good," he murmurs, only pulling back long enough to thrust two fingers into me.

Between him massaging my clit, the perfect way his fingers are fucking me, and the feel of his beard scratching my heated flesh, a climax quickly works its way up. I've had plenty of orgasms over the years, but not a single one has prepared me for the expert way Nate rubs my inner walls and flicks my clit.

I want it to last forever, for him to spend hours eating me out—that's how good it feels—but my body is too worked up, and it's been too long.

And when he pushes the flat of his tongue against my swollen nub, I explode. The most intense orgasm I've ever experienced hits me like a tidal wave, wave after delicious wave, as my entire body coils and then comes undone. I scream out Nate's name as spots cloud my vision, so I close my eyes.

Nate doesn't stop until I'm so sensitive and wrung out that I lazily push him off me, unable to handle another second of his mouth on me. My heart is pounding in my chest, and I briefly wonder if you can have a heart attack from an orgasm.

When he sits back on his haunches, his beautiful brown eyes

meet mine while he makes a show of licking my juices off his lips, and my stomach knots at the thought that tonight is all we have. Tomorrow, I have to go back to the hotel and deal with the rehearsal and dinner afterward. Saturday is the wedding. Maybe we could spend some time together on Sunday if he's not busy. But then Monday, I leave. I have a car scheduled to pick me up at four in the morning because I have an early flight. And that will be it. Nate will go his way, and I'll go mine.

"Get out of your head," Nate says, climbing up my body. "It's just you and me in this moment. All the other shit will be there tomorrow."

He presses his mouth to mine, parting my lips so his tongue can delve in, giving me a taste of myself, while I reach down and wrap my fingers around his shaft.

He's already hard, and I'm wet, so it doesn't take much to guide him into me. He's thick and long, and he stretches me like he was made for me.

When he's all the way in, I hook my legs around his waist, and he starts to fuck me with the same amount of passion he ate me. Every thrust is deep and purposeful, meant to bring me pleasure as well. Nate is the most selfless lover I've ever been with, and I'm already envious of the woman who will get to spend her life with him.

My orgasm starts to build again, and I feel Nate's cock start to swell inside me. We're both close, our bodies working with each other to bring us pleasure.

"Paige," Nate whispers against my lips, his facial hair tickling my flesh. "I don't want to ruin the moment, but you feel so good, and I just realized it's because I forgot to put on a condom. Fuck, baby, please tell me I can come in your perfect cunt."

Shit! I knew it felt too good to be true. I suck at taking birth control, and I hate the thought of something being put inside of me, so I've always insisted on guys using condoms to prevent pregnancy.

"I'm sorry," I mutter. "I'm not on anything. You have to pull out."

Nate groans but nods in understanding. Then, he picks up his pace, fucking me deeper, harder, and for a moment, I think he's going to say *fuck it* and come in me. And when my climax hits and I come for the second time, I don't even think about the consequences until he pulls out and takes his shaft in his hand. He strokes it a few times, and then ropes of cum spurt out, painting ribbons of white across my belly.

"I need more," he murmurs, dropping his hands on either side of me, not giving a shit that with his body pressed against mine, his cum is spreading all over us. "More of you. Tonight can't be the only night I get with you. I'll take any day or night you'll give me. Please."

The desperation in his voice causes me to choke up. I've never had a man want me like this—like I'm the air he needs to survive—and it makes me want to throw my fears out the window and give him everything…all of me. Because this is what I've always wanted. To be someone's everything. And in this moment, as Nate looks at me, it's as if I'm just that to him.

But I know this is the oxytocin and dopamine talking. Tomorrow, when we're no longer orgasm-drunk, we'll be thinking clearly.

So, I say the only thing I can say even though it hurts like hell. "Tonight is all we can have."

Nate sighs but nods because he respects my boundaries enough to accept them even if he doesn't agree with them.

"Then I'm going to make the most of it." He presses a kiss to the corner of my mouth and then sits up. "First, we shower, and then we'll call for new sheets because you soaked the hell out of them when you squirted."

"What?" I gasp, scrambling back.

Sure enough, in between us is a huge wet spot.

"Oh my God," I groan in embarrassment. "I swear that's never happened."

"Good." Nate smirks. "That means none of those other assholes were able to make you come as hard as I did."

He's not wrong.

"On second thought." He glances from the wet spot back up to me. "We'd better keep the sheets on the bed for now because I have every intention of making you squirt all over my face again."

Without giving me a chance to argue, he scoops me up into his arms and carries me to the shower, where he makes me come again before he does exactly as he promised and makes me come all over his mouth…twice more.

And the entire time, I have to keep reminding myself that tomorrow, despite wanting to keep Nate forever, I'm going to have to let him go.

CHAPTER NINE

Nate

I SHOULD BE ASLEEP. IT'S NEARLY SIX IN THE MORNING, AND I've yet to go to sleep. But my brain won't shut down long enough for me to fall asleep. This happens when I'm immersed in a project or there's an issue that needs to be handled.

As the COO of Bradford Hotels, I'm the go-to man. My dad might wear the CEO title, but I'm the person everyone goes to when they need an approval or have a question. So, everything tends to rest on my shoulders.

And when something's wrong, when there's a situation that needs my attention, my brain goes into overdrive. It doesn't stop until I've figured out a solution, and then I crash.

Right now, my brain is in overdrive because I have a situation that I can't control—Paige. She's lying next to me, her head tucked into the crook of my arm, her body and limbs half thrown over me, like she's the most adorable octopus.

She started off sleeping on her side of the bed, but then she gravitated toward me. It's been a long time since I slept in a bed with a woman, even longer since I allowed one to cuddle with me. And I'd be lying if I said I didn't notice how perfectly she fits against me.

Which is why I can't sleep. Because it's been less than forty-eight hours since I met her, and I already know I could fall in love with her. The woman makes it too damn easy with her soft smiles and melodic laughs and the way she wears her heart on her sleeve. She was kicked to the ground, but she's strong and positive, and she refuses to let anything keep her down. She got up, shook herself off, and held her head up high.

One day, some guy is going to see how amazing she is, and he's going to get to keep her, unlike me. Because we live four hours away from each other. Four fucking hours. An hour by plane. But Paige has a life in Houston, and I have one in Dallas, and no matter how much I try to solve that problem, it comes back to the fact that one of us would have to move. And neither of us is in a position to do so. Which means when we get back to the hotel in a couple of hours, I have to let her walk away.

"Why aren't you sleeping?" Paige murmurs, her voice raspy from sleep.

She stretches her arms and legs, and when they glide across my body, her eyes widen as she realizes she's spread out across me.

She tries to move, but I tighten my hold around her, needing a few more minutes with her body wrapped around mine before I'm forced to let her go.

As if she knows what I'm doing, she sighs into me and lets me have the time I need. And then her hand slides down my shirtless torso—since she stole my shirt to wear last night after the second time we had sex and showered—and under my boxer briefs. She wraps her fingers around my shaft and languorously strokes it up and down, using the pre-cum beading on the tip of my head to create a bit of friction.

She pulls my shorts down enough to expose my entire length, and I close my eyes, enjoying the feel of her hand on me, trying to burn her touch into my brain for the nights after she's gone and I'm left with only my memories.

I'm so lost in my own head that I don't realize she's moved down until her lips wrap around the crown of my cock and she takes damn near the entire length of me down her throat.

My eyes pop open, and my gaze goes straight to the gorgeous woman who's on her knees, bent over me, sucking my dick like she's on a mission.

Her shirt has bunched up, showing her pert, bare ass—because I told her if I was going without a shirt, then she was going without underwear, and she agreed.

As if she can sense I'm thinking about and looking at her ass, she shakes it teasingly, and I give it a good, hard slap, making her moan around my cock.

"You like that?" I ask, massaging the area I just slapped.

A muffled, "Yes," comes out of her, so I do it again, this time on the other cheek, earning another moan out of her.

"If we had more time, I'd beg you to let me take this ass," I tell her, imagining the way her tight hole would gape open as I pushed my entire length into her. The way her ass would jiggle as I fucked her from behind.

The thought has my cock swelling, and before I come down her throat, I reach up and pull her face off me and drag her up my body so she's straddling me.

"Hey." She pouts. "You were close."

"And I'll be damned if I'm going to finish in your mouth."

"Well, you can't finish in *me*," she sasses. "At least that's a hole that won't end with me pregnant."

She's being cheeky, but my mind immediately goes to Paige, swollen with my baby, and suddenly, I'm angry. Not at the thought of her pregnant, but at the fact that it'll never happen—at least not by me, thanks to the universe working against us and putting us hours away from each other. The idea of another guy getting to come in her, filling her with his seed, has me damn near seeing red.

She's mine.

But she's not.

Needing a release for the frustration and anger flowing through my veins, I grab Paige's hips and lift her off me so she's on her hands and knees, facing the headboard, with my damn shirt covering her perfect ass.

"Take the shirt off," I demand, needing to see all of her.

My words come out harsh, but I can't help it. I hate when shit is out of my control.

She wastes no time sliding the shirt over her head, exposing her smooth, flawless, tanned skin, and then she looks back at me, her brows furrowed in concern.

"I hate this," I growl, answering her unspoken question. "I need more fucking time."

I reach under her and roughly thrust two fingers into her warmth, and she groans in response.

"We don't have more time," she whispers, her tone laced with regret, which only adds to my aggravation.

I'm a rich man. There are very few things I don't have at my disposal and even less I can't get my hands on if I'm willing to pay to have it. But Paige is unavailable, and no amount of money will change that.

I reach out and fist her long hair, pulling her head back enough so that I can lean over and kiss her sweet lips. She moans into my mouth at my roughness, and my cock hardens.

"I wanna fuck you," I murmur into her ear, "hard and deep. I wanna make you scream and come all over my cock. Tell me I can fuck you how I want."

"Yes! Please, Nate, fuck me."

I thrust my fingers in and out of her a few times to make sure she's ready while I memorize the way she feels, the sounds she makes, and then I replace them with the head of my cock.

I don't go slow. I shove into her tightness, not stopping until I bottom out, and then I start to fuck her just as I said. Hard, fast, and deep. In this position, with her ass in the air, I'm able to hit her G-spot perfectly. And before long, her pussy is gripping my shaft, and she's coming, soaking my cock with her sweet juices.

For a split second, I consider not pulling out and filling her with my seed. The vision of her round with my baby flashes before my eyes, but I can't do that to her. It wouldn't be fair to either of us. I knew going into this that we could never be more. She made it clear, and I have to respect it even if I hate it.

So, when my balls tighten, despite wishing I could coat her walls with my cum, I pull out and jerk myself off. Ribbons of white splatter onto her pert ass, and I take a moment to memorize the way she looks—perfectly fucked.

She dips her head and tilts it back so her satiated green eyes meet mine, and my heart squeezes in my chest because I know this is where our story ends.

And, fuck, does that suck.

⋈

"Mr. Bradford, I don't think it's possible to—"

"Don't tell me it's impossible. Everything is possible. You just have to find a way, and if you can't, I'll find someone who can."

I hang up and slam my phone on the desk, refusing to look at Nolan, who's no doubt staring at me like I've lost my mind. And he wouldn't be wrong. I have.

I never raise my voice. It doesn't matter how mad I get, how fucked up shit gets, I always handle it like a professional. But right now, I'm not myself.

It's been twelve hours since Paige and I arrived at the hotel and said our goodbyes. She's here until Monday morning, but I didn't ask to see her again because I could see it in her eyes that it would be too hard.

But now, I can't stop thinking about her. Wondering how she's doing. She had to go to the wedding rehearsal and then dinner, where her asshole ex would be. He'd texted her to let her know that he'd be bringing his new girlfriend to the dinner and wanted to give her a heads-up so she wasn't blindsided.

I wanted to offer to go with her, suggest she bail on the wedding and we could go somewhere else, anywhere else, but I kept my mouth shut because she was determined to see that stupid fucking wedding through.

So, instead, in the lobby, in front of the elevator, I kissed her, selfishly needing one last taste, and then wished her the best.

And then I went up to my room and tried to work. Only instead, I'm yelling at people and thinking about Paige.

"Maybe you should head back early," Nolan suggests. "I can handle things here."

I appreciate his offer, but the thought of leaving before Paige tears me apart.

"I'm going to get a drink at the bar."

I need some air. And secretly, I'm hoping maybe I'll run into

Paige. It's a long shot, but we are staying at the same hotel, so anything's possible.

When I get down to the bar, it's busy since it's a Friday night, and almost all the seats are taken. I'm about to head back up to my room, not wanting to be around other people, when brown hair with blonde highlights catches my attention. I would recognize that hair anywhere.

I move to the side so I can get a better look at her just in time to see her tilt her head back and down a shot. She slams it on the bar top and then grabs another, swallowing it in one go.

I should walk away, leave her alone, because we already said our goodbyes…but then a gentleman walks over to her, and I can't hear what he's saying, but I can see the sleazy expression on his face.

I'm going to have a word with the bar manager about letting assholes hit on women who have been drinking. This isn't a fucking club. It's an upscale bar in a luxury five-star hotel.

Paige shakes her head and turns her body away from him, making it clear she doesn't want whatever he's selling. She downs another shot, and the guy says something else. Another shake of her head, and then she twists her body in the other direction, attempting to leave. Only her foot gets caught on the leg of the barstool to her right, and she trips, her high heel flying off her foot and under the bar.

I rush over to help her, and she looks up at me with glassy eyes. She's drunk.

"Nate," she slurs. "Are you here to save me?"

Her smile is wobbly, and my heart sinks. The rehearsal must've gone badly.

"I can't seem to find my shoe," she says, looking down at her bare foot. "It must be here somewhere." She tries to bend down to find it, but in her drunken state, she almost falls over.

"C'mon," I say, guiding her to a chair. "Sit right here, and I'll get your heel."

She plops down and smiles softly, and once I know she's not going to tip over, I go back over to the bar and find her heel. I also notice she left her purse hanging on the back of the chair, so I grab that as well.

"Here you go," I say, getting on one knee and lifting her foot so I can put it on her since she's most likely too drunk to do it herself. I'd suggest she take the other one off, but with her luck, she'd step on something and cut her foot.

When I lift her foot to slide her heel on, Paige giggles loudly.

"My prince," she says. "It's just like in the fairy tale."

When I give her a questioning look, she huffs. "*Cinderella*," she clarifies. "She loses her glass slipper, and the prince finds it. He puts it back on her foot, and they live happily ever after."

Her smile morphs into a frown. "Only you can't be my prince because we don't get a happily ever after." Tears prick her eyes, and my heart feels like it's being clenched with barbwire.

"C'mon," I say, standing, since there's nothing I can say to make this better. "Let's get you up to your room."

She nods and tries to stand, but it's not happening. She's drunk too much, and tomorrow, I'll be firing whoever served her this much alcohol.

Reaching down, I lift her into my arms and carry her through the hotel and up to her room.

On the way, she confirms my suspicions when she tells me that the dinner was horrible and she has nobody.

"I don't wanna go to the wedding tomorrow," she whispers, making my heart bleed. "Everyone has someone but me."

The sadness in her voice damn near sends me to my knees.

I know her room number, so once we're there, I find her key card in her purse and open the door. She's half asleep by the time I lay her in her bed. I take her heels off so she's comfortable, but I leave her clothes on, not wanting to do anything without her permission.

"I wish you were my prince," she murmurs, tears sliding down her cheeks as I tuck the blanket around her.

"I do too," I whisper, swiping my thumb along the apples of her cheeks as her eyes flutter shut. "Now, sleep, Princess. I've got you."

Then, I get comfortable in the chair in the corner of her room and watch her sleep until the sun begins to rise and I know she'll be okay. I have Nolan bring me up two pain relievers, and I leave them on her nightstand with a bottle of water. I set the alarm on her phone for nine a.m., so she can sleep in and still have enough time to get ready for the wedding.

And then I go up to my room to get ready because I'll be damned if Paige is going to spend another moment alone with those assholes. Paige doesn't know it yet, but she now has a plus-one for the wedding.

CHAPTER TEN

THE WEDDING VENUE IS BEAUTIFUL. THE DECORATIONS are tasteful. The bridesmaid dresses complement the color palette—and surprisingly aren't ugly. Because I came from out of town, I couldn't try on my dress until last night at the rehearsal, but it fits perfectly.

Marina apologized profusely for me having to walk down the aisle with John, but because their wedding party consists of five couples, it would be rude to ask another couple not to walk down the aisle together.

So, I had no choice but to walk arm in arm with John while Phoebe guiltily stared at us from the sidelines. He tried to apologize again, but I told him to save it. After this is over, I have no intention of ever seeing any of these people again. London is no longer my home—and if I'm honest, it hasn't been since my mom died. It's time to move forward, and when I get on the plane on Monday morning, I plan to do just that.

Last night was hard, coming to the realization that I not only wasted years with John, but because of the distance, Nate can't be in my future either.

It's not that I'm desperate to be with a man, but it hurts to keep letting people in, only for them to disappoint, die, or disappear.

I gave my mom my heart—and she left me.

I gave it to my dad—and he no longer wanted it.

John stomped on it.

And Nate…well, I think he would gladly take it, but I can't give it to him because I have no doubt that if I do, what's left of my fragile organ will end up shattered. Maybe it could be different with Nate, but relationships are already hard as it is, let alone adding distance to the mix. So, instead of setting us up for failure, it's best that we don't attempt it.

When I leave here and go back home, my plan is to focus on myself. I've spent so much time trying to make other people happy that I haven't considered what I need and deserve.

With my mom, it was all about her because she was sick—yet she still gave up and died.

With my dad, I tried to be a good daughter, hoping I would be enough for him after my mom passed away—but he still got himself a new family.

With John, I put my career and feelings on the back burner, wanting to be everything he needed in a partner—but he still cheated on me.

And with Nate, sadly, I'll never find out.

"Do you, Paul Sullivan, take…"

As the bride and groom recite their vows, I tune them out, not in the mood to listen to two people profess their love for one another.

Instead, my thoughts go back to last night. I was in such a

poor mood after seeing John and Phoebe that I went straight to the bar to have a drink—which turned into several more.

It wasn't the fact that they were together that had me upset. The truth is, they barely touched each other all night. It was that they—and what feels like everyone else—get to create a life with the person they love.

My best friend, Ana, found her husband when she was only supposed to be using him to get control of her dad's company. Now, they're married with two precious little ones and beyond happy.

My other friend Kira was hired as a nanny by Kingston's CFO, Ryder. They fell in love and are about to be married next month. They found the person they wanted to spend their life with, and they get to be with them.

Meanwhile, I found someone I could see a future with. A man who is so good that he brought me back to my room and took care of me while I was drunk, left pain relievers and water on the nightstand, and had breakfast and coffee delivered this morning, but instead of getting to see where things go, I have to get on a plane and try to forget he ever existed.

"I now pronounce you husband and wife. You may kiss the bride," the officiant announces, zapping me out of my self-loathing thoughts.

I exhale a sigh of relief that this ordeal is half over. My goal is to go to the reception and be announced with the rest of the bridal party and then skip out when no one is looking. I doubt anyone would notice anyway.

Marina and Paul kiss, and everyone claps, and then we all file out so we can take pictures before the reception starts.

As I stand next to John, forced to smile, I consider getting drunk again to numb the pain of the loneliness I feel.

"You look beautiful," John whispers, making me roll my eyes. "I was hoping we could talk…"

"There's nothing to say," I mutter, keeping my smile plastered on my face.

The pictures thankfully go quickly, and soon enough, we're being announced. The bride and groom have their dance, followed by the bride dancing with her father, and then the bridal party is called to the dance floor.

One dance, I remind myself, and then I can get the hell out of here.

John places his hands on my hips, and I wrap mine around his neck, and even though our bodies are close, I've never felt so alone in my life. As we sway to the song, I can't help but look at how happy everyone is. The bride and groom are laughing and kissing, so deeply in love and looking forward to what the future holds. Couples are talking and smiling, dancing.

I don't even realize I'm crying until John squeezes my arm, and I look up at him.

"I'm so sorry," he murmurs. "I fucked up. I was lonely and—"

"These tears aren't for you," I snap, angrily swatting them away.

"Look, I know—"

"Excuse me," a masculine voice cuts in. One I'd recognize any-where. It's deep and throaty, and I have no doubt I'll be fantasizing about it for months after I leave London.

I glance over and find none other than Nate standing in front of John and me, dressed sharply in a black suit. His hair is styled, and he's trimmed his beard. He looks like sex on a stick.

"Who are you?" John asks, not even attempting to hide his jealousy.

"Paige's date," Nate states without sparing John another

glance. "You look devastatingly gorgeous," he tells me, his eyes staying trained on mine. "May I have this dance?"

"It's for the bridal party," John spits out.

"I'd love to," I say to Nate, backing out of John's hold and going straight into Nate's arms.

He gives me a soft smile, wraps his arms around me, and glides us away from John, leaving him standing there, looking dumbstruck.

"What are you doing here?" I whisper as we slow dance.

"I heard you needed a date," is all Nate says before he leans down and kisses each of my cheeks, where my traitorous tears were still lingering.

I should probably push him away and tell him this can't be happening because spending more time with him will only hurt more when I have to leave, but the fact that he showed up without me asking has my heart swelling inside my chest.

So, instead of arguing, I place my head against his shoulder, inhaling his warm and sensual scent, and murmur, "Thank you."

"Anytime," he says, tightening his hold on me. "And I wasn't kidding when I said you look gorgeous. The way this dress accentuates your curves…" He glides his hands down to my ass and gives it a squeeze. "I'm tempted to find the closest restroom and fuck you against the wall."

His words go straight to my lady parts as I imagine him doing just that, and I glance around the room, wondering if I can spot a restroom.

Instead of finding one though, my gaze lands on John and Phoebe sitting at the table. John is glaring daggers my way, and Phoebe is looking from John to me with hurt etched in her features.

"Ignore him," Nate says. "He fucked up, and now, he's regretting it."

"But why?" I ask, confused. "He did this. He wanted her. He *chose* her."

"Because"—Nate palms the side of my face, tilting it up so I'm looking at him—"you're not the kind of woman men get over. Your smile, your laughter, your sexy body…everything about you is addictive. That asshole left and found a warm body to try to fill in your absence. But now that you're here, he's wishing he hadn't fucked up."

Nate leans in closer and presses an open-mouthed kiss on the sensitive part of my neck. "He's watching us," he whispers as he trails kisses along my jawline. "Wishing he hadn't done what he did." He kisses the corner of my mouth. "Because that woman sitting next to him is nothing more than a cheap knockoff. She'll never be you, and he knows that."

Nate runs his tongue along my bottom lip and then the top, and I groan into his mouth, wanting more than he can give me on this dance floor.

"Let's get out of here," I murmur against his mouth.

Not needing to be told twice, Nate guides me off the dance floor and toward the doors. But instead of exiting, he veers to the right, straight for the restrooms.

He pulls me inside, locks the door, and then lifts me up, setting me on the edge of the counter.

Normally, I wouldn't be down for a restroom fuck, but this one is luxurious, marble sinks and floor and walls. It smells like a mixture of cleanliness and baby powder, and the thought of fucking Nate in here while everyone is right outside the door has me squirming in my spot.

Nate doesn't waste any time gripping the silky material and lifting it up to my hips, exposing my panties.

"Fuck, I should've brought you back to your room," he mutters. "The things I want to do to you…"

He shakes his head as he reaches behind me, delves his fingers into my hair, and pulls me in for a hard kiss that warms my insides.

As his skilled mouth ravages mine, I have no doubt that I could kiss this man every day for the rest of my life, and it wouldn't be enough.

The chemistry between us heats as I reach down and unbutton Nate's pants, taking his dick out and stroking it while he pushes two fingers into me.

"Fuck me," I groan, needing to feel him inside me.

There's no reason for foreplay. We're both turned on and ready.

Nate removes my panties, stuffs them into his pocket, and then grips my hips, pulling me to the edge. When he thrusts into me in one fluid movement, it stokes the flames that have been building between us, setting my body on fire.

Nate kisses me like he fucks me—deeply, passionately—like the world is about to end and this is the last time he'll be able to be with me like this. And I guess, in a way, it is.

"Stay with me," he growls into my mouth, as if he can hear my unspoken thoughts. "Reach between us and stroke your clit."

I've never been with anyone so attuned to my feelings and desires, and it's both a blessing and a curse because when I'm with him, I feel more seen and heard than I've ever felt in my life, and I doubt I'll ever find anyone like Nate. He's going to be the man I compare every guy against in the future. He'll be the one I let get away.

I find my release first, and Nate deepens the kiss to muffle the scream that rips through me as I come undone. And then, at the last second, he pulls out and backs up, coming in his hand.

"Thank God you remembered," I murmur through a pant, earning a laugh from Nate as he walks over to the sink next to me to wash his hands and clean himself up.

I hop off the counter and use the restroom, and when I come out, I find him leaning against the counter, somehow looking even sexier than he did when he approached me on the dance floor.

"What do you say we get out of here and go get something to eat?"

My stomach drops at his question because I want to say yes, but I know I can't. I wasn't even supposed to see him today, let alone be with him like this.

"I can't," I murmur, shaking my head. "It's already going to be too hard."

Before I can finish my sentence, Nate eats up the space between us and pulls me into his arms. "It doesn't have to be." He tips my chin up. "Please," he pleads softly. "I know it sounds insane, but I've *fallen in love* with you, Princess."

Princess…

My thoughts are transported back to last night.

"I wish you were my prince."

"I do too. Now, sleep, Princess. I've got you."

But he can't be my prince because we live too far apart, and when I get on the plane, we'll have hundreds, if not thousands, of miles between us.

"No." I shake my head and step out of his touch. "This was only temporary. We both knew this. You don't live near me. Sure, we'll start off strong. We'll video-chat and text, and we'll make plans to see each other. But life will get in the way, and shit will happen. And days of not seeing each other will turn into weeks and then months."

"I'm not him," Nate reminds me, as if I don't already know how different the two men are. "I'm fucking rich. I can fly from—"

"No!" I cover his mouth. "It can't happen. My heart already hurts, and you're still standing in front of me. Imagine how badly it will hurt when I have to go weeks and months without seeing you. And when does it end? Who moves to be with who? Are you in a place to move to be with me?"

Nate opens and then closes his mouth, his features morphing from a look of hope to defeat because he knows I'm right.

"Please don't do this." I reach up and place my hand on the side of his face. "If things were different…" I sniffle back a sob.

"Okay," he whispers. "I'll let you go, but only because you want me to."

I nod in understanding, then get on my tiptoes and give him a soft kiss on his cheek. "Thank you for reminding me of the magic," I whisper. "In another lifetime, you would've been my Prince Charming."

And then I walk out of the restroom without glancing back—because I know if I look at him, I might cave.

When I get back to my room, I spend the night and the next day crying, wishing Nate would show up, but knowing he won't because he respects my decision.

On Monday, when I get to the airport, with my luggage in tow, I reach into my purse to grab my passport, but when I pull out my wallet, I find a business card–sized paper in there.

> *Princess, keep this in case you change your mind.*
>
> *—Your Prince*

My heart pounds in my chest. I know if I flip it over, I'll find Nate's information. It will probably have his last name, his phone number, the company he works for. And for a second, I consider keeping it. I don't have to look at it now. I can slip it into my wallet and save it.

But then I remember how much time I wasted with John, trying to hold our relationship together while we were thousands of miles apart. The resentment, the bitterness, the cheating.

And without flipping the card over, I drop it into a garbage can.

It's for the best, I tell myself.

Nate and I will always have London, but that's all we can ever have.

CHAPTER ELEVEN

Two Months Later

"L ET'S GO." ANA PULLS THE COVERS OFF ME AND GLARES daggers my way.

"Did you break into my house?" I groan, swiping at the edge of the covers so I can pull it back over me.

"You gave me a key," she says dryly.

"In case of an emergency," I mutter.

"And you refusing to get out of bed is an emergency." She sighs and sits on the edge of my mattress. "You do this every weekend, and I miss my best friend. You work your ass off during the required hours, and then you hide away in your house every night and weekend."

"I'm tired," I choke out.

"No, you're heartbroken," she argues.

"It was only a fling. Not long enough to be heartbroken over."

"The heart doesn't know time. It knows feelings, and you caught feelings for this guy. But you made your choice to walk away. You threw away the card with his information, and now, it's time to move on."

"I'd rather sleep," I grumble. "I'm tired, and I don't feel good."

"Do you think you've caught something?" she asks in concern.

Yeah, I've caught something all right. And if my calculations are correct, in November, my sickness will end when I push a baby out of me.

I've been throwing up almost every day for the past few weeks. I'm not an idiot. I know what this means. But I'm choosing to remain in denial. Because if I am pregnant, what the hell am I going to do?

"I'm fine," I say, not wanting to voice my concerns yet. That will make it real.

"Okay, then get up. Today is our book club and barbecue."

Damn it, I forgot about that.

Every month, we read a new romance novel and get together to talk about it, along with Kira, and Kira's husband, Ryder. After we've discussed it, we go online—Ana has an online group, where they all read it as well—and talk about it with the group.

After I'm showered and dressed, I follow Ana back to her place in my car so I can drive home later. When we walk in, Kira, Ryder, and Ana's husband, Julian, are sitting on the couch, chatting, while the kids are running around and playing.

"Hi, Auntie Paige!" Kingston, Ana and Julian's almost two-year-old son, calls out from where he's setting up his train tracks. The boy is obsessed with trains.

"Hey, King."

Julian comes over and gives me a quick kiss on my cheek, and then Ana, Kira, Ryder, and I head into the library so we can start our book club discussion.

Waiting for us is a table filled with food. My stomach growls since I haven't eaten today, but I make it a point to take it slow, hoping it will all stay down.

"I knew she was pregnant," Kira says, snapping me from my thoughts.

"What?" I breathe. *How the hell could she know I'm—*

"I knew Sadie was pregnant," Kira clarifies, referring to the female main character in the book we read. "The second she threw up, it was obvious."

"Yeah," Ana agrees. "The first couple of months, I couldn't keep anything down."

"Ugh, and my breasts were sore," Kira adds.

"And I was an emotional mess," Ana says with a fake shiver. "I swear, I cried over everything."

Throwing up—check.

Sore breasts—double check.

Emotional—fuck!

"I think I'm pregnant," I blurt out, tears filling my eyes.

"What?" Ana gasps at the same time Kira says, "How?"

"Wait…" Ana's eyes go wide. "The guy in London? Nate?"

"Who's Nate?" Ryder finally jumps in.

"You met a guy in London?" Julian steps into the room with Emilia, their eleven-month-old daughter, on his hip.

"Yeah," I admit. Kira and Ana already know about him, but the guys don't. "After I caught John cheating, I went to the hotel where the wedding was being held…"

I explain how I met Nate and we hit it off. When I get to the part about how I threw away his card, Julian and Ryder both curse under their breath. Every time I tell this story, it never gets easier.

"I thought I was saving myself from more heartbreak," I whisper, tears stinging my eyes. "But now, if I'm pregnant…" My hand protectively goes to my stomach even though there's nothing there yet. "He or she will never know their father."

The tears slide down my cheeks, and Ana and Kira are both on me instantly, pulling me into a hug.

"Maybe you're not even pregnant," Ana says, trying to be positive. "When was your last period?"

"In February, before I left for London for the wedding."

"That was two months ago," Ryder points out. "Have you had any symptoms?"

"Only all the ones Ana and Kira mentioned," I mumble, knowing I'm screwed. "I always wanted a family, but not like this." I shrug, feeling helpless.

"Don't go thinking the worst," Kira says. "If you are pregnant, we can try to find him."

"Really? How?" I ask. "I have a couple of selfies we took, joking around, and the name Nate. Hell, Nate could be short for Nathan or Nathaniel. I know he's a businessman of some sort, but I don't even know the field he works in. Oh, and he's long-distance."

"If you're pregnant, we could do a reverse image search," Julian points out.

"But first, we need to know *if* you are pregnant," Ana says. "And lucky for you, I have plenty of tests left over from when Julian and I were trying for Emilia."

After checking on the kids, who are playing in the playroom with their nanny, Diana, we go to Ana's bathroom so she can grab a test.

When she hands it to me, my stomach knots.

"I'm scared," I admit.

"We're right here," Ana says. "Oh! How about we all take one?"

"I'm down," Kira says. "We've got you, Paige."

The three of us take turns peeing on a stick, leaving them on the counter next to each other. We're waiting for the timer to go off when Julian comes in with Emilia, who's whining to be fed.

We wait while Ana breastfeeds her daughter, and then the three of us and Emilia pile into the bathroom. But before any of us can get a look at the results, Emilia kicks her foot out, wanting to be let down, and the three pregnancy tests go flying off the counter and onto the floor.

"Emilia," Ana scolds her daughter with zero heat in her voice. "Give me a second so I can give her back to Diana."

She leaves the room, and Kira and I stare down at the tests still on the floor. One is facing up and reads NOT PREGNANT. Another one reads PREGNANT, and my heart sinks.

Kira flips the last one over since it fell screen down, and it reads PREGNANT.

"Oh shit," I whisper at the same time she snorts out a laugh.

"So?" Ryder asks, leaning against the doorframe. "How did it go?"

"Well, two of us are pregnant," Kira says with a smirk.

"Two?" Ryder lifts a brow. "Who all took a pregnancy test?"

"We all took one to support Paige," Ana says, walking back into the room with Julian since this is apparently a group activity.

"I was just telling Ryder that two of them are positive," Kira says, "but because Emilia knocked them off the counter, we don't know who's pregnant."

"It'd better not be you," Julian says with a chuckle to his wife.

"It's definitely not me," Ana says with an eye roll. "You had a vasectomy."

"That doesn't mean you can't get pregnant." There's laughter in Julian's tone, but Ana glares.

"Are you trying to say I'd cheat on you?"

"No!" Julian pulls her into his arms. "I'm trying to say maybe my sperm is so strong that it made it through and still managed to knock you up."

Ryder laughs, and Julian says, "What are you laughing at? One of those positive tests could be Kira's."

"I sure as fuck hope so," Ryder says with love shining in his eyes at his wife, which reminds me that if one of the positive tests is mine, I don't have a loving husband to do this with.

I'm on my own, and unless I find Nate by some miracle, I'll be raising this baby alone.

"I have more tests," Ana announces. "And this time, we'll write our names on them."

She grabs a Sharpie, and after we write our names on our tests, we take turns going pee again—which isn't easy since we all just went.

Six minutes later, Ana's test reads NOT PREGNANT, Kira's reads PREGNANT, and mine, of course, reads PREGNANT.

Kira screeches in excitement while Ryder hugs her, telling her how excited he is. And Ana walks over to me, still staring at my positive test.

"What are you going to do?" she asks softly, rubbing her hand up and down my arm.

"I don't know." The words cause a dam to break deep inside me, and as Ana pulls me into her arms, I cry harder than I've ever cried.

I want this baby. I already love him or her. But I don't want to do it on my own. I've always wanted a family, but in my head, it in-cluded a doting husband who loves me. Not me as a single mom, raising a baby alone.

"I know, right now, it sucks," Kira says, reining in her excite-ment to be a friend. "But I did it on my own, and, yes, it was hard, but I promise you, your baby will not be loved any less. Not only will they have you, but they'll have all of us as well. And"—her hand goes to her belly—"we'll be pregnant together. Based on the dates, we're only a month apart."

"Thank you." I give Kira and then Ana a hug. "I really appreciate you both. And I'm so happy for you, Kira."

"Send me the pictures you have," Julian says. "Let's see if we can find this guy."

He grabs his laptop, and I email him the two pictures I have—one from the top of the Tower Bridge and the other in Bath, each of us holding a scone to our mouths. I deleted them when I got home, but then in a moment of weakness, I restored them. Now, I'm thankful I did because if I don't find him, I have nothing of him but these two pictures to show our son or daughter one day so they know who their father is even if they can never meet him.

Julian spends the next hour trying to get a match. Several pop up of similar-looking guys, but each one he shows me isn't Nate.

Since the book club discussion was interrupted and the mood has been ruined, we agree to have it another day. We all munch on the food while the kids play, and after we eat, I tell everyone I'm going to head home.

"Are you sure?" Ana asks. "You could stay here. We have a guest room."

"I really appreciate that," I tell her, grateful to have such wonderful friends. "But I think I need some time alone to think about everything."

"I'll keep looking," Julian says. "There are thousands of pictures on there."

"Thank you. I'm going to look as well," I say even though the chances of finding him are slim.

When I get home, I call the hotel and ask to speak to a manager. I explain my situation and ask if they could see if a Nate stayed there.

The woman is nice, but she's no help because even if she could search by the first name, due to privacy laws, she can't give out any-one's information.

After I've changed into my pajamas, I get comfortable on the couch and pull the site up that Julian told me about. I upload one of the photos, and while I scroll through picture after picture of men who aren't Nate, I cry. And when I feel like I'm all cried out and still haven't found Nate, I close my laptop and take a deep breath.

This might not be how I wanted to raise a baby, but this is the reality of my situation. And it could be worse. I own a beautiful house, I have a great career, and I am more than capable of taking care of this baby. And I'll do everything in my power to make sure he or she is loved enough for me and Nate.

At the thought of Nate smiling, laughing, and begging me to give him a chance, I start to cry again.

This is my fault. I'm growing Nate's baby in my belly, and because I refused to exchange information, he'll never know.

That leads me to crying again.

Tomorrow, I tell myself. Tomorrow, I'm going to stop crying and deal with my reality.

But tonight, I'm going to cry.

CHAPTER TWELVE

"I F I HAVE TO HOLD YOUR HAND EVERY STEP OF THE WAY, I might as well appoint myself operations manager and save the company thousands on what we pay you. Next time, do as Valerie told you, and this won't happen."

I press the speaker button on the office phone and slam the receiver down, ending the call.

"Is he fucking serious? I explicitly told him that I needed that meeting set for this week."

"Actually, you barked it," Dustin says dryly. "The same way you've been barking orders for the past two months since you got back from London."

I give him a look that would send others scrambling out of the room, but my brother isn't the least bit affected.

"If people would do their jobs—" Speaking of which…"Where is Nolan?" I glance around for my assistant, who seems to be MIA.

"He's probably hiding from you, like the rest of the staff is,"

Dustin drawls. "And stop your bullshit and save it for someone who doesn't know you."

He leans back and threads his fingers behind his head—his telltale sign that a lecture is coming. I might be the eldest and the COO, but that won't stop my brothers from putting me in my place when need be.

"When are you going to accept that you fell for this woman and go after her?" he asks. "I get it. You agreed to no-strings with her, and you want to respect her decision, but, Jesus, bro, you can't continue like this. You're alienating everyone around you with your moodiness, and this isn't how we run the company."

"He's not wrong," Carmine says, strolling in since the door was partly open. He has a seat in the visitor chair next to Dustin and throws his ankle onto his knee. "I just caught Courtney crying to Nolan in the break room. Something's gotta give. If you need time…"

"Fuck that." Dustin scoffs. "He's had two damn months. He needs to either move the hell on or find her 'cause this moody bull-shit isn't cutting it. The employees are noticing and starting to talk." He hits me with a pointed look. "This is not you, Nate. You're not the asshole who yells at women and makes them cry."

Fuck, he's right. I know he is. But I can't help it. Since Paige walked out of my life, I've been on edge, annoyed at the situation, and taking it out on everyone around me.

"And what is he going to do when he does find her?" Carmine argues.

"I don't know." Dustin throws his arms up. "But he needs to do something because the vibe in this place is not it."

Before Carmine can respond, I cut in, having had enough of them discussing me.

"*He* is in the damn room," I say with a sigh. "And you're right," I tell Dustin. "I need to do something."

My brothers and I don't argue ever. So, for us to be in my office, bickering like we're kids, it's enough for me to open my eyes and accept that I'm not okay and I need to handle my shit.

"Like what?" Carmine asks carefully, concern etched in his features.

My brothers know that Paige lives in Rosemary, thirty minutes outside of Houston—yes, I looked her up because I couldn't help myself—and in order for us to be together, one of us would have to move, and she made it clear that she's not moving, nor should she have to.

"I don't know," I admit. "But I can't continue like this."

I found Paige's social media pages a few days after I got back and was desperate to see her face—after making the mistake of not taking any photos of us with my phone. Every night, I check and refresh, hoping to see a new post, but unfortunately, she doesn't post much, aside from advertisements for Kingston and the various places she's traveled to for work.

Her last post was a photo dump from London—which didn't include any pictures of us, despite her taking a couple, but it did include all the places we'd visited together—with the caption: *Forgot how magical it is here.*

As I swiped through them, remembering our short time together, I was so damn close to messaging and begging her to talk to me. But I left her my contact information, so if she wanted to talk to me, she would reach out. It's been two months, and she hasn't, which tells me all I need to know—she's moved on.

"What if we had a way for you to see her—" Dustin says.

"I already told you—"

"In a business capacity," he finishes.

"What the hell are you talking about?"

"This." Dustin tosses a manila folder he's holding onto my desk and stands. "If you want to see her, there's your way in."

I glance from him to Carmine, who shakes his head. "For the record, I think this is a bad idea, and the only reason I'm going along with it is because Dustin bullied me into it."

"Fuck you." Dustin laughs. "You're the one who brought it up to me!"

"No, I was simply presenting you with the proposal since you're the money man," Carmine argues. "You're the one that insisted we share this with Nate."

"Share what?" I ask, opening the folder.

Only once I do, I no longer need either of them to explain because right there in black and white is the solution to my problem.

"You're welcome." Dustin smirks. "Now, quit being a fucking dick and go get your woman."

CHAPTER THIRTEEN

One Month Later

"THE HOUSE IS BEAUTIFUL." I GLANCE AT KIRA, WHO'S grinning happily, her hand on her belly despite her being only eight weeks along.

She said because she's already had one baby, it's common to show quicker, but I can't help but wonder if maybe something is wrong with me—or maybe I'm not actually pregnant. I have an appointment tomorrow morning with my OB/GYN, so I'll find out then.

"Thank you," Kira says. "I was surprised when Ryder suggested moving since our old place was plenty big enough for our growing family."

"It is," I agree, "but it's not about the size of the house that makes it feel like a home."

I moved more times than I could count, growing up, so I know firsthand that not every house feels like a home. Hell, the house my dad bought in Florida with his wife was the most beautiful, over-the-top house I'd ever lived in, but it never felt like home. Then again, I bought a house I loved, decorated it how I wanted, and it still doesn't feel quite like home.

"I can't wait to decorate the baby's room," Kira gushes. "I told Ryder there's no way we're waiting to know the gender." She laughs, but when she glances at me, she immediately stops.

"Don't do that," I say. "We're friends, and I'm so happy that you're happy, and I don't want you hiding it because my life is a mess." I look from Kira to Ana. "Neither of you."

Both women nod in understanding.

"How are you doing?" Ana asks softly.

"I'm okay," I lie, not wanting to bring Kira and Ryder's house-warming party down with my negativity.

"Don't do that," Ana says, repeating the words I just said to Kira. "You don't want us to hide our true feelings. Well, we don't want you to hide yours either."

"What do you want me to say?" I choke out, my emotions getting the better of me. "I messed up. I hooked up with a stranger, and now, I'm pregnant."

"First of all," Ana says, "you didn't *hook up* with a stranger. You met a man and fell for him. Don't belittle the time you spent together. We've listened to you talk about him, and it wasn't just a one-night stand."

"And even if it had been," Kira adds, "there is nothing wrong with that. After the shit your asshole of an ex pulled, you deserved to get laid."

"Damn right she did," Ana agrees.

"Well, it doesn't matter what it was because the outcome is

the same. I'm pregnant, and in less than six months, I'll be a single mom."

Tears fill my eyes, and I close them, trying to stop the liquid emotion from seeping out, but like every time I think of Nate, they spill over.

"This just isn't how I wanted this all to go down," I rasp. "And the worst part isn't that I'll be a single mom. I can handle that, especially since I have two of the best moms I know as friends." I smile a watery smile at Kira and Ana. "It's that Nate's out there somewhere with no clue that there's a baby with his DNA growing in my belly. I don't even know if he wants to be a dad, but because of my stupidity, I took the choice away from him, and there's nothing I can do to fix it."

Sobs rack my body as both women pull me into a hug, telling me it's going to be okay. And I want to believe them, but right now, it feels like I'm at my lowest point. I'm emotional and terrified, and I just want to crawl under my covers and go to sleep for a long time even though I know it won't solve anything.

My phone rings in my back pocket, and we break apart, so I can check it. I hired a PI to try to find Nate, so every time the phone rings, I rush to answer it in hopes that it's him with some information.

"It's my dad," I say when I look at my phone.

"Answer it," Ana encourages, knowing I haven't told my dad the news yet.

He called me right after I found out, and I didn't answer. Since then, he's been calling every few days, but I haven't had the courage to tell him I'm pregnant and I have no idea where the dad is. I think a part of me is afraid this might be what drives him away for good.

"Okay, I'll meet you guys out back."

Kira and Ryder are barbecuing, and everyone is spending the afternoon by their pool since it's a beautiful day.

"Hey, Dad," I say as I step outside to the front of the house. There's a cute bench near the door, so I have a seat on it.

"Paige." He sighs. "I've been worried about you."

The way his concern sounds genuine has me flinching because we both know he doesn't really care. And honestly, I don't even know why he continues with these monthly calls or why I answer them.

I tell myself that he's the last connection I have to my mom, to the family I once had, and if I cut him off completely, that will be it.

But, as I sit here, with my own baby growing in my belly—a baby I can't fathom ever not wanting—I question why I keep allowing this cycle to continue. My mom is gone, and she heard what he said about me, so I don't believe she'd ever fault me for completely removing him from my life.

"Paige," he says again, snapping me from my thoughts. "Are you okay?"

"I'm pregnant," I blurt out.

"Oh," he says. "Well, congratulations. Is John excited?"

"It's not John's," I admit. "We broke up, and I was with someone else. It was an accident, but I'm still thrilled."

And as the words leave my mouth, I realize I really do mean that. Sure, things are messy, I have no idea how to find Nate, and I don't know what the future holds, but I'm thrilled to be a mom.

My thoughts go back to when my mom was alive and the relationship we shared. She loved me more than anything in this world, and even though my dad didn't want me, she did, the same way I want this baby.

"Well, that's okay," Dad says. "As long as you're happy, that's all that matters. I know you're busy, but I was thinking we could visit you. It's been a long time, and I'd love to see you. And the girls would love to meet their sister."

Soon after Kristin was born, Ashleigh came along. The girls must be close to being teenagers, and I've yet to spend any time with them, aside from the few times I saw Kristin when she was a baby.

I don't get it. For a man who flat-out said he didn't want me, why does he always do this? Why does he call and beg to see me? It doesn't make any sense. I consider calling him out on it, but sitting on a bench in front of Kira's new home isn't the place to do so. I also read that stress isn't good for the baby, so there's that.

"I can't," I tell him. "Work is crazy, and now, I need to start getting ready to be a mom. And since the dad isn't in the picture—"

"What do you mean?" he asks. "Where is he?"

"I don't know," I admit truthfully. "But it doesn't matter. I'm going to be a mom, and I need to focus on that."

"Okay," Dad relents. "But if you need anything…"

If I need anything, I'll do what I've been doing since my mom died—handle it myself.

"Thanks," I say. "Have a good rest of your weekend."

"Love you," Dad says like he always does.

But rather than say it back, like I usually do, I hang up.

Because fuck him. Fuck him for agreeing to have me when he didn't want me. And fuck him for continuing this fake relationship for years after Mom died. He might think he's doing right by the woman he loved, but all he's doing is hurting me.

So, I'm done. I'm done with people who don't want me, who don't think I'm enough. I don't need anyone but myself. And soon, I'll have this baby. And that's enough for me.

"Right there is your little one." Dr. Mays points at the tiny, alien-looking baby on the screen, and my heart clenches in my chest because, holy shit, I'm pregnant. "And this"—she clicks a button, and a second later, a whooshing sound fills the room—"is your baby's heartbeat."

Ana squeezes my hand while Dr. Mays continues to go over everything about the baby, reminding me that I'm not alone as tears track down my cheeks, hitting my ears since I'm lying down.

I'm pregnant. I'm really freaking pregnant, and I'm going to be doing it alone. My thoughts go back to my time with Nate, and even though I'm missing him like crazy and I wish he were here to see this, I also love that we created this baby during our time together.

For those five days, I was enough. Every laugh, every smile, every kiss was enough. He showed me more passion during our time together than any man I've ever been with, and even though I'll probably never find him, I love that I'll get to keep a piece of our time together with me forever.

Did I want to do things properly? Of course. But there's no point in focusing on what could've been. This is where I'm at, and I'm going to spend my life loving this baby the way my mom spent every day she was alive loving me.

"Are you okay?" Ana asks once the doctor has given me copies of my ultrasound and excused herself to see her next patient with the reminder to schedule my next appointment for four weeks from now.

"I'm overwhelmed and scared," I tell her truthfully as I sit up on the medical bed. "I'm mad at myself for throwing away Nate's number and annoyed that I've paid a PI to find him, yet he's found nothing. It's like Nate doesn't even exist, which makes no sense"—I point at my bloated belly—"because, obviously, he does. But I'm also excited to be a mom."

"It's one of the best feelings in the world," she says. "And you and Kira are only four weeks apart! This is going to be so much fun. You guys are giving me serious baby fever, so I'll be living vicariously through you both."

I slide off the bed and get dressed and then head out to the receptionist to make my next appointment. Since I'm exactly twelve weeks, she makes it for one month from now. When she gives me the day and time, I glance at my calendar.

"I have a meeting at eleven. Can we do it for nine?" That should be enough time for me to get to work and prep before the meeting.

"You should just take the day off," Ana suggests.

"I can't. It's with that hotel we're partnering with."

"Oh, Bradford Hotel," Ana says. "Julian is excited about that. He thinks it's going to be a serious game changer if we can get the marketing right."

"Well, that's what you have me for." I shoot her a playful wink, and she bumps her hip against mine.

"Damn right," she says. "I don't know what I would do without you, in and out of the office."

"Good thing you'll never have to find out."

When I get home, I pull out the scrapbook I've started and put one of the images from today's ultrasound in it. I spend the evening titling it, writing my thoughts, and decorating the page. When I was younger, Mom and I kept a scrapbook for every place we moved to. I haven't made one since she passed away, but after finding out I was pregnant, I pulled out all the stuff and then went to the store to pick up a new book and materials.

Page one: My trip to London and the time I spent with Nate.

He might not be here, but I'll be damned if our baby ever thinks he or she wasn't wanted. I might not know Nate on a deeper level, but I felt his heart, and I'd like to believe that if the circumstances were different, he'd want this baby as much as I do.

Which is one reason why I'm kind of glad—okay, maybe *glad* isn't the right word, more like *okay*—that Nate doesn't know. If he found out and told me he didn't want this baby, it would break my heart. So, maybe, in a way, it's for the best that he's not in the picture. I can pretend he would've wanted me and the baby and never know any different.

Ignorance is bliss, right?

CHAPTER FOURTEEN

Paige

One Month Later

Cathy: Where are you?

Cathy: Please tell me you're on your way.

Cathy: If you're not here soon, we're going to have to start without you.

I should've known better than to schedule a doctor's appointment before a meeting, but in my defense, the last appointment went smoothly. Unfortunately, the same can't be said for this one.

Despite my scheduling it for first thing in the morning, there was an emergency, and I was told it wouldn't be too long, so I chose to wait. And as the minutes ticked by, I considered rescheduling and going to work, but by the time I went up to the desk to do so, I was told Dr. Mays was ready for me.

But once I was brought back, they had to do blood work and

get a urine sample, and then the nurse needed to discuss my lab results, which came back slightly anemic, so they'd like to add an iron supplement to my prenatal pill.

While I waited for the doctor to come in, I tried to call or text my assistant, Cathy, but I had zero service. So, I had no choice but to take a calming breath and enjoy listening to my baby's heartbeat. The doctor said the baby's heartbeat was strong and I looked great. I scheduled my next checkup for twenty weeks, which will also be an ultrasound, and then hauled ass out the door.

The moment I had service, my phone blew up with texts. I called Cathy back, but she didn't answer. So, I focused on getting to the office as quickly and safely as possible.

I fly through security, flashing my badge, and take the elevator up. I don't know if it's the stress or the cologne the guy standing next to me is wearing, but the second the doors open, I detour to the restroom to throw up.

Jesus! I read morning sickness usually only lasts for the first trimester. Guess I'm one of the unlucky ones because I'm still getting sick damn near every day.

Once I've washed out my mouth and brushed my teeth, I head back to the conference room. It's not until I walk inside that I realize I have no clue what meeting this is for. Let me tell you, pregnancy brain is a real thing.

"Good morning," I breathe, stepping into the room and praying my brain will remember what we're doing here. "I'm sorry I'm late."

"Don't worry," Cathy says. "Mr. Bradford is running late as well. Traffic. He's coming straight from the airport."

I sigh in relief. "Good, because I swear this pregnancy has fried my brain. What is the meeting for?"

Cathy, who has two kids of her own, chuckles. "You think

pregnancy brain is bad? Wait until the baby comes. Baby brain is even worse."

I groan, unable to even imagine how this could get any worse. "At least I won't be throwing up every damn day."

"No, you'll just have a sweet little baby throwing up on you," Cathy says with a laugh.

Tom and Jill, two of my marketing leads, laugh and nod in agreement. It's nice to work for a company where people are understanding. The previous company I worked for would've found a way for me to be fired the second they found out I was pregnant.

"Thanks, guys. I can't wait," I say dryly. "Now, refresh my brain."

The team is getting me caught up to speed when Janet, the receptionist for our department, opens the door. "Good morning. Mr. Bradford is here."

"Send him in, thanks," I tell her.

"I'm shocked the COO is coming to discuss this himself," Cathy says.

"Yeah, normally, the CMO would handle it," Tom chimes in. "And you know he's capable since they're brothers. But he insisted that—"

His words are cut off as the door opens, and Mr. Bradford strolls through, along with another gentleman. Words are spoken, but I can't focus on anything other than the man standing in front of me.

Brown hair, styled neatly, that I ran my fingers through. Stubble along his jaw that I felt against the inside of my thighs. Whiskey-colored eyes that I looked into as I came over and over again.

My heart squeezes in my chest, and my stomach tightens. I open my mouth to speak, but a bout of nausea has me racing out of the room and into the nearest restroom to throw up.

Holy shit, he's here.

Nathan Bradford, the COO of Bradford Hotels, is Nate. My Nate!

And then it hits me…the hotel in London. Him being able to get me a room.

He wasn't just there on business. His family owns the damn hotel!

CHAPTER FIFTEEN

"I'M SO SORRY," CATHY, THE WOMAN I'VE BEEN SPEAKING TO on the phone to coordinate this meeting, says. "Morning sickness can be rough."

She continues to speak, but everything she says comes out sounding like the adults in *Charlie Brown* episodes because the only thing I can hear is, "Morning sickness can be rough." It repeats over and over while I try to compute what she just said. What this means.

I know what morning sickness is. My brother and sister-in-law have two kids. I run a company filled with women who get pregnant all the time. But what I can't seem to wrap my head around is why Paige Abrams would have morning sickness.

Is there another type of morning sickness that I'm unaware of? Because unless there is, that means that Paige—*my fucking Paige*—is pregnant, which means I'm too late.

I started planning this partnership two months ago with Evan,

Kingston's COO. I was hoping it would happen sooner, but there's a lot involved when dealing with multimillion-dollar contracts.

It's been four months since I saw her, and the entire time, while I've been thinking about her, she was moving on.

"Sorry about that," Paige says, walking back through the door. "It must've been something I ate."

It's a lie I don't call her out on because this isn't the time or the place, and if she's moved on, there's nothing I can say or do. Hell, for her to be pregnant, it must be serious. I waited four damn months, and I was too late.

"Paige Abrams." She extends her hand and smiles, but it's not the smile I love. It's the fake, forced one she gives when she's upset, but doesn't want anyone to know. "Thank you for coming all this way."

"Nathan Bradford," I say, taking her hand in mine. "It's a pleasure to meet you."

She flinches at my greeting, confirming that she remembers me.

"We're looking forward to doing business with you, Mr. Bradford."

"Please," I say, releasing her hand even though I don't want to lose the connection, "my dad is Mr. Bradford. Call me Nate."

She nods and walks past me, her floral scent hitting my senses—the one I tried to memorize, but my memories didn't do it justice.

"Our team has put together some marketing ideas we think will work wonderfully with the collection we'd like to pair with your hotel."

Everyone has a seat, and Paige takes charge, going through their marketing pitch. The idea is genius. Kingston Limited will be creating an exclusive Hotel Collection for Bradford Hotels, where guests who wish to purchase the package will experience different cocktails throughout their stay at our hotel.

I already looked over the marketing plan on the plane ride over and know they came up with damn good ideas, so I don't feel too bad when I tune out what she's talking about and spend the next half hour focusing on *her*.

Her hair has grown out a bit, and she's lightened it with more blonde. It's up in a tight ponytail, reminding me of when I took her from behind and she moaned when I tugged on her hair, begging me for more.

Her makeup is professional, and her lips are plump and glossy. I'd bet if I kissed her, she'd taste as sweet as I remember. She's wearing a simple white button-down blouse and a black pencil skirt, and aside from it being a bit snug on her, she doesn't look pregnant. Which has me wondering if maybe her assistant was wrong. Maybe it was something Paige ate, and she hasn't moved on and gotten pregnant.

"Mr. Bradford," Paige says, snapping me from my thoughts.

With the way her brow is raised, I have a feeling this isn't the first time she's called my name to get my attention.

"Nate," I remind her. "And everything sounds great. If you can send over the numbers, we can go over them and get back to you later this week with any questions."

"Speaking of which," Paige says, "out of curiosity, is there a reason why you came instead of…"

She glances down to find his name, but I answer before she has a chance.

"Carmine Bradford." I grin when her brows furrow. "He's the head of marketing. And my brother Dustin handles the finances. Our dad is the CEO, and I'm second in charge. I know it gets a little confusing since all four of us share the same last name."

"Right," Paige says. "So, will we be working with you or with Carmine?"

"You'll be working with both of us," I tell her, knowing this isn't standard procedure. "Carmine wasn't available to come, so I came in his place. I'll be in town until we finalize the deal and get it all worked out. And then he'll take over from there."

Paige's eyes go wide. "You're…staying in town?" she chokes out. "A partnership like this can take weeks to finalize."

Everyone's gaze volleys from hers to mine, and I assume they're confused as to why she's questioning me because they don't know what we know—she doesn't give a shit about who's handling the deal. She wants to know why I'm here when the COO doesn't handle shit like this. Why I wasn't shocked to see her when I walked in. Why I'm insisting on staying for as long as I am.

"That's okay," I tell her. "I've booked a room at the Bradford Hotel in Houston." I stand and drag my gaze away from her to Cathy. "You have all my information. Once you email my assistant everything, we'll look it over and discuss it, and then we can schedule to meet again."

"Perfect," Cathy says. "I'll show you out."

"Actually," I say, "I have a couple of things I'd like to discuss with Miss Abrams."

I meet Paige's nervous gaze.

"Of course." She forces a smile onto her face and rounds the table. "Why don't we discuss it in my office?"

"Perfect." I give the other associates a smile. "It was wonderful to meet all of you, and I look forward to working with you on this partnership."

I follow Paige out of the conference room and down the hall. She stops at the receptionist's desk and asks her to cancel her lunch appointment.

The receptionist looks like she wants to ask why, but Paige doesn't give her a chance to before she heads down the hall with me following.

When we get to her office, she stands at the door for me to go in first, and then she closes the door behind her.

Once we're both alone, I bring up the elephant in the room, not wanting to beat around the bush. "You're pregnant."

Her eyes bulge, and her hand goes to her stomach. "How did you…"

"Your assistant. When you ran out, she said you had morning sickness."

Paige sighs. "Sorry. I didn't mean to lie…"

"It's okay," I tell her, removing the space between us. "I came here, hoping to see you, but I was too late. I spent two months fighting with myself to respect your wishes for me not to contact you and then another two preparing the deal with Kingston so I could have a reason to see you. I should've just messaged or called. But I didn't, and you moved on."

"You did all this just to see me?" She crosses her arms across her chest, and I can't help but glance at the way her breasts rise slightly, straining against her top. "So, the partnership with Kingston, it's all a ruse?"

She purses her lips, and I shake my head, gesturing for her to have a seat on the sofa. She does so reluctantly, and I sit across from her, itching to touch her but keeping my distance because she's not mine to touch.

"The deal is legit," I tell her. "My brothers bid on it because we genuinely wanted to work with Kingston. But once you reached out, because they knew who you were to me, they gave me the option to handle it so I could come see you in person…"

"And then you could say it was business," she finishes, a small smile curving in the corners of her mouth. "I was wondering why you requested me personally when my team generally handles these types of partnerships."

"I thought I had it all figured out," I say with a humorless chuckle. "But I was so focused on seeing you that I didn't even consider that you might've moved on."

"What?" She looks at me in confusion. "Moved on? What are you talking about?"

"You're pregnant." I nod toward her belly.

"I am," she says with a laugh. "But spoiler alert: you don't have to be married or even be in a committed relationship to get pregnant. Apparently, all you need is two people attracted to each other in London...or maybe Bath."

She smirks, and it takes me a second to wrap my head around what she just said.

London...Bath...

We were together in London and Bath.

And now, she's pregnant.

"Holy shit," I breathe. "You're pregnant?"

"I think we've established that," she says with a small laugh.

"Why didn't you tell me?"

If she got pregnant during our time together, that would make her—I do the math in my head—four months along. Yet I never heard from her once.

Does that mean...

Was she going to...

"Were you so hell-bent on not reaching out because of the distance that you were going to raise our baby alone?"

Paige's face falls, and my first instinct is to go to her side.

"Did something happen? Is the baby okay?"

"The baby is fine," she says softly. "But I don't have your number," she rushes out. "When I found the card in my purse at the airport, I knew I would be tempted to call you, so I threw it away. And then a few months later, when I found out I was pregnant, I regretted it.

I swear I searched for you, but all I had was the name Nate and a couple of pictures of you. I even hired a PI, who couldn't find anything. He was a total waste of money."

"I'm a private person," I admit. "My goal is to become the CEO, so I keep my business private. Nothing destroys a company quicker than a scandal."

She nods in understanding.

"So, you're really pregnant with my baby?" I ask, still in shock.

"Yep."

"And you're not seeing anyone else?"

"Nope. The only person I've been with is you."

Jesus, I was hoping to simply see her, but now, the stakes are so much higher. Not only is Paige sitting right in front of me, but she's also pregnant with my baby. It's like fate. I fantasized about getting her pregnant and now here she is, carrying my baby.

"Can I take you out to dinner?" I ask, thinking that's the best way to start figuring out where we go from here since we're currently sitting in her office and she still has a half day of work left.

"I think that would be a good idea."

CHAPTER SIXTEEN

Nate

"Sʜᴇ's ᴘʀᴇɢɴᴀɴᴛ?" Dᴜsᴛɪɴ sᴀʏs ᴏᴠᴇʀ ᴛʜᴇ ᴘʜᴏɴᴇ. "Hᴏʟʏ shit!"

"What are you going to do?" Carmine asks, a helluva lot calmer than Dustin.

"I don't know. I've only just found out. We're going to dinner tonight to talk."

I considered keeping the news to myself, but my brothers are my best friends, and I needed to tell someone. This is huge. The woman who I could see a future with is pregnant with my baby. So, the second I got back to the hotel—after letting Nolan know I'll be staying here until further notice and he's to handle things in Dallas—I conference called them so I could share the news with them at the same time.

"Well, shit," Carmine says with a chuckle. "You went there to get a woman and ended up getting an entire damn family. Mom and Dad are going to be thrilled to learn they're going to be grandparents again."

Fuck…our parents.

"You can't say anything to them," I say. "You know how Mom is. She'll be begging to meet Paige, and right now, shit is complicated."

"Yeah, well, I suggest you *uncomplicate shit*," Dustin says, never beating around the bush, "because in less than six months, you're going to be a dad, and the mother of your baby lives four hours away and didn't want to keep in touch with you, let alone raise a baby with you."

I release a harsh breath, knowing he's not wrong. And my mind goes back to my ex. She cheated on me because I hadn't given her enough attention. She strayed because I had been neglecting her. And yet we lived together in the same city, in the same house. How the hell am I supposed to make this work with Paige when we're living hours apart?

"We'll figure it out," I tell him, refusing to compare Paige to my ex. "But in the meantime, I'm going to be staying here for a while. Nolan's already been informed that he'll be my eyes and ears in Dallas. All meetings will need to be online for the foreseeable future. I already planned to be here for a few weeks, but now, with this new information, I have a feeling my trip is going to be extended because there's no way I'm leaving without Paige and me figuring out how this is going to work between us. It's no longer just us we need to consider, but our baby too.

"Fuck, we're about to have a baby."

Dustin and Carmine both bust out a laugh, and without waiting for either of them to say something that I'm sure will piss me off, I hang up.

At six o'clock on the dot, I pull up to Paige's house. It's smaller than a lot of the homes in the neighborhood, but no less cared for. Remembering that when Paige and I were spending time together in London, she told me it was the first home she ever purchased—and that she did it on her own—has me smiling, proud of her. It's clear she works hard for everything she has, and to be the CMO of a multibillion-dollar company like Kingston is huge.

If I had to guess, that piece-of-shit ex of hers was jealous. He didn't like the fact that she probably made more money than he did, and instead of supporting her, he put his career rather than their relationship first.

"Are you going to stand out there all night or knock on my door?" Paige calls out, making me laugh because I was standing at the end of her sidewalk, lost in my thoughts.

"Sorry," I say, giving her my attention.

Unlike the professional attire she was wearing earlier today, she's dressed in a flowy red-and-white polka-dot wraparound dress, showing off the swells of her breasts. Her hair is down in waves, and her lips are glossy.

My gaze descends to her toned, tanned thighs and calves and land on her black heels.

She looks fucking stunning, and I have no idea how I'm going to get through an entire dinner without touching or kissing her... or sneaking off to the bathroom and fucking her.

You need to take things slow, I remind myself. *Just because you're ready to hit the pavement running doesn't mean Paige is.*

"My eyes are up here." Paige says it in a serious tone, but her eyes are filled with mirth.

"I can't help it," I say, extending my hand with the flowers I picked up on my way here. "You look gorgeous."

Blush tints her cheeks, and I can't help but smile, loving that I still affect her.

"Thank you."

She takes the bouquet from me and brings them up to her nose to inhale the scent. Since they're already in a vase, she sets them on the foyer table without inviting me in, and then we head out in my rental to the restaurant where I made a reservation.

I'm not familiar with the area, but after doing some research, I found a small Italian restaurant with good reviews. Not wanting to be disturbed, I booked us a private booth.

The drive to the restaurant is filled with small talk, neither of us mentioning the baby. Paige tells me about work and how everyone is buzzing with excitement about the partnership, and I fill her in on what I've been up to since I got back from London. It feels natural, light, similar to the way it felt in London. Like, even though we barely know each other, we're comfortable with one another.

I'm hoping the vibe continues once we sit down for dinner, but the second the waiter walks away after dropping off our drinks, Paige gets straight down to business.

"I know my being pregnant is a shock to you," she begins after taking a sip of her water, "but I want you to know that you have options."

"Options?"

She can't possibly be talking about what I think she is.

"Yes," she says, straightening herself like she's in a business meeting instead of discussing something as intimate as her having my baby. "If you don't want to be a dad, I won't force you to be one. I know firsthand what happens when a man is forced, and that's the last thing I want for my baby."

Her hand goes protectively to her stomach, and before I can respond, she continues, "When I was fourteen, right before my mom chose to stop her chemo treatments, I found out that my dad never wanted me." She says it so matter-of-factly, like it's a speech she rehearsed. "Apparently, Mom always wanted to be a mom, so my dad gave in to what she wanted. After she died, he barely spoke a single word to me."

She swallows thickly—the first emotion she's shown since she started talking. "He moved us from place to place, and then one day, he found another woman and started a new family with her…one he actually wanted."

Up until now, she was doing a good job at holding in her emotions, but when her voice cracks on the last few words, I know she's more affected by what her dad did than she wants me to believe.

"Paige," I say, in shock at the turn of events because this isn't at all how I saw this conversation going.

"Please," she pleads, "let me get this out. That's why we're here—to discuss the baby—and you should know where I stand before you make a decision."

I sigh in frustration but nod for her to continue. I hate what's coming out of her mouth, but maybe I need to hear it all so I know where she's coming from, and then I can assure her that I'm nothing like her dad.

"I only saw my dad a couple of times after I left home, and then, after college, I moved to London, hoping to be closer to my mom. I wanted to feel that magic," she says, smiling sadly. "But as you know, I couldn't feel it. I felt like I was alone in this world. My mom had given up, my dad didn't want me, and John didn't want to settle down."

At the mention of her ex, my jaw clenches, but I keep my mouth shut, letting her get this all out.

"I've watched my friends fall in love and start families, and I wanted that," she admits with a watery smile that does shit to my insides because how this woman doesn't see what I see blows my mind and fuck everyone who made her feel like this.

"All I wanted was to be enough." She sniffles back a sob, and it takes everything in me not to move to the other side of the table and pull her into my arms. "To be enough for my mom to want to live. For my dad to want to be my dad. For John, who I gave my heart to, and in return, he cheated on me."

She bursts out with a humorless laugh, and it shatters my heart because while I knew what John had done fucked with her head and heart, I didn't know how deep her insecurities ran.

"I've never been enough," she says with a shake of her head, "and now, I'm pregnant."

She takes a sip of her water, her hand trembling, and then places it back down. Out of the corner of my eye, I spot the waiter heading over to take our order, so I shake my head, silently letting him know not yet. With a quick nod, he lets me know he understands and walks in the opposite direction.

"This isn't how it was supposed to happen," Paige whispers. "It was supposed to be magical. We were supposed to fall in love and get married, create a home together and then have a baby. I was supposed to be someone's *enough*. But now, everything's forced. Just like my mom forced me on my dad, this baby is being forced on you."

Holy shit. I'd think she was playing a horrible joke on me if I didn't know how damn serious she was right now.

I'm still trying to wrap my head around everything Paige has dropped on me when she adds more to the mix.

"And then there's the issue that you don't live here, and I can't— no," she corrects, "I *won't* move to wherever you live because I've had to move so many times, and there's no way I'm giving up everything for someone else again. I have a job I love, a house that's mine. I have friends who care about me. And for the first time, I'm making myself a priority."

Her beautiful emerald eyes well up with tears, and I realize, in this moment, that I didn't come prepared for tonight. I was so lost in my own head, excited to be in the same city as Paige, shocked—in the best way—that she's pregnant with my baby, that I thought we'd, what…pick up right where we'd left off? Fuck, I was so stupid. I'm a businessman, I know better than to think with my emotions, but with Paige, it was just so easy to turn it all off and let my heart guide me.

"I'm glad you found me," she says softly, her glassy eyes meeting mine, "because I felt so guilty when I wasn't able to tell you about the baby. But I need you to know that you are not obligated to be in this baby's life, and I'd rather you walk away now than hurt him or her later on. I don't want or need anything from you, and if you decide to sign over your rights, I promise this will stay between us. As you mentioned, you prefer your life to be private, and a baby scandal wouldn't be good for your reputation."

When she releases a harsh breath and her shoulders sag and she doesn't attempt to speak again, I know she's done. And that's good because after all that, I have a few things I need to say as well.

"First of all," I begin, forcing myself to remain calm, "your dad and John and anybody else who didn't think you were enough, who didn't make you a priority, are goddamn fools because you and this baby are more than enough. You deserve to be someone's priority, and I have every intention of making you mine."

She opens her mouth to say something—probably argue—but she had her time to speak, and now, it's mine.

"You are everything I've ever wanted," I continue without letting her cut in, "and that was before I found out that you were carrying my baby. Hell, when we were in London, I'd be lying if I said that I didn't fantasize about *not* pulling out and filling you with my seed on more than one occasion."

Her cheeks turn the most beautiful shade of pink, and I shrug because it's the damn truth. Too many times when we were together, I wondered what it would be like to make her mine, to fill her with my babies, and to live a life with her by my side. I just didn't think it was actually a possibility.

"And while I hate that John cheated on you because you deserve way better than that, selfishly, I'm glad he showed his true colors when he did because it's what led you to me."

"I think it was me tripping over the cobblestone and nearly getting run over that led me to you…but yeah," she mutters, making me laugh.

"That too," I agree. "But regardless, their loss is my gain."

"But what are you gaining?" she asks. "We live…where do you live?"

"In Dallas."

"Great," she chokes out, fresh tears filling her eyes and spilling over. "We live four hours away from each other, and I'm pregnant."

Having enough of not being able to hold her, I round the table and sit in the chair next to her, pulling her into my arms. Thankfully, she comes willingly.

"Don't cry," I murmur into her hair, holding her tightly as she sobs into my chest. "We'll figure it out, but the one thing you need to know is that I want this baby very much. I've always wanted to be a dad, and I can't think of a better mother for our child than you."

Paige cries for a few minutes, and once she's calmed down, she sits up and excuses herself to the restroom to freshen up. While she does that, I move back to my seat and let the waiter know we'll order once she returns, in case she doesn't want to stay. But when she comes back, she tells me she's starved, so we order.

Once the waiter is gone, Paige takes a piece of bread from the basket and, after taking a bite, grins. "I can't believe you haven't bolted yet," she says with a small laugh.

It's meant as a joke, but I answer her seriously, "There's nowhere I'd rather be. Hell, I couldn't even make it two months of respecting your wishes before I was seeking you out."

She huffs a laugh and nods. "So, what now? I mean, you're here, but it doesn't change the fact that you live hundreds of miles away, and then there's—"

"Breathe," I say, hating that she keeps working herself up. "Stress can't be good for you or the baby. We'll figure it all out. Now, you tell me about your pregnancy. I've already missed the first…four months?" I guess.

"I'm sixteen weeks," she confirms. "I actually went to my appointment this morning. That's why I was running late for our meeting."

She reaches into her purse and pulls something out. When she hands it to me, I recognize it as a sonogram picture. I stare at it for several seconds, letting it soak in. I'm going to be a dad, and Paige, the woman I fell in love with in London, is going to be a mom.

"That's from my three-month appointment," she says. "I'm due in November, and I get to see her…or him at my next appointment."

"You think it's a girl?" I ask, glancing up from the picture.

"I don't know." She shrugs. "I don't really care one way or another, but when I found out, all I could think about was how close I was with my mom when she was alive and how excited she would be. I wouldn't mind a little girl who I could go on adventures with."

"I hope she has your green eyes and your big heart," I admit, handing the image back to her.

"You can keep it," she says. "I have others."

"Thank you. If it's okay, I'd like to go to the next appointment with you."

"Or I can video it for you," she offers, confusing me until she adds, "Seems like a waste of a trip to fly all the way here to go to an appointment."

"I'll already be here," I remind her, which makes her brow furrow.

"I doubt it's going to take a month to finalize the details of the partnership with Kingston."

She's right—it won't, especially since most of the major details have already been handled. Kingston doesn't fuck around. But I'm not going anywhere. Wherever she and our baby are is where I'll be.

"I'll be here," I say simply.

Then, because I don't want her to ask questions that I don't have the answers to—like what am I going to do about the company I run in Dallas—I change the subject.

"How has the pregnancy been so far?"

I remember Carmine's wife, Penny, talking about cravings and hormones and all types of things when she was pregnant with my niece and nephew.

"It's been good," she says, perking up. "The morning sickness, as you witnessed, has been rough, but it's slowing down. Most women stop getting nauseous by twelve weeks, but not me." She glances down and rubs her belly lovingly. "I read that the sicker you are, the stronger the pregnancy, so I keep reminding myself of that every time I upchuck my breakfast."

I snort a laugh. "And cravings?" I ask as the waiter sets down our salads.

"Oh my God," she says, her eyes bright, "so many. For

starters…" She stabs her fork into her salad and shows me the pickles she asked for in her salad. "Pickles. It's so cliché, but I'm addicted. Chocolate-dipped pickles, sweet pickles, spicy pickles. The other night, I was dipping pickles into my Ben & Jerry's Phish Food ice cream." She groans as she brings her fork to her mouth. "Pickles are just so good."

We spend the rest of dinner keeping the topics at surface level, and the more we talk, the more I'm reminded of our time together. Paige is sweet and funny and so damn smart. When I tell her about an issue I'm having with one of our vendors, she gives me a perspective I didn't consider, and I mentally note to email Dustin when I get back to my hotel.

⋋⋌

"Thank you for dinner," Paige says when I walk her to her door. "It was delicious."

"As good as your pickle ice cream?" I joke.

"Umm, no," she says with a laugh. "Nothing is better than Phish Food and pickles."

We both go quiet, unsure where we go from here. So much was said, yet nothing has been resolved.

"Can I see you tomorrow night?" I ask.

I was hoping she might invite me in, but she yawned a few times on the drive to her house, so I imagine she's exhausted and she'll want to shower and get some rest.

"Sure," she says. "Just call or text, and we'll figure something out."

She's about to open her door, but before she does, I lean in and press my lips against her cheek. Her skin is soft, and her scent is sweet, and all I want is to lift her into my arms and carry her into her house so I can spend the night holding her. But I don't think she's ready for that, so instead, I tell her good night and wait until she's inside and she's locked the door before I go to my car.

Then, I do the hardest thing I've ever had to do. I drive away from the woman I'm in love with while I try to figure out how I can make her mine.

⬦

Dad: Why did I overhear Dustin say that you got a woman pregnant?

Dustin: Dad knows. Sorry.

Carmine: Mom knows about Paige being pregnant.

Jesus, it only took less than a day for everyone in my family to find out. It shouldn't surprise me though. With us working together and being a close-knit family, we rarely keep any secrets from each other.

Since there are three missed calls from my mom, I call her back.

"Nathan," Mom says when she answers, "tell me it's not true. Tell me you didn't hook up with a woman and get her pregnant."

"Mom," I sigh.

But before I can finish whatever I'm about to say, the call abruptly ends, and a second later, she calls back, using FaceTime.

Damn it. I knew this was coming, which is why I wanted to tell her in person.

I click Accept, and the second her frowning face pops up, she says, "So, it's true. You got a woman pregnant."

"Yeah," I admit. "But she wasn't just a hookup. She's the woman I've been talking about that I met in London. I love her."

I haven't said the words to Paige since the one time I told her I'd fallen in love with her and I was begging her not to walk away before we parted ways. But it's the truth. I fell for her in England, and every day since, my feelings have only deepened. I thought maybe it was all in my head until she walked into the office and I knew what I felt was real. And that was before I knew she was carrying my baby.

"Okay," Mom says slowly. "So, you found her?"

It's not a secret that I've been pining after the woman I met in London. Mom told me on more than one occasion to reach out if I thought she was the one.

"Yeah, she works for the company we're doing business with in Houston."

"That's why you're there?" she says, connecting the dots.

"I came to handle the partnership so I could have an excuse to see her again, but I had no idea she was pregnant."

"Cary," Mom yells, "get in here. Our son apparently forgot all the sex ed we'd taught them and got a girl pregnant."

"Jesus, Mom," I groan. "It's not like that."

Once Dad joins her, I spend the next few minutes explaining Paige's and my time together. Our chemistry. The way I knew she was the one, but she wasn't having it because of the distance. When I'm done, Mom has hearts in her eyes because she's a romantic and Dad's brows are pinched together because even though he's my dad, he's also a businessman.

"So, what are you going to do?" Dad asks.

"Marry her, of course," Mom answers. "Didn't you hear him? He's in love with her."

"I'm going to spend some time here and figure it all out."

"What is there to figure out?" Mom asks, confused.

"Honey," Dad says, "she lives and works four hours away."

"So? Can't she move here?" Mom questions. "She's going to have his baby."

To her, the decision is easy. She's been a wife and a mom her entire life, and she's content with that, so it's hard for her to understand why Paige wouldn't simply move to Dallas to be with me.

"She has a life in Rosemary. A home…a job she loves. Friends…"

"But you live here," Mom mutters, her features etched with concern as she pieces the puzzle together. "Nathan, you're not… you're not moving, are you? You have the company and your family, and your father is supposed to retire at the end of this year."

"I know, Mom," I say, choked up with emotion. "But Paige and this baby are now my family too."

Mom's eyes fill with tears. "But how will I get to watch my grandbaby grow up?"

"Don't freak out, please," I say. "Paige is only four months along. We're going to figure it out. And no matter what happens, we'll make sure you have plenty of time to spend with your grandchild."

Mom nods. "When can I meet her? Maybe if she comes here and gets to know all of us and sees your beautiful home, she'll want to move here."

It's doubtful, especially after she made it clear she needs to put herself first, which includes not moving anywhere for anyone.

"I'll talk to her," I say. "But if she comes to visit, you can't push her to move there."

"I won't," Mom promises. "But you said it yourself. She doesn't have any family there. So, maybe once she meets ours, she'll want to move here."

"Maybe," I agree, knowing it's not going to be that easy.

"Keep in touch," Dad says. "We love you."

"Love you too."

I hang up and lie back in my bed, wishing I were with Paige at her house instead of in a hotel room. I think about what my mom said, her worry over me possibly having to move.

The truth is, until Paige, the only future I could see for myself was in Dallas as CEO of Bradford Hotels. But now, when I think about my future, the only thing I know for certain is that it includes Paige and our baby.

CHAPTER SEVENTEEN

Paige

"Hey, Paige. There's a delivery for you."

I glance up from the email I'm typing and find Janet standing in my doorway, along with a gentleman holding a lunch box.

"Thanks, Janet."

She retreats, and I move toward the gentleman.

"Paige Abrams?" the gentleman verifies.

"That's me."

He smiles and then sets the lunch box on the edge of the sofa. He unzips it and pulls out a container of Ben & Jerry's Phish Food ice cream, followed by a jar of pickles.

"For you," he says, like it's perfectly normal to deliver pickles and ice cream.

Before I can ask who these are from, he says, "Oh! There's a message too."

He pulls a folded piece of paper out of his pocket and hands it to me.

"Thank you," I say, confused—but delighted—that someone has sent me my two favorite items.

I grab a ten-dollar bill from my purse, but the gentleman shakes his head.

"No can do. I was already tipped and told not to accept one from you."

He nods once and then exits my office, leaving me with my ice cream, pickles, and a note.

After storing the goods in my mini fridge, I sit down and open the note.

Princess,

I look forward to dinner tonight. Here are a few essential items to help get you through your day.

XO,

Your Prince

My thoughts go back to our time in London, the night I got drunk…

"I wish you were my prince," I murmur, tears sliding down my face as Nate tucks the blanket around me.

"I do too," he whispers, swiping his thumb across my cheek to wipe the tears away as my eyes close. "Now, sleep, Princess. I've got you."

"What's wrong?" Ana asks, making me jump.

When I glance up, she's blurry, and I realize I was tearing up at the memory.

"Nothing," I say with a laugh, trying to play it off. "You know how it is. Pregnancy hormones are going to be the death of me."

Ana nods in understanding and sits in the visitor seat across from me. "I get it, but generally, there's a reason for crying."

"I found Nate."

Ana's eyes bulge. "What? When?"

"Yesterday."

"And I'm only now hearing about this? And only because I came to you! What the hell, Paige?"

"It was all so much," I say with a sigh. "One minute, I was running late from my checkup, and the next, I was standing in the conference room, staring into his whiskey-colored eyes. For a second, I thought I was imagining shit."

"I bet!" she exclaims. "How did he find you?"

"He always knew how to. He had my full name, and I told him I worked for Kingston. I just thought he'd respect my wishes when I told him what happened in London needed to stay in London."

"Well, thank God he didn't listen! So, he just showed up?"

"Not quite. He's Nathan Bradford…with—"

"Holy shit! Bradford Hotels!" Ana shrieks, bouncing in her seat. "They're partnering with Kingston."

"I know," I say with a laugh.

"Of course you do." She rolls her eyes. "Sorry, I'm just so excited. You found your baby daddy!" She eyes me skeptically. "Which has me wondering why you aren't more excited."

"I am," I say with a half-smile.

"Oh, yeah, I can tell you're just jumping for joy." Her brows pinch together. "Wait, is that why you were crying? Did he say something? Do something? I'll murder him in his sleep."

"Easy there, killer." I chuckle. "I wasn't crying. I was tearing up because he had pickles and ice cream delivered with a note, and it made me emotional."

"Awww, that's so sweet. So, I'm assuming that means he knows about the baby?"

"He does. I told him after our meeting, and then we went to dinner to talk."

"Okay…and?"

"And he's excited. He's always wanted to be a dad…"

"But…" she prompts because she knows me too well.

"He lives in Dallas."

"Oh." She deflates.

"Yeah," I agree. "He says we have time to figure it out, but I don't know how that's possible when he runs an entire company four hours away from where I live and work. And even if we take ourselves out of the equation, what will that mean for our baby?"

Tears of frustration fill my eyes, and Ana rounds the desk to pull me into her arms. I stand, and we hug for several minutes while I get it out.

Once I'm calm, she says, "Don't stress about this, Paige. I know it's easier said than done, but things have a way of working themselves out. I know that firsthand."

I sniffle back a sob and nod. "I know. It's just so hard. Spending time with him last night felt so natural. It was like we picked up right where we'd left off in London. Only there's this giant elephant in the room."

"How did you guys leave things?"

"He asked me to dinner again and then had my favorite ice cream and pickles delivered to me this morning."

"That's so sweet." Ana swoons. "Just like in a romance book. Speaking of which, we need to figure out when we're having our book club meeting." She pouts. "We haven't rescheduled it since you and Kira found out you were pregnant."

"Yes, that's definitely at the top of my priority list," I joke.

"It should be. Reading is the ultimate escape."

"Yeah, well, right now, I need to deal with my reality."

We talk a little longer about Nate and then move on to how her little ones are doing, which leads to her inviting me over for a barbecue this weekend.

"You should invite Nate," she suggests. "It will give us a chance to get to know him. Regardless of what you guys decide, he's your baby daddy."

"Will you stop calling him that?" I laugh. "You make it sound so scandalous. But we'll see. I don't know what his plans are. He says he's staying in a hotel for the next few weeks, but I don't know if he's planning to fly back home."

"Okay, well, it's an open invitation," Ana says, standing. "And you'd better update me on your date tonight. I'll be in my office tomorrow morning with breakfast and coffee."

With a wink, she strolls out.

I pull my phone out and type in Nate's name—as I input it yesterday, when he asked to exchange info. Then, I type out a message.

Thank you for the ice cream and pickles.

Within seconds, he texts back.

You're welcome. See you tonight.

The thought of dressing up and going out to dinner after working all day sounds exhausting, so I send him back a text, ignoring how intimate it sounds.

I was thinking we could order in tonight instead of going out.

Sounds good. Text me once you're ready for me to come over. I'm just at my hotel, working remotely.

◇

"Do I dress up or dress comfortably?"

I texted Nate that I'm home and he's welcome to come over whenever he wants, but when I started to take off my work clothes, I realized I had no idea what to put on, so I video-called Ana.

"You're at home and pregnant. Nobody will judge you for dressing comfortably."

"Yeah, but…"

"But what? You're attracted to him, so you want to look your best because you're pregnant and horny and you haven't gotten laid in four months?"

"Jesus, Ana," I grumble. "You got all that from me barely saying two words?"

She shrugs. "I don't know Nate, but I know Julian, and he doesn't care what I wear if I'm willing to give it up."

She waggles her brows, and I groan because she isn't wrong. A part of me is worried about the baby's and my future, but the other—horny—part of me remembers how good Nate was in bed and wonders if he'd be interested in scratching my itch.

"God, this is so complicated." I groan into my hand.

"Is it though?" Ana asks. "You like him, and he likes you…"

"And he lives over two hundred miles away."

"Oh, I meant the sex." She grins innocently when she's anything but.

"Goodbye," I mutter dryly. "I need to go figure out my clothing situation."

"I vote for pajamas," she says with a laugh. "Oh! Or something sexy, like lingerie."

"Goodbye," I repeat.

"Tomorrow morning, breakfast. I can't wait to hear all the juicy details!" is the last thing she says before I click End on the call.

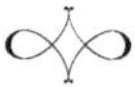

"Did I misunderstand?" Nate glances down at my heels and then lets his gaze roam up my body with an appreciative but confused look. "I thought we were ordering in."

Despite wanting to wear comfy pajamas—and sexy lingerie was a hard no—I went with a cute plaid skirt, a stretchy, long-sleeved black top, and heeled black boots. Nate and I are still getting to know each other, and I didn't want to appear like a slob who's letting myself go only a few months into my pregnancy.

John hated when we had people over and I dressed for comfort instead of to impress. He'd always say that people judged based on looks and the last thing you wanted was for people to think lowly of you because of how you dressed.

But the second I look at Nate—dressed in a pair of gray sweats, a white T-shirt that molds to his sculpted body, and a pair of Crocs—I immediately chide myself for letting dumbass John get inside my head.

Oh well. It's too late now.

"No." I shake my head. "You didn't misunderstand."

Without waiting for him to respond, I open the door wider so he can come in, and then I show him around my place since it's his first time being in here. It's a three-bedroom, two-bath home, and since it's only me, I use one room as a home office and the other as a guest room that's never been used since I don't really have any family coming to visit and the few friends I have live nearby.

"I'm planning to turn that room into the nursery," I tell him.

"You have a beautiful home," he says. "It's exactly how I pictured it."

"Thank you," I say, trying to hide my wince as we walk back out to the living room. My boots might be cute, but they're sure as hell not comfortable.

"Come here," Nate says, sitting on the couch and patting the spot next to him.

Once I join him, he lifts my feet into his lap and then unzips and pulls one boot off and then the other, making me audibly sigh.

As he massages one of my feet, I lie back on the couch and enjoy it. Being pregnant has changed my body. I haven't put on a bunch of weight yet, but I'm sore, and my feet tend to swell. I looked it up, and the pregnancy sites say it's due to water retention.

"I think we're passed dressing up for each other," Nate says with a soft smile as he works the arch of my foot expertly. "You should be comfortable when you're pregnant, and I don't care what you wear. Besides, wearing shoes this tall seems dangerous. What if you fall?"

"Trust me, I'm a pro at wearing heels." I wave him off. "My ex always said we're judged by the way we look and dress. He wouldn't so much as go to the grocery store without dressing properly. I guess his views kind of rubbed off on me."

"I get it," Nate admits. "In our line of work, everything is about appearances. But here in your home, when you're with me, I want you to be comfortable." He releases one foot and starts working on the other. "This is a judgment-free zone. Besides"—he smirks—"I know how gorgeous this body is under the clothes. I don't give a fuck what you wear."

"Trust me, that body you remember is changing." I lift my shirt and expose my newly protruding belly. "So, hopefully, you memorized it because I don't think it will ever be the same."

Nate stops massaging my foot and sets it aside, then leans in, placing his hand on my belly. "You're carrying our baby in here. Whatever changes occur will only make you that much more gorgeous." He dips his head and presses a soft kiss to the spot just on top of my belly button. "I can't wait to watch you grow with our baby."

He glances up at me, and my breath hitches at the way his eyes shine with awe and love. A look nobody has given me since my mom was alive. Sure, John said he loved me, and he was attracted to me, but he never, in all the years we dated, looked at me like I was… everything.

"Thank you," I choke out, my emotions getting the better of me.

"You don't have to thank me for being honest," Nate says, sitting back up and scooting closer so my legs are sprawled across his lap. "Now, what should we order for dinner?"

"Oh my God, this is sooo good," I moan, taking a bite of the chicken chow mein straight from the container.

After we decided on Chinese, since I couldn't pick one dinner, Nate ordered a little bit of everything. At the time, I thought he was crazy, but as I chow down on the various foods in front of me, I happen to think he's a genius.

"Try this," Nate says with a chuckle, lifting a crab rangoon to my mouth. "They're delicious."

I take a bite and moan as the perfect mix of cream cheese and crab hits my taste buds. "So good," I agree.

Once I've chewed and swallowed my bite, I grab a piece of the honey garlic chicken and pop it into my mouth. It's sweet, and the chicken is tender yet crispy.

"Try this." I fork a piece and lean over to give Nate a bite, but before it reaches his mouth, the honey-covered chicken falls off my fork and rolls down the front of his white shirt. "Shit," I say, jumping up. "I'm so sorry. Let me see if I have a shirt for you to change into."

"It's okay." He laughs. "I doubt you have anything that will fit me."

I actually know for certain that I do, but that will mean…

I glance at his shirt that's now covered in stickiness, debating if I should just let him stay like that or if I should try to wash it or…

When he attempts to wipe the honey off and it smears, making it worse, I head to my room, yelling over my shoulder, "Give me a minute, and I'll try to find you something."

I grab the shirt from my drawer and bring it out to him. "Here, this should fit you."

He glances down at the gray shirt with the Aspen skiing logo that's identical to the shirt he wore during our time in London and smirks.

"You stole my shirt?" he asks, but it's a rhetorical question because he already knows I did. He wore it to bed, and after we made love, I put it on and kept it.

"Just take the damn thing," I say with a huff, my face heating from embarrassment.

I extend my hand out for him to take the shirt, but instead of him grabbing it, he tugs on the fabric, jerking me toward him until I'm situated on his lap, my legs straddling him.

"I love that you kept a piece of me," he murmurs, his face only a breath away from mine. "Tell me, Princess, did you sleep with it on?"

His gaze locks with mine, and the fire in his eyes has me squirming.

"Yes," I admit, making him growl under his breath.

He brings the shirt up to his nose and inhales, and I cover my face with my hands.

"You haven't washed it," he murmurs. "It smells like me…and you."

"Yeah, yeah," I mutter. "I'm a freaking weirdo who stole your shirt and slept with it every night without washing it because it smelled like you."

"Nothing about that is weird," he says, lifting my chin so I'm forced to look at him. "You remember the silky underwear you wore to the wedding? The pair I pocketed?"

I nod, remembering that when I left, I was pantyless, but I was too upset about having to end things with Nate to give it much thought. I went back to my room, changed, and then sulked for the rest of my time in London.

"They're currently in my drawer at my house…unwashed." He smirks devilishly, and my insides knot. "I can't even tell you how many times I've smelled them to get a whiff of your essence."

He glides his hand around to the back of my head and entangles his fingers in my hair. "I've done nothing but think about you the past four months." He tilts my head to the side and then leans in, audibly inhaling my scent. "About the way you smell." He runs his nose along my neck. "Your soft, smooth skin." As he peppers kisses along my jaw, warmth spreads through my body. "Your sweet taste," he murmurs against my lips, giving me a chance to back away.

When I make no move to stop him, he takes that as my approval, and then his mouth connects with mine in a searing, toe-curling kiss. And just like that, my body goes from warm to on fire as I get lost in everything that is Nate.

His fingers tighten in my hair as he deepens the kiss, and I shift slightly, turned on and desperate for the connection only Nate can give me.

When my pelvis grinds against his and I feel his hard length between my legs, only my panties and his sweats creating a barrier between us, I gasp and pull back.

"What are we doing?" I breathe, wondering how the hell we went from eating Chinese to devouring one another.

"Most people call it kissing," Nate says with a boyish grin.

"You know what I mean." I glare as I try to climb off him.

He releases my hair to grip my hips to prevent me from moving. "Stop. I know," he says. "But we don't have to have it all figured out. Right now, I'm just so damn happy to have you back in my arms when, four months ago, I thought I'd never get to see you again, let alone kiss you."

He kisses me once again, and when I squirm in his lap, unable to hide how turned on I am, he says, "Let me take care of you."

And because I'm pregnant and horny and in need of a release, instead of saying no, like I probably should, I say, "Okay."

CHAPTER EIGHTEEN

Nate

THE SECOND SHE SAYS OKAY, I TIGHTEN MY HOLD ON HER and stand, carrying her to her room. Sure, we have things to figure out, but right now, the only thing I want to focus on is giving Paige pleasure. I could feel it when we were kissing, how wound up she was, and I remembered, on several occasions, the way my brother would brag about how horny his wife was when she was pregnant.

At the time, I could've done without that info—and I told him as much—but now, I'm thankful for his overshare.

"You wore this little skirt for me?" I ask when I lay her on the bed.

She nods slowly, her eyes filled with desire.

"Did you consider the easy access when you put it on?"

I flip the skirt up, exposing her simple black cotton thong that has a tiny wet circle soaking through the material.

Spreading her legs, I pull my sticky shirt over my head, dropping it onto the floor, and then bring my face right up to her center, in-haling her scent. Fuck, how I've missed her. When my nose rubs along the wet spot, Paige groans, wiggling her hips in frustration.

That's okay because I'm about to make her come so hard that she'll be more than relaxed.

But first...

"Take your shirt off, baby," I tell her. "I need to see those perfect tits I've been fantasizing about."

Even in the dimmed light, I can see her face flush, but she does as I asked, lifting her shirt over her head and undoing her bra.

I crawl up her body, my mouth watering at the sight of her tear-dropped tits and dusty-rose-colored nipples.

I don't waste any time, taking one hardened peak between my lips, while I cup her other tit in my hand, rolling her nipple between my thumb and forefinger.

Paige gasps. "Careful. They're sensitive."

I nod in understanding, then change my tactic, circling my tongue around her areola. She sighs in pleasure, so I do it to the other one, making it a point to gently suck on the tip while watch-ing to make sure she's enjoying it.

As I suck and lick her nipples, she squirms under me, her legs wrapping around my waist and her material-clad cunt rubbing against me, desperate for the friction to get her off.

At one point, Paige moans so loudly from my sucking that I'm almost positive I could get her to come from nipple stimulation alone, but I want more than that. I know firsthand that my woman is a squirter, and I have every intention of getting her to soak this fucking bed.

When I pull back, she scrunches her nose in displeasure, and I can't help but lean in and give it a kiss. Then, I kiss the corner of her mouth.

"Don't pout," I murmur against her lips. "I'm going to make you come."

I kiss her quick and hard, needing a taste of her, and then force myself to break the kiss so I can give her what she needs.

Wanting to reacquaint myself with her body, I trail kisses down the center of her breasts and her torso. When I get to the protruding area where she's carrying our baby, I stop and give it a kiss. I've wanted to be a dad for so long, and this beautiful woman is giving it to me. She doesn't know it yet, but she's already mine, and soon, I'm going to make it official. I'm going to put a ring on her finger and make her my wife, and I'm going to give her and our baby every-fucking-thing.

"Nate," Paige says, reaching down and gently tugging on my hair. "You okay?"

"Yeah." I chuckle, realizing I was staring at her stomach while I was lost in thought. "I can't wait to see your stomach grow."

She snorts out a laugh. "That makes one of us. Growing leads to stretch marks and—"

"And you'll still look beautiful, if not more so because they'll be due to you carrying our baby. You have no idea how much I want this," I admit, voicing my earlier thoughts. "It's because of you, I'm going to be a dad."

Her eyes turn glassy. "Well," she says through a watery smile, "you kind of had something to do with that. Granted, it was the fun part, but you were still part of it."

I bark out a laugh, falling even harder for this woman. She's funny and kind and smart, and I hope our baby is just like her.

"I'm about to have some more fun."

Before she has a chance to respond, I dip my head and press an open-mouthed kiss to that wet spot that's only gotten wetter.

I pull her thong down her legs and then spread her lips so I can taste her. She's dripping fucking wet, and as I glide my tongue up her center, I suck her juices into my mouth, her essence hitting my taste buds like electricity that shoots through me and straight to my cock.

"Oh God," Paige moans, tugging on the strands of my hair. "Yes, right there."

She tightens her legs around the sides of my face, and when I lick up her slit again, my beard scratches the insides of her thighs, eliciting a loud moan out of her. I know from our time in England that she loves my facial hair. I do it again and again, each time stopping and sucking on her swollen clit.

She's close—so fucking close—and when I reach between us, gathering her juices onto my finger, and then push one into her tight ass, she detonates, coming all over my face and the bed. I would love to watch it happen, but I refuse to stop massaging her clit, until she's pushing my face away, her head moving back and forth as she mutters that it's too much.

I love satiated Paige just as much as I love turned-on Paige, especially knowing I did that to her—made her come so hard that her eyes are hooded over, and her entire body is lax.

She sighs in contentment, her eyes fluttering shut, and with one last kiss to the hood of her pussy, I climb off the bed so I can go clean up.

"Where're you going?" she slurs, drunk off her orgasm.

"To clean up," I murmur, giving her a kiss so she can taste herself on me.

Her tongue darts out, and she moans, loving the taste.

As I'm pulling back, her eyes crack open. "What about you?"

"I'm good, Princess."

Yeah, my cock is hard as granite and begging to be back where he belongs—in Paige's tight warmth—but this isn't about me. It's about her, and I'll gladly make her come every time she lets me if it means getting to be with her in some way.

When I get into the bathroom, instead of washing my hands and face, I decide to take a quick shower since I'm covered in her juices and my cock is painfully hard.

I'm soaping my body when the air turns cold, followed by a naked Paige stepping into the shower to join me.

"What are you—"

The words are caught in my throat when Paige drops to her knees, takes my cock in her hand, and strokes it.

I glance down at her in shock, ready to tell her she doesn't need to do that, but before I can speak my thoughts, her emerald eyes meet mine as she opens that pretty mouth and damn near swallows my entire length.

I haven't had sex since England, so, with her wet mouth gliding up and down my shaft, it doesn't take long for my balls to tighten and me to shoot my load down her throat.

I try to warn her it's happening, but she never stops, never takes her eyes off mine, while she milks every drop of cum from my cock. Then, like the little minx she is, she gives the crown a small kiss and stands.

"Marry me," I say, half joking.

Her eyes go wide, and then she barks out a laugh. "That good, huh?" She smirks, knowing damn well what she does to me.

I wrap her in my arms and nuzzle my face into her neck. "I missed you," I admit, "so damn much."

Her body tenses, but she thankfully doesn't pull away. And then she shocks me when she murmurs, "I missed you too."

Paige might be hesitant regarding us, but I'm going to do everything in my power to show her that what happened in London was meant to be. Paige and this baby are mine, and I'm going to make sure she knows that.

After we shower, I throw my sweats back on, sans shirt, while she puts on a pair of tiny cotton pajama shorts and tank, no bra.

She offers to wash my shirt, and I take that as an invitation to stay the night. So, while she throws a load into the washer, I clean up the mess from dinner and then meet her back in her bedroom, leaving the shirt she stole from me on her dresser.

As we're climbing into bed, my phone goes off with a text, and since it's kind of late, I check it in case it's an emergency.

> **Mom:** Can you please reconsider coming home this weekend for your dad's birthday? You can bring Paige.

"Your mom knows about me?" Paige squeaks, having seen the text from over my shoulder.

"Of course she does," I say, pulling her into my arms. "My whole family knows about you."

"Oh my God," she groans, dropping her head into her hands. "They must think I'm the worst hussy ever, hooking up with a stranger and getting pregnant."

"Hey," I say, pulling her hands away from her face and tilting her chin to look at me. "Nobody thinks you're a hussy. Don't ever say shit like that again. What we had in London meant everything to me, and when we had sex, it was two consenting adults who had feelings for each other…one of whom still does."

Paige's eyes widen at my admission. "I do too," she admits sheepishly. "I never stopped having feelings for you, but that doesn't change the fact that we live four hours apart."

"Actually, it does," I say. "Because it means we'll figure this all out. Starting with a trip to Dallas."

"What?"

"You read what my mom wrote. She wants to meet you, and she knows I'm not going without you."

"What? Why not?"

"Because I meant what I said. I'm not leaving you."

"You're going to have to leave me sometimes," she sasses.

"Probably, but I just got you back in my arms, so it won't be anytime soon."

"You should go," she argues. "It's your dad's birthday."

"Only if you go with me. And trust me when I tell you that they're champing at the bit to meet you. We're a close family, one that you and our baby are now a part of." I run my hand along the underside of her belly. "Be prepared for my mom to spoil you. I swear she's closer to my sisters-in-law than her own sons, and she barely goes a few days without seeing my niece and nephew. She's beyond excited to have another grandbaby to dote on."

When I notice Paige's eyes have turned glassy, I palm the side of her face. "What's wrong?" I try to think about what I said that would have upset her, but I come up blank. "Talk to me, please."

"I'm sorry," she whispers, tears filling her eyes and spilling over. "It just made me think about how my mom will never get to meet my baby, and my dad…well, he's barely a dad, so I have zero expectations of him being a hands-on grandpa."

"Your mom might not be here, but she's looking down at you, and fuck your dad. He doesn't deserve to have you or our baby in his life."

I swipe a tear that's resting on her cheek, then lean in and kiss the corner of her mouth. "Come to Dallas with me, Princess," I murmur against her lips. "My family is going to love you. Hell, I'm almost positive they already do, and if you let them in, they can be your family too."

"Okay," she agrees softly. "I'll go to Dallas with you."

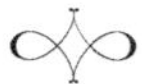

"Hey, Paige, what's this?"

I lift up the big black book from the table when she pokes her head out of the kitchen, where she's making us breakfast and coffee before she heads to work, and I go back to my hotel to shower and get dressed and then meet her at the office to discuss the Kingston Hotel Collection.

"That's my scrapbook," she says, disappearing and then reappearing with a tray of food and coffees. "I started it when I found out I was pregnant."

She sets the tray down and hands me my coffee. We both take a sip, and once she's done, she grabs the book and sets it in her lap. "My mom and I used to scrapbook."

"You'd make one everywhere you went, a new page for every adventure," I recall. When she looks at me in confusion, I add, "You told me about them in England. You guys have never been snowboarding, so one day, when you're not pregnant, I'm going to take you."

I shoot her a playful wink, and she shakes her head.

"You remembered."

"Of course," I scoff. "I remember everything you tell me."

She points to a bunch of thick books on her bookshelf. "I still have them all, the scrapbooks…and when I'm missing my mom, I look through them to remember the magic."

She opens up the book in her lap, and the first picture is of three pregnancy tests—two positive and one negative. "That one's mine," she says with a laugh, pointing at one of the positive tests. "Ana and Kira took tests with me. I was freaking out, and even though I already knew I was pregnant, I was hoping I was wrong."

She frowns, and I pull her into my arms.

"I wish I could've been there."

"If you had been, I don't think I would've been as nervous as I was," she admits. "I had thrown away your number and had no way to find you, and the thought of raising our baby alone was devastating."

"I get it. I've always wanted to be a dad, to have a family like the one I grew up in, but I always saw it happening a certain way."

"Do you feel like you've been robbed of that?" she asks softly.

"No." I lift her chin and look into her eyes that hold so much emotion. "Because it would mean it wasn't with you, and I'm so glad that what we did in London ended with a baby. It's just further proof that our time in London wasn't meant to be over."

"Maybe," she murmurs. "But it also means everything else is up in the air."

"Everything else will be figured out," I remind her.

"So, who else is pregnant?" I ask, pointing to the other positive test.

"Kira," Paige says with a laugh. "She's due four weeks after me."

"That's nice you have someone to be pregnant with."

"Yes." She grins. "Honestly though, I've been so busy at work that we haven't had a whole lot of girl time. I should text her and Ana to hang out soon. Ana's throwing a barbecue this weekend, but I'll be in Dallas with you."

"Ask them for a rain check," I insist. "I want to get to know the people in your life."

She nods and then turns the page, where I see two pictures of us with the caption **Made in London.**

"That's cute."

"Thanks. I was so thankful I at least took a couple of selfies of us so the baby would be able to see what you looked like."

"And now, they'll know me."

"Because of you," she says, leaning into my side. "Thank you for not listening to me."

She goes through page after page, each one documenting a week of her pregnancy. There are images of her belly, her favorite foods, and the sonogram pictures she's taken from her appointments so far. It's clear from the pages she's made how much she already loves our baby, and I have no doubt she's going to be an amazing mother.

"Make sure you send me the date and time of your next appointment," I remind her when she closes the book.

I have no intention of leaving, but I still want to make sure that it's in my calendar so Nolan doesn't schedule any meetings or phone calls for me during that time.

"Will do."

CHAPTER NINETEEN

"OH MY GOD, STOP IT!" I PLAYFULLY SLAP NATE'S HAND off my thigh. "We're supposed to be discussing the marketing strategy for the Kingston Hotel Collection."

"And we are," he says, running his hand up my bare thigh. "But how do you expect me to sit here and focus when my baby mama is dressed in this sexy-as-hell pencil skirt, showing off all this skin."

He licks his lips, his gaze homing in on my legs as I cross them, trying not to let his touch or words affect me.

Ever since he gave me that orgasm, I can't stop thinking about him giving me another. It took everything in me to leave for work this morning instead of begging Nate to play hooky with me and spend the day in bed. We should probably be taking things slow since so much is at stake, but I can't help it. I'm pregnant and horny, and I have a man who loves to please me.

"Focus," I groan as his fingers glide along the seam of my panties. "We need to get your feedback so I can submit the changes to my marketing team before we leave in"—I glance at the clock—"two hours."

Shit! Where the hell did the time go? "I still need to get home and pack, and we need to get to the airport two hours before the flight."

"Calm down." Nate chuckles. "We have plenty of time. The great thing about having a company jet is that it waits for you." He shifts my hair to the side and leans in, giving the column of my neck soft kisses. "Ever since you walked me into this office, dressed professionally, in those heels, I've been fantasizing about bending you over that desk, lifting your skirt to your hips, and fucking you until we both come. What do you say?" Nate runs his tongue along the sensitive part under my ear. "Want to make my fantasy come true?"

Jesus, I told myself I would have more restraint than this. I already caved regarding the mutual orgasms last night and justified it by telling myself that I wouldn't actually have sex with him until we figured out the important things, like where we're going to live and raise our baby, if we're going to even be together…

But the thought of Nate fucking me on my desk has me throwing all my common sense out the window. I mean, we've already had sex—hence the baby in my belly—so will it really make a difference if we do it again? I don't see why either of us has to be deprived of any possible orgasms while we're figuring things out.

"Fine," I breathe, not caring that I sound as turned on as I am. "Lock the door. But we need to make this quick."

The corners of Nate's mouth spread into a beautiful, boyish grin, and then he's up, locking my office door while I head over to my desk to make sure my papers don't go everywhere when we do this. I've only just leaned over to move my files to the side when Nate rounds the desk and grips the curves of my hips.

"Organizing your desk defeats the purpose of desk sex," he murmurs into my ear.

"Oh, have you had it much?" I glance behind me and raise a brow.

"Never," he admits. "But in my fantasy, the papers go flying from me fucking you so hard."

He spins me around and crashes his mouth against mine. He tastes like the perfect mixture of coffee and passion and something that is just him. His tongue massages mine, and I sigh into the kiss, my body craving more.

Without breaking our kiss, Nate lifts me onto the desk, my ass crushing and wrinkling the files under me. He pushes my skirt up to my hips, tugs my panties down my legs, and then drops to the ground, his head disappearing between my thighs.

I'm about to remind him that this was supposed to be quick, when his fingers part my lips and his tongue lands directly on my clit, making me throw my head back in pleasure.

I'm horny and sensitive, and I come so quickly that I'd be embarrassed if I wasn't so busy wanting Nate inside me.

"Fuck, I love the way you come for me," he says, helping me off the desk.

He kisses me again before he turns me around and gently runs his hand up my back, silently telling me to bend over.

The sound of him unzipping his pants fills the otherwise silent office, and then the cold air hits me when he lifts my skirt over my ass and spreads my legs.

"I've fantasized you just like this a million times," he murmurs, "but none of them did you justice. Having you here, your ass and pussy bared for me."

He goes quiet, and I wait with anticipation for what's to come, knowing Nate is going to make it good. I was only with him for a short time in London, but I learned quickly that he doesn't do anything half-assed, including pleasuring me.

His fingers wrap around my ponytail, and he tugs my head back as he carefully leans over me to whisper in my ear, "Now that I have you back, Princess, I'm never letting you go."

And then he thrusts into me, filling me so deliciously full that we both moan in unison.

Fuck, I've missed this. Missed *him*.

He gives me a few seconds to adjust to him, and then he starts to move. While his thick length slides in and out of me, his hands are everywhere—gripping my hips, running along my back, tangled in my hair. It's not often I can come from intercourse alone, but the way Nate's hitting me in all the right places sends me straight over the edge.

As if he can sense it coming, he reaches around and covers my mouth with his hand, quieting my moans as my walls grip his cock, sending him right over the edge with me.

"You okay?" he asks, pulling out and spinning me around.

I glance down at the cum dripping down the inside of my thigh, and when I look up, I find him looking as well, his own eyes hooded with lust.

"Fuck, if you weren't already carrying my baby, I would consider shoving my cum back inside you in hopes that you would end up pregnant."

His words both shock me and turn me on. "Breeding kink much?" I half joke.

"Breeding what?" he asks, raising a questioning brow.

"In my romance books, some guys have breeding kinks," I explain. "They want to get the heroine pregnant and enjoy…filling her with their cum."

My cheeks heat as the words leave my mouth. It's definitely easier to read a romance with a breeding kink than to explain it.

Nate's gaze darkens slightly, and he nods slowly. "Yeah," he murmurs. "I definitely have a breeding kink when it comes to you. Do you know how many times I considered not pulling out when we were together in London?"

"What?" I gasp. "So, this is your doing?" I point to my belly.

"Hey, I pulled out every time." He smirks.

"Yeah, but apparently, you manifested this."

"And I'm completely okay with that. I can't wait to watch your belly grow with our baby. You're only just starting to show, and it's the sexiest thing I've ever seen."

"You're good for my ego," I mutter. "Now, move so I can get cleaned up."

Since I have a bathroom connected to my office, we use that, and then after packing up anything I might need for the weekend since we'll be leaving town, we head out.

We're almost to the elevators when my name is called.

I turn around and find Ana sauntering my way with a knowing grin on her face.

"Hello," she says, extending her hand to Nate. "I'm Anastasia Parker. We haven't officially met."

"I'm Nathan Bradford," Nate says, shaking her hand.

"Oh, I know who you are. You're the man who knocked up my best friend and is taking her to Dallas instead of to my barbecue this weekend."

"Ana!" I splutter, glaring at her.

But, of course, she ignores me, her eyes staying trained on Nate, who doesn't look uncomfortable at all. If anything, he looks proud of himself.

"That would be me," he says. "I've heard a lot about you. I look forward to working with you and Kingston as well as getting to know you on a personal level as Paige's best friend."

"Good," Ana says. "Because as her best friend, I'm a bit protective of her."

"I don't blame you," Nate says, not missing a beat. "I met her asshole ex. But I can assure you that I'm nothing like him and only have Paige's best interests at heart. Something you'll see once we get to know each other better. We're leaving to visit my family in Dallas for my dad's birthday, but once we return, we need to all get together."

Ana nods, stunned, and even though I've seen the difference between Nate and my ex, right now, it's even more clear. Where John only cared about himself, Nate genuinely cares about me, which means getting to know the people who are closest to me.

When Ana finally finds her voice, she says, "I can see how you got into her pants so quickly."

"Ana!" I exclaim, unable to hold back my laugh because I get it—Nate is a smooth talker.

Nate chuckles and nods, and then the elevator dings.

"We have to go," I say. "I'll be back on Tuesday, but if you need anything…"

"Enjoy your weekend." Ana leans in and kisses my cheek. "And next time you want to have office sex, remember that your office shares a wall with mine. You got me all worked up with all that moaning, and then I had to convince my husband to get me off." She pulls back and smirks. "Have fun, you two!"

It's not until we're in the elevator with the doors closed that Nate bursts out laughing. "I like her."

It's like Nate knew I was nervous to meet his family. On the flight over, instead of sitting in the chairs or on the couch, he brought me straight back to the private bedroom, where he spent the flight pulling the stress straight from my body in the form of two mind-blowing orgasms.

By the time we arrived, I was so high from the orgasms that I didn't have a stressful bone in my body. The only thing I wanted to do was curl up in bed and cuddle with Nate.

But unfortunately, the nap will have to wait because we're only stopping at his place long enough to freshen up before we head to Dallas Steakhouse to meet his family for dinner. His dad's birthday barbecue will be taking place tomorrow with their entire family and friends as well as several close colleagues, but tonight is his dad's actual birthday, and dinner will only be with immediate family—and me.

Like Ana, Kira, and me, Nate, his parents, and two brothers all live in the same gated community, each home on a big enough piece of land that allows them a bit of privacy. My home is only on a quarter acre, but Kira's and Ana's homes are on several acres.

Nate points out where his brothers and parents live, and then we pull up to his beautiful ranch-style home that reminds me of a modern cabin. The exterior is framed with dark wood and complemented with the most gorgeous stone. He pulls into one of the two garages and places his hand on mine—something I've come to learn means to stay put so he can open my door.

The first time he did it in London, I was confused. The second time, I figured he was just being a gentleman and it would eventually stop. But Nate insists on opening my door every single time I get in and out of the car, and maybe my expectations are low after dating John, but every time Nate does it, I swoon that much harder.

"This is home," Nate says when he opens the door and gestures for me to go in first.

The inside is just as beautiful as the outside with its exposed wooden beams and floor-to-ceiling stone fireplace. It's not cluttered, but it's clearly lived in. I spot several framed photos on his shelves, and my heart clenches in my chest because, unlike me, Nate has a family.

I scan the various pictures that are filled with laughing and smiling faces, and I miss my mom that much more. It might've only been the three of us, growing up, but Mom made sure I had the best life, filled with love and laughter.

"How long have you lived here?" I ask, setting my purse down. "It's beautiful."

"Sold my condo a few years ago and built this place. I wanted to be near my family."

"It's a lot of home for a single guy."

"Yeah." He chuckles softly. "I was hoping, one day, to have a family of my own."

Of course he was, and he was planning to move her in here, near his family, where they'd live close enough to walk over to each other's houses, to have barbeques and pool parties.

"Hey," he says, palming my cheek. "It's just a house...a dwelling."

"It's bigger than my place and closer to your family."

"I don't give a shit about the size of the house," he says, locking eyes with me. "And you're my family too."

"Yeah, family who's taking you away from your other family," I mutter.

"You're not taking me away from anyone," Nate argues. "We're going to figure this out. Even if it means we live in Rosemary and keep this house so we can visit."

"That's a waste of money."

"What's the point of me busting my ass to make a damn good living if I can't use my earnings to ensure we're close to family?" He glides his thumb down my cheek and then leans in and presses a tender kiss to my lips. "We'll figure it all out, I promise," he murmurs against my lips. "The important thing is that I found you and we're together. Everything else can and will work out. I just need you to trust me."

He kisses me again, this time his tongue sliding in to deepen the kiss, and warmth spreads throughout my body. For so long, I've felt alone. Even when I was with John, I felt like I was doing it all on my own, but when I'm with Nate, it's like I actually have someone in my corner, a partner who thinks about me. Maybe, instead of assuming the worst, I need to give him the benefit of the doubt.

"Okay," I murmur against his mouth. "I'll trust you."

His entire body sags in relief. "Thank you. Now, let me show you around, and then I'll give you time to freshen up before we head to dinner."

Nate takes me on a tour of the house. Aside from the state-of-the-art kitchen and living room, he has three additional rooms that he uses as guest rooms and an office. He has an in-home gym, which completely makes sense because, my God, the guy is fit. He has an outdoor kitchen and grill and a pool and hot tub, which I tell him we will be going in sometime this weekend.

The tour ends in his room that, like the rest of the house, is clean and lived in. He has a family photo on his dresser and a beautiful piece of art hanging above his bed that's the perfect mix of country chic, which seems to be his decorating style.

When I yawn, exhausted from…well, being pregnant—I mean, do I need any more reason than that? I'm literally growing a human—Nate chuckles.

"Why don't I draw you a bath?" He points to his luxurious spa bathtub, complete with jets. "You can relax while I finish up some work."

I was about to suggest he join me, but at the mention of him needing to work, I simply nod, not wanting to get in the way of his work. I've learned from my previous relationships that men don't like clingy women, and the last thing I want is Nate feeling like I'm dragging him down or away from his responsibilities.

"Sounds good." I force a smile and kiss his cheek. "Go do your COO things."

CHAPTER TWENTY

"I UNDERSTAND THEY WANT SEVEN PERCENT BUT—" DUSTIN starts to argue, but his words are cut off by the sound of his alarm going off. Since he's late to everything, his assistant insists on him using alarms for everything. "Shit, we're going to need to table this," he says, standing. "I need to head home to get ready for dinner."

I glance at my watch, shocked to learn that I've been working for quite a few hours and Paige hasn't appeared.

"I need to get ready as well," I say, standing.

"Paige is with you, right?" Dustin asks.

"Yeah, she was in the bath…" Like, three hours ago. "We'll see you tonight."

I click End on our video chat and head straight for my bedroom since the last time I saw her, she was in my bathtub, soaking in the tub.

But before I make it into the bathroom, I'm stopped in my tracks by the sight of her sleeping in my bed. She's curled up and beneath the sheets with her face nestled into the pillow. It's the first time I've had a woman in my home, in my bed, and I love that it's her.

I pull my phone out to take a picture, wanting to capture her in this rare moment of peace. Between the stress of us and our future, carrying a baby, and working hard at Kingston, she's getting pulled in different directions, and I worry it's all too much. Decisions need to be made, but I wasn't lying when I told her that she can trust me. She might not have had the best track record with men in her life until now, but that stops with me. I will always put her and our baby first.

After taking a couple of pictures, I pocket my phone and sit on the edge of the bed, leaning over Paige so I can kiss the corner of her mouth. She sighs in contentment, and my heart swells in my chest.

Not long ago, my entire world revolved around work. My only goal was to become CEO of my family's company. But the moment Paige stumbled into my life—literally—my priorities shifted. I'd forgotten what it was like to connect with someone on a deeper level. To laugh and joke and be intimate with them. And now that I have it, I won't do anything that will put me at risk of losing it—of losing her.

"Why are you staring at me?" Paige asks, her voice raspy from sleep.

"Just trying to figure out how the hell I got so lucky to call you mine," I tell her honestly.

She smiles lazily, only half of her mouth quirking up. "That's so damn cheesy, but I love it." She fists the front of my shirt and pulls me down to her. "What are the chances of me convincing you to give me an orgasm before we have to go?"

"That depends…can you be quick? Because we need to leave in about twenty minutes."

"What?" Paige shrieks, pushing me back and sitting up. "Why would you let me sleep that long?"

"I didn't even know you were asleep," I say with a laugh.

"Ugh!" She groans, throwing her legs over the side of the bed. "I didn't mean to, but your bed was too comfy."

"Look at the bright side. After dinner, you can come right back to my comfy bed, where I can spend the next twelve hours making you come as many times as you want."

I smirk, and Paige blushes.

"You can't say things like that or I'll be begging you to cancel dinner. I'm already worried about meeting your entire family."

"Not my entire family," I remind her. "Only my parents, brothers, and their wives. Tomorrow, you'll meet the rest of my family, including my adorable niece and nephew."

"You're not helping," she mutters as she closes the bathroom door behind her.

I know she's nervous about meeting my family, especially since she's not close with the only family she has left—her dad—but my family isn't judgmental, and I have no doubt that once she gets to know them, she'll realize her worry is for nothing.

⬦

"What do you mean, you haven't seen your father in almost ten years?" Mom stares at Paige in horror. "What parent lets a child go that long without seeing them?"

"Well, in his defense, he used to ask me to go home..." Paige murmurs.

"No," Mom says, "that doesn't defend him. You were obviously upset, and he should've come to you. He should've tried harder. You already lost your mother..."

Mom pulls Paige into a hug since she's sitting next to her at the dinner table. "You're so strong," she coos. "Losing your mother and then your father. You went to college and then got your MBA all on your own. You should be so proud of yourself."

"Thank you," Paige says.

"I know you're independent and used to going through life alone, but you have us now," Mom tells her matter-of-factly. "We're your family. Anything you need—and I mean, anything—you just ask."

"Thank you," Paige whispers as Mom continues to hug her.

I can't tell if she's annoyed or sad or now regretting coming to dinner since I'm sitting on the other side of her and her face is tucked into my mom's chest, but my answer is given when the hug ends and Paige turns to me, and with a small smile on her face, she says, "I really like your family."

"Good, because they really like you," I murmur so only she can hear.

Dinner was spent with everyone getting to know Paige. They didn't ask her anything to make her feel uncomfortable, keeping it about the baby and how she likes living in Rosemary. Carmine talked to her about the Kingston-Bradford partnership since he's supposed to be the point of contact, and they hit it off immediately, talking about marketing through half the meal.

Then, Paige shocked me when she started asking the questions. It's not that I don't think she's social, but I wasn't sure how it would go since there's only one of her and so many of us, so I'd imagine it could be a bit intimidating. But she was comfortable enough to ask Carmine and Penny about their kids, which stemmed into a conversation about parenting, which unfortunately led to Paige admitting she lost her parents years ago in different ways.

"I'm glad you convinced me to come," she says with a smile.

"Me too." I lean over and kiss the corner of her mouth.

"And I'm really glad this will be our baby's family."

Her words cause my heart to both warm and squeeze in my

chest. The former because I love that she's so accepting of them, and the latter because even though she's so accepting of them, her home is four hours away from them, which means so is mine.

And with that thought, it hits me—I'm going to need to move to Rosemary if I want a future with Paige. And I do, more than anything else in this world.

And just like that my decision is made—I'm moving to Rosemary.

"I wish my mom were here," Paige admits, laying her head on my shoulder as we watch the fountains dance to the lights. "She would've loved your mom."

After we had dessert and everyone said good night since we're going to see them tomorrow at the barbecue, I asked Paige if she'd like to go for a walk with me. Downtown can get busy, but there's a walkway along the water, where I sometimes go for a run, that's beautiful at night. She spotted the fountains immediately, so we had a seat on the bench to watch them.

"Do you think she would've liked me?" I ask, curious since they were so close.

Paige looks up at me and grins. "She would've warned me away from you. Told me you were too good-looking and you would break my heart."

I know she's only half joking, but I lean in anyway and speak so she can hear me clearly over the sound of the water. "I would've proven her wrong…shown her not to judge a book by its cover because there's no man who will love her daughter like I will…like I do."

Paige's eyes go wide. "L-love? You mean hypothetically, right?"

"No," I admit truthfully. "I love you, Paige." I glance up so I can look into her striking green eyes. "I fell in love with you in London, and I told you so, and it's only grown since then." I place my hand on her bump and kiss her lips before backing up slightly so I can look at her again. "I'm going to show you every day how much I love you and our little one."

Paige's eyes water as she nods in understanding. I don't expect her to say the words back. Even if she feels them, she's too scared about our future. But I need her to know how I feel. I love her, and if I have it my way, I'll get to spend the rest of our lives showing her how much.

◇

"Wow, you have a big family," Paige says, sitting in a chair I saved for her. "Your mom introduced me to them as her daughter-in-law."

"Give it time, and she'll be insisting you call her Ma."

My mom knows no boundaries. Once you're part of our family, you're in it for life. Valerie and Penny are both close with their moms, but it didn't stop mine from insisting they call her Ma, claiming they were the daughters she never had.

"Oh, she already did," she says, her eyes glassy with emotion. "Right after she told me she can never replace my mom, but she already loves me like one of her own." She glances out at everyone laughing and talking and mingling. "I've always wondered what it would be like to be part of a big family."

"It's not all rainbows and sunshine," I tell her. "People disagree, and arguments happen. One Thanksgiving, my aunt Linda stopped talking to my uncle Barry, and the whole ordeal got canceled. Half the family ate at my parents' while the other half ate at my uncle Barry's."

"But they obviously made up since they're all here now," Paige points out.

"Yeah, they always make up. That's what families do. They fight, and they make up."

"My dad and I never fought," Paige says softly. "Sometimes, I wish we had. Then, we could have gotten it all out, you know?"

"It's not too late."

"It feels like it is." She shrugs and then changes the subject. "Are we doing anything tomorrow? Valerie and Penny asked me to go to breakfast with them."

"Ahh, yes. Tomorrow is their monthly girls' brunch. My brothers and I usually go golfing, and the girls go to brunch at the country club. I can skip it, unless you want to go."

"I do," Paige says. "I'd like to spend some time with them since our time here is limited."

"We can come back anytime you want," I tell her, tugging her chair closer so I can wrap my arm around her. "I know Rosemary is your home, but here, with my family, can also be your home."

CHAPTER TWENTY-ONE

Paige

"UNCLE NATE!" ANNEMARIE, NATE'S THREE-YEAR-OLD niece, yells. "Come and throw me in!"

"Me too!" Dylan, her two-year-old brother, adds. "Throw me in!"

Nate looks between the kids and me, torn on leaving me, so I say, "Go! Go play with your niece and nephew. I'll be fine right here."

"Or you could go in with me." Nate waggles his brows. "You know I'm dying to see you in that swimsuit you put on this morning."

"Uncle Nate, please!" Annemarie begs.

"Go play, and I'll think about going in."

"Fine," he says, standing and pulling his shirt over his head, exposing his washboard abs, chiseled chest, and sexy tattoos. He drops his shirt onto the table and then reaches down to tie his board shorts that came loose.

The act has my gaze sliding down his abs and landing where

that perfect V, along with his happy trail, dip into the front of his shorts like the biggest tease.

Nate leans down, gives me a quick kiss, and then takes off running toward the pool—his backside almost as perfect as his front—yelling, "Cannonball," as he jumps in and makes a show of splashing the kids.

"Might want to wipe that drool," Carol, Nate's dad's assistant, says with a smirk. "You know, they say it's bad for the mom-to-be to be craving anything. When I was pregnant, my husband insisted on making sure I got everything I craved. His mother said if a pregnant woman doesn't get her cravings fulfilled, the baby will come out drooling."

I bark out a laugh at the gray-haired woman who's old enough to be my grandmother. "Is that so?"

"Yep. So, if it's your baby daddy you're craving, make sure it's being fulfilled."

She winks at me, and I laugh harder, seriously loving this family.

"Well, in that case"—I glance at Nate, who's taking turns throwing his niece and nephew into the water—"I'd better go get my fill."

I wink back at her, and she nods in approval.

I'm about to head over, but my bladder screams in protest, so I take a detour inside to use the bathroom. One thing I won't miss about being pregnant is the constant need to go pee, and from what Kira and Ana have told me, it's only going to get worse as my pregnancy progresses.

Once I've washed my hands, I head back out, but before I get to the doors leading outside, a masculine voice says my name, stopping me in place.

I look back, assuming my name was being called by Nate—maybe he followed me inside—but the next spoken words have me realizing my name wasn't called...it was mentioned.

"She doesn't want to move here, and Nate isn't going to force her."

I glance around the corner and see Dustin and his wife, Valerie, standing in the kitchen, talking. It must've been Dustin who said my name.

"You could always step up as COO," Valerie says.

"Yeah, except I like my position, and I'm not sure I'd be able to run Bradford the way Nate does. He's going to work remotely for now. Besides, if anyone should be stepping into that position, it's you. You've been working under him for years now."

"I'm nowhere near ready for that," Valerie says, shaking her head. "I thought when Nate became CEO, I'd move up as COO and be trained by him. I don't want to step into that position and fail."

"Then, we'll have to bring someone on board." Dustin sighs.

"But it's always been a family-owned and -run company," Valerie points out, making my heart sink.

"What choice do we have?" He pulls his wife into his arms. "In order for Nate to be with Paige, he has to move there."

"But he's worked so hard, and he was so close to becoming CEO. Where will he work?"

"I don't know." Dustin shakes his head. "And it sucks. I mean, he's busted his ass to make this company what it is. But I get it—if I had to choose between you and my job, I'd choose you every damn time." He kisses her softly, and she sighs into him. "All we can do is support his decision. He's going to work remotely for the time being, and we'll figure it out as we go. You know Nate. He wouldn't leave the company hanging."

"He must be devastated," Valerie murmurs. "I hate this for him."

Tears prick my eyes at their words. At the fact that I'm causing this because of my own insecurities. I want to support Nate and move to Dallas so he doesn't have to leave everything and everyone he loves behind, but I can't do it. I can't give up my entire life and move to Dallas. What happens if we don't work out? Then, I'm left with nothing. I've put so many people first, and I was left with nothing every single time. I hate that he's in this position, but I can't put him first.

Which only leaves one option…

We need to end whatever this is between us and focus on raising our baby together. It sucks that we'll have to co-parent long-distance, but it's done all the time. We'll figure it out.

I step outside since I have nowhere else to go and I don't want Dustin and his wife to know I overheard. I'm about to have a seat back at the table where I was sitting before when Nate calls my name.

"Come in the pool," he says with a smile, swimming to the edge. "The water's nice."

I consider saying no, but the last thing I want is to draw attention to myself in front of his entire family. Nate won't stop until I tell him what's wrong, and at his family's home, in the middle of his dad's birthday barbecue, is not the place to have this conversation.

We need to get through this weekend, and then once we're back in Rosemary, I'll tell him that I've made the decision to keep things between us strictly about the baby.

We'll finalize the Kingston-Bradford collaboration, and then he'll go back to Dallas with his family and his job, and we'll figure out how to co-parent long-distance.

"Paige," Nate yells again. "You going to come in, or do I have to come and get you?"

Several people chuckle, their eyes on me, so I nod and stand.

"I'm coming," I tell him, forcing a smile onto my face.

I take my cover-up off and fix my newly purchased maternity bathing suit. I'm still on the smaller side, but my belly has popped, and I now officially look pregnant as opposed to bloated. I went with a two-piece, hoping it will give my belly room to grow since the summer in Texas is hot and we spend a lot of time in the water.

As I walk over to the pool, Nate gives me his full attention, his eyes alight with lust, mixed with love, and my stomach knots because Nate loves me. He's attracted to me. He not only wants me, but he also wants this baby.

A little over four months ago, I walked in on my boyfriend having sex with my friend, and I questioned if I was enough. If I was pretty enough, good enough in bed, enough to be loved. Yet every time I'm around Nate, he does nothing but show me just how *enough* I am.

To my ex, I was one woman in a room filled with many others. But when Nate looks at me, it's like I'm the only woman in the room.

And despite how he makes me feel, I can't have him because it's not fair to either of us. He might be willing to give up everything to be with me, but I'm not going to let him do that.

When I get to the bottom step, Nate encircles his arms around me, and I wrap my legs around his torso. The backyard is filled with well over fifty people, but when I'm with Nate, it feels like everyone else disappears and it's just us.

"I love this," he says once we're in the middle of the water.

"What?" I run my fingers through his wet hair, trying to memorize everything about him. I only just got him back, and I'm already going to have to give him up.

"The feel of your stomach against mine." He grins. "I read that the baby will start kicking soon. I can't wait to feel him or her."

He presses his lips to mine, and I sigh into him.

"What else did you read?" I ask curiously. I didn't even know he'd been looking up stuff about the baby and my pregnancy. Imagining him googling pregnancy questions makes me smile on the inside.

"A lot of stuff." He shrugs. "Like, at twenty weeks, we can find out the sex." He grins. "What do you think? Should we find out?"

I've thought about it, but the idea of finding out stresses me out. It'll make it that much more real. It means we can start buying things, decorating the nursery, which means we'll have to decide where the nursery will be. Which means having a conversation about where we're going to live. But now, I know where we're both going to live, and it won't be together, which means...

"Paige," Nate says, quirking a brow. "If you don't want to find out the sex..."

"We can find out," I whisper, trying and failing to keep my emotions in check.

Maybe I should just move to Dallas to be with him. It would solve all our problems. He has a beautiful home and a good job. He loves me and this baby. And I love him.

But then what happens when he doesn't want me anymore?

What happens when I'm no longer worth sticking around for?

When he wants a new woman to warm his bed? A new family to play house with?

Where will I be left then?

Before I can stop myself, tears well in my eyes, and Nate notices immediately.

"Hey," he says, "what's wrong?"

"Nothing," I tell him, hating that I couldn't keep my emotions in check. "I just..." I can't get the words out, so instead, I bury my face in his neck and hold him tight.

I know he's confused, but he simply holds me, letting me silently cry in his arms.

Cry for the relationship that was doomed from the start.

For the baby who's going to be pulled in two directions.

For our hearts that I have no choice but to break.

Because I'm terrified that he's going to resent giving up everything to be with us.

Because I can't let him give up everything to be with us, yet I can't find it in me to give up everything to be with him. And fuck if that doesn't make me a horrible person.

"Paige," Nate says softly. "I think you're having a panic attack, Princess."

It's then that I look up and realize he's carried us out of the water and into the house. I'm sitting on his lap on a chair in the kitchen.

"I'm sorry," I cry. "I'm okay."

"No, you're not," he says with a shake of his head. "Talk to me, please. Tell me what's wrong so I can make it better."

"You can't," I whisper.

"Try me."

I open my mouth to let it all out, but before I can get the words out, Dustin and Valerie appear.

"Hey, is everything okay?" Dustin asks carefully.

"Yeah," I choke out, pushing off Nate and standing despite him trying to keep me in his lap. "I was just having a moment. This pregnancy is going to be the death of me."

I force out a laugh, and Valerie joins, but neither Nate nor Dustin joins in, both too intuitive for their own good.

"Can you give us a minute?" Nate asks.

"Yeah, of course," Dustin says. "We're about to sing 'Happy Birthday.' Come out as soon as you're ready."

"Actually, we should go outside with everyone else," I say, not wanting to be left alone with Nate. "We can talk later."

Nate looks like he wants to argue, but thankfully, he nods in agreement, and I sigh in relief, not wanting to have this conversation until we're back in Rosemary, where I'll be safe to wallow in self-pity in the comfort of my own home.

CHAPTER TWENTY-TWO

Nate

EVERYTHING WAS GOING WELL UNTIL IT WASN'T. PAIGE WAS having a good time—until she wasn't.

One minute, I was horsing around with my niece and nephew in the pool while Paige was talking and laughing with Carol, and the next, Paige was distraught. I don't know what changed, but whatever it was, it has Paige pushing me away.

She avoided me the rest of the trip, feigning headaches and exhaustion. And since I didn't want to upset her, I let her get away with it. But now, we're pulling up to her house, and I'm going to find out what the hell is going on.

Without asking if she's up for company, I grab her luggage and mine and follow her into her house. She's quiet as she turns off the alarm and then flicks the lights on.

I think I'm going to have to pry whatever is wrong from her, but then she turns around and says, "We need to talk," and my stomach drops because those words coming from her can't be good.

She gestures for me to sit on the couch, and then she sits across from me on the love seat, solidifying I'm not going to like whatever she's about to say.

"Your family is wonderful," she says with a small frown that contradicts her words.

"They are," I agree. "And they really like you."

"I like them too," she says, her voice a bit wobbly. "And I'm glad they're going to be a part of our baby's life."

"Of course they will be," I say, unsure where the hell this is going.

"And I think it's good that you guys are close because…" She takes a deep breath like she needs to hype herself up to say the next words, and I hold my breath, knowing it's going to be bad. "I think…no, I *know* it will be best if we figure out how to co-parent long-distance."

I let her words ruminate in my brain for several seconds so I can make sure I'm calm when I ask her what the fuck she's talking about. Because from what she just said, I'm getting the impression that she just broke up with me. Only we're not together, so I'm assuming she's trying to make it clear that we're never going to be together, and she just decided for me that I'm going to take my ass back to Dallas and co-parent with her from there while she remains here.

And that's not fucking happening.

"And why is that?" I ask.

"Because we both know—"

"Whoa," I cut her off. "Don't put words or thoughts into my head. We both don't know shit. You know what you *think* you know, and I know what I fucking know. So, try that again, but this time, only speak for yourself."

She widens her eyes, taken aback by my harsh words, but I don't care. Nobody has the right to tell me what I want, even her.

"Fine," she says. "I want you to go back to Dallas. I don't want to be the reason you lose your job and your family and your entire life over there. Your family needs you, and I don't want to be the person who pulls you into a different direction."

"You don't get to decide that," I say. "You made the decision not to move to Dallas. You made it clear this is where your home is. Your job, your friends, your house. It's here in Rosemary, and I respect that, so I've made the decision to make it my home as well. I want to be with you. I love you, fell in love with you in London, and it's only grown since then. But I can't make you want to be with me.

"Regardless, Rosemary will be my home because it's where you and our baby will be living. So, if you're pushing me away, thinking it's going to send me back to Dallas, you can *think* again. Because I'm not going anywhere."

"You're being ridiculous," Paige says with tears in her eyes. "If you quit your job at Bradford, how will you pay your bills?"

"I have plenty of savings, and I'll find another job. Hell, maybe Kingston has a position for me." I smirk. "I heard they're a good company to work for."

"That's not funny," Paige chides. "I'm being serious, and you're—"

"Also being dead serious." I get up and move from the couch to the love seat next to her. "I'm not going anywhere, Princess. While I appreciate you thinking you're looking out for me by pushing me away so I'll go back to Dallas, it's not happening. I already spoke to my dad and brothers. I'm going to be working remotely while I show Dustin the ropes."

"He doesn't want to be CEO," she points out.

"Why do you say that?"

I know Dustin isn't keen on the idea, but I don't know when he would've told Paige that.

"Because he likes finance," she mumbles, looking down.

"We'll handle it."

"Which wouldn't be necessary if you stayed in Dallas."

"It's not happening," I say, trying to keep my tone even.

Paige is hormonal and emotional, and everything she's saying is coming from a good place. She met my family and likes them, and she doesn't want me to lose them to be with her. And if I were to guess, it has something to do with her insecurities. She can't make me her priority because she did that with her ex and he hurt her. She's been hurt by her dad. She lost her mom. Paige is scared. She can't move to Dallas and risk having her heart broken again, so I'm going to have to show her that her heart is safe with me.

"Everything will work out," I tell her, framing the sides of her face. "You just have to let me in."

"I think you're making a big mistake," she whispers. "And if you want to move here, I can't stop you, but I'm not asking you to, and I don't want to be the reason."

She lifts her chin stubbornly, and I swear I fall even harder for her. She thinks she's pushing me away, but her caring this much about me walking away from my job and family only shows just how much she cares.

"That's okay," I tell her as I stand. "I have all the time in the world to convince you to be with me." I lean down and kiss her cheek. "I love you, and I'm not going anywhere."

Except to my hotel because there's no way Paige is going to let me spend the night here tonight. Not while she's on a mission to push my ass back to Dallas.

⋈

"...if there are no other questions, I think that about wraps it up." Paige grins at everyone in the conference room, waiting to see if anyone has anything to add, and when they don't, she nods. "Okay, have a good weekend and rest up because we have a busy few months ahead of us."

She winks playfully, and everyone chuckles, knowing that while she's half joking, she's also serious. It's been a busy week, but we've managed to finalize the Kingston-Bradford partnership. Contracts have been signed, and we've hammered out the details. Now starts the hard part for the marketing teams. It's one thing to come up with the ideas, but it's a whole other to put them into motion. This is the part where Carmine will take over, and his team will handle Bradford's part from Dallas while Kingston's team will handle theirs from here.

It's also the time when I'd be heading back home, only I have no intention of leaving despite Paige completely shutting me out.

I've asked her to dinner every night this week, and she's turned me down, giving me every excuse under the sun. But I'm not going to give up, and once she sees I'm not going anywhere, she's going to give in.

"Hey, Paige," I say once everyone has filed out. "Any plans this weekend?"

"Just catching up on some work and sleep," she says cautiously. "You?"

"Same. Any chance I can convince you to go to dinner with me tonight or tomorrow night?"

"Sorry, I can't," she says, not even bothering to come up with an excuse.

"All right, well, I'll be around if you change your mind."

I give her arm a squeeze and then head out, trying to figure out a way to get her to spend some time with me since I'll no longer have a reason to hang around the office after today.

I'm racking my brain with ideas when I spot Ana sauntering through the office, and a thought comes to me.

"Hey, Ana," I say, rushing toward her.

"Hey," she says with a forced smile that screams pity, telling me she knows that her best friend is freezing me out.

"Can we talk somewhere a bit more private?" I ask, not wanting anyone, including Paige, to overhear.

"Sure."

She guides me over to her office, and once inside, she says, "So, how are you?"

"I'd be better if Paige stopped pushing me away," I tell her, getting straight to my point.

"Yeah, I heard about that. She's just scared. She's been through a lot, and she's trying to save herself from another heartbreak."

"I get it. So, are you in favor of me sticking around, or are you Team Send Nate's Ass Back to Dallas?"

Ana laughs. "I'm Team Paige." I sigh, ready to give up until she adds, "which means I want her to be happy, and I think you could make her happy. The question is, are you willing to work for it?"

"I'm willing to do whatever it takes to prove to her that I'm in it for the long haul. Even if she wasn't pregnant, I'd be here. I sought her out before I knew she was carrying my baby. I love her. I fell in love with her in London, and I want a life with her."

"And you're really going to give up your life in Dallas to be with her?"

"I've already let my family know. I'm working remotely while we figure it all out because I'm not going to leave them in a bind."

"Of course not," she agrees.

"I was hoping to convince Paige to live with me, but she's not there yet, so I think I'm going to start looking for homes closer to her in Rosemary. The drive from Houston is rough, especially during rush hour.

"And I've had my assistant put together a résumé for me. I'm going to apply to several companies. It most likely won't be the same position I have now, but I'm sure I'll find somewhere I can put my degree and experience to use."

"Wow, so you're really serious about moving here?" Julian asks, strolling into his wife's office. He gives her a quick kiss, then faces me.

"Yeah," I tell them both. "I am. My family says I'm a cranky bastard when I'm not with her so…" I shrug. "The problem is, she doesn't want to move to Dallas, but she also doesn't want me to move to Rosemary."

Julian laughs. "That's a woman for you."

Ana playfully smacks his chest and glares up at him, but he simply kisses the tip of her nose, completely unfazed.

"I want that." I nod toward them. "I want the wife and kids and home, and I want it with Paige. I knew I wanted it the moment after she tripped and fell in front of my hotel and I carried her inside. I asked her if she was hurt, and she looked up at me and said, 'Other than my pride, no.'

"I looked into her green eyes and knew I could fall for her. And I did. A few days in London, and I was a goner. I know that sounds crazy, but…"

"No, it doesn't," Ana says, her eyes glassy. "Julian and I fell fast and hard."

She looks at her husband, who nods in agreement.

"Paige is reacting to her past," Ana says. "She's been burned so many times."

"I know," I tell her. "And I'm going to prove to her that I'm not them, that she can trust me with her heart and I'm not going to break it like those other assholes, but to do that, I need her to let me in. The problem is, the deal with Kingston is done, so I have no reason to be around her."

"There's a barbecue this weekend," Julian says.

"Didn't you have one last weekend?"

"We have a lot of kids and birthdays," he says with a laugh. "It's Fourth of July and Violet's birthday. She's Ryder and Kira's daughter. I'm extending an invite to you. Bring a gift. She's turning six, and she likes anything pink."

He shoots me a wink, and I laugh.

"You got it. Thanks. I really appreciate it."

"Don't hurt her," Ana says, her tone serious. "She's one of the best people I know, and she deserves to be happy. If there's any chance you don't mean everything you said, let her go. Co-parent and let her find someone who can love her."

I get what she's saying. I understand she has her friend's back, and I'm glad that despite Paige not having any family, she has friends like these. But…

"That's not even an option," I tell her honestly. "Unless Paige flat-out says she doesn't want me, I'll be damned if I'm letting any other man love that woman. She's mine."

CHAPTER TWENTY-THREE

"WHERE'S THE BIRTHDAY GIRL?" I JOKINGLY PRETEND to look everywhere but at Violet, who laughs.

"I'm right here, Auntie Paige."

Violet waves her hand in the air to get my attention, and I fake gasp.

"Oh, there you are."

She's wearing her adorable pink and white polka-dot bathing suit since it's a pool party and her hair is up in two high pigtails.

"I heard you're six, but you look at least twenty-one."

Violet rolls her blue eyes that are identical to her mom's, and I wonder if my baby will have whiskey-colored eyes like Nate or green eyes like me. The thought tugs at my heart because Nate and I created a baby. A little miracle who is growing inside of me and is half me and half him.

"I'm not six for five more days," Violet says, snapping me out of my thoughts. "We're just celebrating today."

"Oh, gotcha. Then, I guess this is for…" I trail off because I spot Nate out of the corner of my eye.

At first, I think I'm seeing shit because I was just thinking about him and his beautiful eyes, and why would he be at Ryder and Kira's house? But then I see my best friend looking at me with guilt etched in her features, and it all makes sense.

"For you," I finish, handing Violet her gift.

"Thank you! I love the wrapping paper," she gushes. "Pink is my favorite color. I'm gonna put it on the table. Mommy said I can't open anything till later."

I force a smile, keeping it in place until Violet's gone, and then I make a beeline straight for the only person—besides Nate himself—who is sure to have answers.

"I didn't do it," Ana says, raising her hands in surrender.

"Didn't do what? Invite my baby daddy to Violet's birthday party, knowing I'm trying like hell to avoid him?"

"I did," Julian says, wrapping his arm around his wife. "Guy was desperate, and I threw him a line."

"A line that wasn't yours to throw." I glare.

"Maybe not." Julian shrugs. "But I've been where he is. I know what it's like to be in love with the woman you want to make yours and she's too damn stubborn to give in."

"I'm not Ana," I mutter. "I'm not…" My words trail off because Nate is now walking over, looking beyond delicious in a pair of red-white-and-blue board shorts, a white collared shirt, and flip-flops.

Maybe it's because I rarely see him dressed like this or because he looks like he should be in a vacation magazine, but as he strolls over, I can't help the way my body warms and my lady parts tingle. I blame these damn baby hormones. They're making me act crazy.

"Hey, baby mama," Nate says, leaning over and kissing my temple. "How are you feeling?"

"Confused," I blurt out, then glare at Julian. "Betrayed."

Julian doesn't even bother to look the least bit guilty when he shrugs and then pulls his wife away, leaving Nate and me alone in the living room.

"Don't be too mad at them," Nate says. "I was desperate."

"So he said. But I just don't get what you're doing here. I made it clear how I feel."

"That you're scared?" Nate quirks a brow. "Yeah, I heard you loud and clear."

"That's not what I said."

"It's what you meant though." He entwines our fingers and pulls me over to the couch.

Since the party is outside, we're alone in here.

"Did you fly all the way here for the birthday party?"

"I never left," he says, shocking me.

It's been almost a week since we finalized the deal, so he has no reason to be here, especially since I made it clear where I stand.

My stomach roils at the thought of him leaving, but I push my feelings aside. This is for the best…for both of us.

"The baby isn't coming for another five months," I point out.

"But you're here," he says with a soft smile. "I'm not going anywhere, Princess. If you're here, this is where I'm going to be."

My heart picks up speed at his words as flashes of my past flit through my memory. Me begging my mom not to give up, crying to my dad not to move us away from London. Pleading with John to choose us over his job. None of them chose me, yet Nate is here, begging me to choose us.

He didn't leave.

He wants to be with me.

He's choosing us.

But then my thoughts go back to the conversation I overheard in his parents' kitchen…

"He's worked so hard." Valerie.

"He's busted his ass to make this company what it is." Dustin.

"He must be devastated. I hate this for him." Valerie.

This is what I wanted. For someone to choose me, yet the thought of him doing so has me feeling sick because is it really a choice when he's being forced? Either move away from everything you love to be active in your baby's life or stay in Dallas and live long-distance from your baby. My hand goes to my belly. I hate all of this and don't know what the right answer is.

"Hey," Nate says, shaking me out of my intrusive thoughts. "What are—"

His phone rings, cutting him off. After he glances at it, he puts it back in his pocket.

"What—"

His phone rings again, and when he pulls it back out, his brow furrows. "Can you give me a second?" He looks at me nervously. "It's my dad, and he never calls twice in a row."

"Of course."

My God, am I such a bitch that he's scared to answer a call from his own family when he's around me? Of course he is because when I'm not pushing him away, I'm forcing him to choose between being here with his baby and being in Dallas with his family. This whole situation sucks.

"Thanks," Nate says. "I'll just be a minute."

He answers and turns his attention to his dad.

I don't know what they're talking about since I can only hear one side of the conversation, but from what I can gather, something has happened with a property they bought with the intention of building another hotel, and Nate's dad needs him to go there to handle it.

Nate argues back and forth with his dad, and my stomach sinks at the thought that he's arguing with him because of me. He doesn't want to leave because of me. Once again, he's being pulled in another direction because of me and our baby. And it's always going to be like this if I can't convince him to stay in Dallas.

Or you could move to Dallas?

Right…give up my house, my job, my friends…and then when he's had enough of me—because let's face it, everyone in my life eventually does—I'll be stuck there, all alone.

Ugh, cue the *woe is me* pity party for one. Why can't I just throw all my inhibitions out the window and jump in headfirst?

"Hey," Nate says when he hangs up, cupping the side of my face. "What's going through that beautiful head of yours? And please don't lie."

"I've never had anyone fight to stay with me," I admit, my voice shaky with emotion. "Everyone in my life has always chosen to walk away. But you actually fight to stay. I'm just not sure what's worse—them choosing to walk away or you being forced to stay here."

"Let's get one thing clear," he says, moving his hand to my jaw and tipping it so I have no choice but to look into his eyes. "*Nobody* forces me to do anything. I'm right where I want to be. With you and our baby."

"And what if there was no baby?" I blurt out.

"What?" He glances down at my stomach in confusion.

"I mean, what if I weren't pregnant? Would you still be here? Choosing me over your job? Over the only home you've ever known? Over your family that you're close to?"

I hate that my insecurities are driving me to ask these types of questions, but I need to know because nothing between us happened the way it was supposed to, and I can't help but fear that he's making his choices because of the baby and not because of me.

"When I took over the Kingston-Bradford partnership, I had no idea that you were pregnant," he says. "All I knew was that I had been missing you like crazy for two months and I needed to see you." His eyes bore into mine, and my heart clenches in my chest. "I tried like hell to respect your wishes, but I couldn't do it. I came to Rosemary to see you."

"And you're staying because I'm pregnant."

"No," he corrects. "I'm staying because I fell in love with *you*. Do I want to be home with my family? I would be lying if I said I didn't. I love my family and my job. But I love you too, Paige. And in life, we have to make decisions—"

"You mean sacrifices."

"No," he says, "*choices*, and I'm choosing you. I can visit my family anytime. I can get a new job. I can live with you, or we can buy a new house. But if I stay in Dallas, I don't get you, and you're everything I want, with or without the baby."

I choke out a sob, and he pulls me into his arms.

"I love you, and I'm not going anywhere."

He's not going anywhere.

He wants to stay with me.

He's choosing me.

But what about his family? By him staying here, his family is left without their future CEO. Bradford Hotels runs the risk of no longer being family-owned and-operated. And all because of my selfishness.

"Hey," he says softly, wiping away a tear I didn't realize had fallen. "What's going on?"

I open my mouth to tell him what I overheard, but before I can get the words out, his phone buzzes in his pocket.

"It's okay," I tell him, forcing a smile. It's bad enough he's going to be leaving his family's company for me. The least I can do is be understanding when they need him. "Answer that. Your family needs you."

"My dad needs me to go to Vegas," he says. "He'd go, but he hasn't handled anything regarding this property, so he wouldn't know where to start, and they're not telling him much over the phone, except they were digging at the site and something happened, causing the county to issue a cease and desist. I'm going to meet our attorney there to get it all sorted. If I could send someone else, I would, but…"

"It's okay," I insist. "It's part of the job."

"I'll be back as soon as I can," he promises. "But while I'm gone, can I call you?"

The pleading in his tone has me saying, "Of course."

I'm so confused about where we stand, but one thing I know is that I need to stop avoiding him. No matter what happens, he's the father of my baby, and we're going to be in each other's life for a long time.

And then a thought hits me. "Will you be back for my twenty-week appointment?"

"That's not for over a week." He scoffs. "There's no way I'll be gone that long. From what my dad said, there's a snag with the county. Probably a permit that wasn't filed correctly. If all goes well, I should be back in a few days at most." He leans in and presses a kiss to my temple. "And when I get back, we're going to talk about us, Paige."

CHAPTER TWENTY-FOUR

Paige

"GOOD MORNING, BEAUTIFUL."

I smile into the phone at Nate. He's been gone for four days, and every day, he's made it a point to video-call me in the morning and evening.

"Good morning," I say back, rolling to my side and snuggling into my pillow. "How's it going?"

Nate's brows pinch together at my question, and my stomach knots at the look of distress on his face.

"Not good," he admits. "When I arrived, they notified me that they had found bones, but this morning, they confirmed they're human."

"What?" I sit up in shock. "Like people bones?"

I scrunch my nose up in disgust, and Nate chuckles.

"Yeah, tests came back positive for human DNA. Everything has been shut down while they investigate."

"Maybe it's for the best. Do you really want to build a hotel on top of a murder scene?"

Nate barks out a laugh and shakes his head. "Yes, we do. Otherwise, hundreds of jobs will be lost on top of the millions of dollars in man hours we've already spent on this project. Right now, we're hoping the bones are from a murder and not part of an Indian burial ground because if they turn out to be from an Indian tribe, we're fucked."

"When will you know?"

"Hopefully in the next few days."

"You still awake?"

"No, you're talking to a sleeping person," I joke, making Nate chuckle.

He has dark circles under his eyes, his hair is a mess like he's been running his fingers through it all day, his suit is rumpled, and his tie is barely hanging on, yet he's calling me to say good night.

I hate that he's being stretched so thin, but when I told him he doesn't need to call me every day, twice a day, he told me talking to me was the best parts of his day, so how could I deny him that? Besides, if I'm honest with myself, it's the best parts of mine as well.

It's been eight days since he left, and I'm missing him more than I thought I would. Since he's come back into my life, the longest we've gone being apart has been the few days I avoided him after the partnership and marketing plan were finalized.

Missing him has me wanting to tell him I want to give us a chance because the thought of us not being together physically hurts my heart, and the idea of him listening to me and going back to Dallas makes me feel sick to my stomach. But then I remember how upset his brother Dustin was about Nate walking away from the company, and I'm at a loss as to what the right thing to do is.

The problem is, Nate being gone and calling me twice a day has given us the chance to talk. While I've been worried about Nate feeling forced into moving to Rosemary—despite him saying he doesn't feel that way—he's done a damn good job of proving otherwise, which is making it really hard for me to continue to keep him at an arm's length. I'm worried that once he comes back, I'm going to selfishly give in and give us a chance because the truth is, that's what I want. I want Nate here, with me, and not just because he's the father of my baby, but also because I love him and can see a future with him. But more than that, I can't see a future without him.

"Sorry I called so late," he mutters. "It's been a crazy day."

"Any news on the bones?"

"Not yet." He sighs and drops onto the edge of the bed. "Tell me something good."

As I'm thinking of something to say, a flutter spreads throughout my belly, and I smile. "I can feel the baby inside me," I tell him.

"What?" His eyes widen. "Like, kicking?"

"It's more like a flutter. At first, I thought it was gas," I admit, my face warming in embarrassment. "But after it happened a few more times, I realized it's the baby." My hand goes to my belly, and I rub it, hoping my little guy or girl can feel how much I already love them.

"That's wonderful," Nate says with a smile. "I can't wait to feel it once it gets stronger."

Speaking of which…

"When are you coming back?" I ask since the ultrasound appointment is in two days.

"I don't know," he says with a sigh. "Everything here is fucked. Our attorneys are working around the clock, but the county is dragging their feet." He pulls the phone back and then sighs again. "Hey, I hate to cut our talk short but—"

"No, no! Go!" I tell him without letting him finish.

He doesn't owe me anything, and this is exactly why I've been pushing for us to focus on figuring out our roles as parents and not on us. It's obvious Nate cares about his family's company—as he should—and asking or expecting him to walk away from it all is selfish. I know he's hell-bent on doing it anyway to prove that he's all in, but when he gets back, we're going to need to sit down and discuss this because I can't imagine Nate being happy, walking away from everything just to, what, take a chance on us? When the fact is, he can be a father in Dallas. It won't be perfect, and a lot of travel will have to take place, but I can't be the reason he gives up every-thing…even if I want to be.

He looks like he wants to argue despite being the one who needs to go, so, before he can, I tell him good night and hang up. And then I spend the rest of the night trying to figure out how to convince him—and myself—that him going back to Dallas is for the best.

"Hey, Paige. We're going over to Kira and Ryder's for dinner. Wanna go?"

I look up from the email I'm typing and shake my head. "Thanks, but I'm a bit tired. I think I'm going to grab takeout and get into my pajamas and binge-watch something on Netflix."

Today has been a shitty day, starting with Nate not calling this morning—like he's been doing every day. He texted that he was sorry things have been a mess and had flowers sent to my office, but it only solidified that I'm doing the right thing by pushing him away.

He's exhausted and burned out. Bradford Hotels means everything to him, and I'm not going to be the one to take it away from him.

Ana nods. "Any news as to when Nate will be back?"

"No, but he said he'll be at my appointment tomorrow."

Although that was before he stopped calling, so, at this point, who knows? And since I don't want to add to the pressure that he's under, I haven't brought it up.

And if I'm honest, I'm nervous to ask and hear him tell me that he can't make it, which will break my heart.

"Okay," she says. "Well, if anything changes, I made sure not to have any appointments scheduled so I'll be free to go with you."

She smiles softly at me, and I'm reminded why Anastasia Parker is my best friend.

"Thank you," I say, pushing back my chair, so I can give her a hug.

But when I take a step around the desk, somehow, my heel must get caught on the carpet because I lose my balance and stumble forward. It happens in slow motion yet not slow enough for me to prevent it from happening.

I try to break my fall by grabbing ahold of the desk, but in doing so, my stomach collides with the corner, and when a huge pain radiates throughout my body, I fall back, landing on the ground in what feels like the worst game of human pinball.

Ana's immediately at my side, calling for an ambulance and then asking if I'm okay. But I can't speak. Words are on the tip of my tongue, but I can't release them.

Julian runs in moments later and tells me not to move.

While we wait for the ambulance to arrive, I clutch my stomach, sharp pains immobilizing me. A myriad of thoughts and emotions flicks through my head and heart—pain, worry, confusion… but the strongest is fear. Fear of losing my baby. It's my job to protect them, and I've failed.

"Do you want me to call Nate?" Ana asks.

"No." I shake my head, feeling like the worst mom-to-be in the world.

I should've been more careful. Nate warned me wearing heels was dangerous, and what did I tell him? That I was a pro. Now, look where I am. Lying on the floor of my office, waiting for an ambulance and praying that my baby is okay.

When Ana gives me a look, I add, "I don't want to worry him. I'll call him once I know…" I choke out the last word, unable to finish my sentence. Not wanting to put my fear out into the world.

Thankfully, the paramedics arrive quickly, and after Ana relays what happened and I tell them my symptoms, they help me onto a stretcher and then take me to the ambulance, where I'm brought to the closest hospital with Ana and Julian following.

Once we arrive, they wheel me into a room and then carefully transfer me onto a bed. Ana texts that they're waiting in the waiting room and to let her know if I need anything. I'm surprised she didn't offer to come to my room, but I'm too worried to give it much thought.

A sweet young nurse greets me, and after I go through what happened, she says, "Well, Ms. Abrams, how about we take a look at your little one, so we can see what we're working with?"

As I nod, my first thought is that I wish Nate were here by my side. And it's with that admission that I know, despite how much I want to do the right thing and push Nate away, I'm going to be selfish and pull him in closer. Because I love him and I want him by my side, no matter what the future holds.

I'm about to text him to let him know what's going on when there's a knock on my door. Assuming it's Ana, I tell her to come in. Only when the door opens, it's not Ana.

It's Nate.

CHAPTER TWENTY-FIVE

"THEY'VE CONFIRMED THE BONES ARE NOT FROM AN Indian tribe," Nolan says over my Bluetooth.

"Thanks." I sigh in relief. "Let's—"

The screen on the dash lights up with an incoming call—Julian Parker. He never calls me. The only reason I have his number saved is because of our companies working together, but our teams are handling the details, so this can't be about the partnership, which means there's only one reason he's calling me.

"I'll call you back."

Without waiting for Nolan's response, I switch the call over.

"Hey, Julian. Is—"

"Please tell me you're on your way here." Ana.

The desperation in her tone causes goose bumps to prickle my skin.

"I'm on my way to Paige's house as we speak."

Her doctor's appointment isn't until tomorrow, but I couldn't stay away from Paige another day. The phone calls weren't enough. And the stress of being away from her was eating away at me. She's the calm to my storm, and I told my dad that I'll be working remotely from Rosemary since there's nothing else for me to do in Vegas.

Thanks to Nolan's update, all we're waiting on now is for the county to give us the green light for construction to continue, and they don't need me there for that.

My plan is to get to Paige's place before she gets off work and surprise her with dinner since I know the code to get inside her house. And now, with the county approving us to continue construction, we have something to celebrate.

"Okay, good," Ana says, bringing me back to the now. "There's something you need to know…Paige fell."

"What? Where is she? Is she okay?"

"We're on our way to the hospital now. We don't know anything, but she's in the ambulance. We didn't want to risk moving her. They're taking her to Rosemary General."

"I'm on my way."

I hang up with her and input the hospital into the GPS. Fifteen minutes. Thank God this town is fucking small.

When I arrive, Ana and Julian are already in the waiting room. I shake Julian's hand, and Ana gives me a quick hug. Then, I go to the nurse at the front desk, needing to get to Paige.

After explaining that she's my wife and she's pregnant, the nurse scans my license and then guides me back to Paige's room. The door is closed, so I knock, and once I hear her soft voice say to come in, I step inside, noting how fragile and scared she looks, sitting in the large hospital bed.

"Nate," she gasps, her eyes widening in surprise. "You're here."

"Fuck, Princess."

I make a beeline straight for her, ignoring the woman who's standing next to her. I give her a kiss on her forehead, inhaling her sweet scent. And when I tilt her chin up, my heart breaks at the raw emotion swimming in her eyes.

"Are you okay?" I murmur, squatting so we're eye level.

"I…" She glances at the woman. "I'm okay but…" The tears welling up in her eyes spill over. "I don't know if the baby is," she whispers.

"It's okay," I tell her, taking her hand in mine. "It's going to be okay."

"You're just in time," the woman says. "We were just about to do an ultrasound to see what we're working with."

I notice she's wearing a white lab coat, and when she twists slightly, her name badge reads Dr. Michaels.

She looks at Paige. "Are you okay with him being in the room?"

"Yes," Paige says. "He's the dad."

"Okay, I'm going to go grab the machine, and I'll be back in a moment."

"What happened?" I ask once the doctor leaves us alone.

"It was all my fault," Paige cries, shaking her head. "You told me not to wear heels—"

"Hey, hey, stop. You look sexy in those heels. I just didn't want you to be uncomfortable."

"I tripped," she mutters. "My heel got caught on something, and I fell. My stomach hit the corner of the desk," she sobs. "It hurt so badly."

"Paige, this isn't your fault," I tell her, hating that she's blaming herself. If something is wrong with the baby, she's never going to forgive herself. "People trip all the time. Even if you had been in the safest tennis shoes possible, you could've tripped."

"But I wasn't in the safest heels. I was in tall heels. If something happened to our baby—"

"Stop," I tell her, grabbing a chair and sitting next to her. She lays her head on my shoulder, and I hold her the best I can from the side. "No matter what that ultrasound shows, this wasn't your fault. Shit happens. But we'll get through it together."

She looks up at me, and I kiss her soft lips that are tinged with salt from her tears.

"I missed you," she says.

"Not as much as I missed you."

"How long are you here for?"

"I'm not going anywhere."

Her phone buzzes from next to her on the bed, and I sit back.

"Why did Ana call me?" I ask.

I assumed it was because Paige hadn't had access to her phone, but she obviously does.

"I didn't want to bother you," she admits with a frown.

"What?" I hiss. "Are you serious? You fell. In what universe did you think calling me to let me know what happened would be considered bothering me?"

And then it hits me. "Did I do something to make you think you couldn't call me?"

"No." She shakes her head. "It's just…you've been busy. You've barely called the past couple of days, and when we did talk, I could see the stress you were under. I didn't want to add to that, especially without knowing what's going on."

She rests her hand on her protruding belly. In the week and a half that I've been gone, she's grown more, her bump even more pronounced, and I can't wait to see all the ways her body changes as she grows our baby.

"It feels like you do that a lot," I say with a sigh.

"What?"

"Take my choices away from me. You didn't call me because you didn't want to bother me, but did you think about how I would feel, not knowing? Had Ana not called me, I would've been at your house, surprising you with dinner, while you're in the hospital, worried about our baby. The same way you keep telling me where I should and shouldn't live and whether I should be with you."

She swallows thickly, and I hate that we're having this conversation right now, but it's one that needs to be had.

"You told me that your dad didn't talk to you after your mom died. He moved you to another country without considering your feelings. He took your choices away, and you didn't like that, did you?"

She shakes her head.

"Neither do I. I'm never too busy for you, Paige. Never. You understand that?" I pinch her chin and look into her eyes, which are filled with sorrow. "I don't care where I am or what I'm doing. You come first. Always. Don't take my choices away. You and this baby are my world. Let me in, please."

She nods in understanding, and we're both quiet for a moment before she breaks the silence.

"What if I lost the baby?" she whispers, fresh tears filling her eyes.

"Don't think like that," I say, squeezing her hand. "There's no use in thinking the worst."

"But it hurt. And...I'd rather prepare for the worst."

I don't agree with that logic, but since that's her way of thinking, I go with it. "*If* something happened to the baby, we'll handle it together." With the hand that's not holding hers, I palm her cheek.

"It's you and me, for as long as you'll have me. I came to Rosemary for you. You being pregnant was merely a bonus."

"I want you," she admits, shocking me. "I realized this week how much I care about you. And even though it's selfish, I want to be with you. I know your family is going to be upset but—"

"Whoa, why would my family be upset?"

My family has been one hundred percent supportive since they found out about her.

"I overheard Dustin and his wife talking at the barbecue," she admits, looking at me sheepishly.

Suddenly, it all makes sense. One minute, she was fine, and the next, she was pushing me away.

"He said they would have to find someone to replace you… someone that's not family, and Valerie said you must be devastated."

Jesus, fuck. I'm going to kill my brother and his wife. I know without a doubt that they both support my decision but…

"Dustin is a numbers guy," I tell her. "He's good at his job. He handles our numbers like the expert he is, but there's a reason why he doesn't want to be anything but our CFO. He sucks at communication, and he's the least eloquent speaker I know.

"And as for Valerie, she's a workaholic, and I say that in the nicest way possible. It's why she and my brother don't have kids. They love their jobs, and for her, the thought of me walking away from the CEO position is unfathomable." I run my knuckles down her cheek. "But I can tell you, they both support my decision."

"They probably hate me for taking you away," she mutters.

"Not even close. Are they upset that I'm leaving? Of course. Honestly, I would be a bit hurt if they didn't give a shit." I shrug. "But Valerie is Dustin's world, so he gets it."

"He told her that," she says. "He said he would choose her. But he doesn't have to."

A tear slides down her cheek, and I catch it with my thumb.

"That's because she works for Bradford, and they've created a life together without having to make choices like we do."

"I hate that you have to choose. That I'm *making* you choose."

"You're not making me do anything. You told me this is where your life is and you're not comfortable moving to Dallas, so I'm choosing to move here to be with you. You've been hurt, and you've lost your trust in others. But I'm going to prove to you that not all of us will hurt you. And one day, you're going to trust me…trust *us*."

"I want that," she admits.

"Good." I lean over and kiss her. "Because I'm going to make sure you have everything you want."

I hold her for a few minutes, until there's a knock on the door, followed by the doctor pulling in a cart.

"Sorry about that," Dr. Michaels says. "We're a bit short-staffed at the moment."

She types away on the screen and then says, "Okay, let's have a look."

Paige lifts her shirt, and the doctor tucks a blue towel in her waistband, then squirts gel onto her stomach.

We sit in silence, both of us watching the screen, though I have no idea what I'm looking for since I've never seen an ultrasound in action before.

Paige squeezes my hand, and I do it back, silently letting her know I'm right here.

The doctor moves the probe around her stomach, spreading the gel all over. She stops every few seconds, clicks and types, and then does it all over again.

Finally, she glances at us with a soft smile, and I sigh in relief because there's no way a doctor smiles like that if she's about to give you bad news.

"Everything looks perfect," she says, making Paige sob in relief. "This is your baby's heartbeat." She turns a knob, and the most beautiful whooshing sound hits our ears. "It's strong. One hundred forty-three beats per minute."

She moves the probe around some more. "This is the face… the hands…the feet."

The screen is gray and black, but the baby is outlined perfectly. I can make out the face, the ribs, his or her little heart beating. Until now, I don't think I fully grasped it…

"We're having a baby," I murmur to Paige, who laughs.

"We are." She giggles.

"That's in you," I whisper.

"It is," she agrees with another watery laugh.

"I'm assuming by the way you're talking, you don't know the gender yet," the doctor says with a grin. "Are we waiting, or would you like to know?"

"You know?" Paige asks, her eyes lighting up.

"I do. Would you like to know?"

"Yes," Paige says, then glances at me. "You still want to know, right?"

"Sure. Would be nice to be able to refer to it as a he or she."

"Okay then," the doctor says. "You see this?" She slides the probe over and points to a blurry area on the screen. "That's a boy."

"Really?" Paige gasps. "We're having a boy?"

"You are," the doctor says. "I know your appointment is tomorrow. And because of what's happened, I'd like you to keep it. It can't hurt to have another ultrasound done, but everything looks good. A woman's body is meant to protect the baby, and when you fell, your body did just that."

She removes the probe and stands. "I'll let them know that you can be discharged, but I do want you to take it easy. Based on the bruise that's already forming, you're going to be sore. If you can, rest for a few days."

Once she's gone, Paige looks at me with a smile on her face and tears in her eyes. "He's okay."

"He is." I bring her hand up to my lips and kiss her knuckles. "And he's perfect."

CHAPTER TWENTY-SIX

Paige

"WHAT ARE YOU DOING?"

I glance up at Nate. "Nothing."

"Really?" He chuckles. "Because it looks like I stepped away for ten minutes to make a call and you decided to bag up all of your heels when you're supposed to be resting."

"Huh…don't know what you're talking about."

I throw my favorite pair of Jimmy Choos into the bag—*It's been a good run. Sorry to see you go*—but before I can grab my Louboutins, Nate snatches the bag away from me.

"Paige, stop," he says gently. "You're supposed to be resting, and this is the opposite of that."

"I've been resting for days," I whine. "And I'm sitting on the floor, which is considered resting." I pout, knowing full well I sound like a baby.

Nate tries to hide his smirk, but I catch it and glare his way.

"I just need to finish packing up this bag to donate, and then I'll rest."

Aside from going to my doctor's appointment the day after I was discharged, Nate has insisted I stay in bed while he waits on me hand and foot, refusing to let me do anything that might cause me stress—including sex.

I learned that the hard way the second night he slept in bed with me and I tried to make a move. He gently took my hands, kissed my knuckles, and told me it wasn't that he didn't want to, but he wanted to talk about us, as well as make sure I was no longer sore before we did anything.

I pouted my best pout, but he wouldn't budge, threatening to sleep on the couch if I couldn't behave myself.

"You're not donating all your heels," he says. "You were scared, and I get it, but you and the baby are okay. When the dust settles, you're going to regret getting rid of all those sexy heels when you're stuck with only your running shoes and flats."

"Fine." I huff, standing with his help, and walk out of my walk-in closet. "But I'm at least getting rid of the pair I was wearing when I fell."

"What do you say we take a little trip?" Nate drops the bag into my closet and closes the door.

"Where?"

Since It's Friday and I'm off until Monday, we could go somewhere, but it can't be too far...

"I was thinking—"

My phone goes off, and when I see it's my dad, I click Ignore. "Go ahead."

Nate's brows furrow. "Whose call did you just decline?"

"My dad." I shrug.

"You should answer it."

"It's going to be awkward. It's always awkward. And I'm supposed to be resting."

Nate chuckles. "Way to twist the doctor's words, but seriously, Paige." He steps into my space and drops his hands onto my hips. "Maybe it's time to talk to him. You're going to be a parent in a few months. What if our son overheard something and he didn't give you the chance to explain?"

"Really?" I groan. "And you talked about me twisting the doctor's words?" When he simply raises a brow, I sigh. "Okay, fine. But, umm…" I swallow nervously. "Will you stay here with me?"

"There's nowhere else I'd rather be."

When I call my dad back, he answers on the first ring.

"Paige, are you okay?"

His words shock me.

"Umm, yeah…" I say, walking out to the living room and sitting on the couch.

"I was worried. I called you several times, and you didn't answer."

I don't know if it's the sound of genuine concern in his tone or the fact that I've already decided to talk to him about what I overheard, but instead of answering, I blurt out, "Why?"

"Why what?" he asks.

"Why were you worried?"

"What do you mean? You're my daughter, and you're pregnant. Of course I'm going to worry."

"But why?" I choke out. "Why do you care? You didn't even want me, so I don't understand why you waste your time worrying about me as if you give a shit."

"What the hell are you talking about, Paige?"

"I heard you," I admit. "All those years ago, when you didn't think I was home, you told Mom you never wanted me. I heard you. You told her that you never wanted me…that you never wanted a family, and the only reason why I was born was because she wanted me!"

I choke out a sob, and Nate pulls me into his comforting arms.

"I just don't understand why you care," I continue. "I thought you'd be relieved that I moved away and never came back, yet you keep calling me every month like clockwork, as if you actually care."

When I stop speaking, I feel the weight lift off my shoulders from the many years of holding on to this information. I probably shouldn't have spilled it all out like that, but I doubt there's a good or proper way to bring up the subject.

The other side of the line is quiet for so long that I pull my phone away from my ear to make sure the call hasn't dropped.

And then my dad speaks…

"Oh, Paige," he murmurs. "Why didn't you say something?"

"Does it matter? You said what you said, and I heard."

"Of course it matters," he chokes out, emotion seeping through each word. "It matters because that was over fifteen years ago, and this entire time, you thought I didn't want you when that's the furthest thing from the truth. Oh my God," he sobs, making my body tense up because I wasn't expecting that kind of reaction from him.

I thought he'd be shocked, maybe embarrassed, but I didn't think he'd be…upset.

"I didn't know," he says. "I didn't understand why you'd pushed me away. I thought it was because you were grieving your mother's death, and then I moved us out of London, which I knew you were upset about. But now, it all makes sense."

"I was grieving Mom, and I was mad that you'd moved us," I tell him. "But I was also upset that you didn't want me. I know Mom and I were closer because you traveled a lot for work, but I thought we had our own special relationship. But then you told her you never wanted me, never wanted a family, and—"

"I didn't mean it," he says, his words making me dizzy.

I take a deep breath, confused because I know what I heard. "What do you mean, you didn't mean it? Why would you say something like that if you didn't mean it?"

Nate tightens his hold around me, silently reminding me that he's here.

"I didn't know you were home," Dad says. "I was mad at your mother. She had just told me she was stopping the treatments, and I was terrified I was going to lose her. So, I said things I didn't mean in hopes that she would change her mind. Her biggest fear was leaving you, so I used it against her. I'm so sorry, Paige. You have to know that I didn't mean it. I love you. You and your mother were my entire world. How could I not love and want you? You are the best parts of your mom and me."

He sobs through the phone, and a lump of emotion fills my throat.

"But you said…"

Oh God. I got it all wrong.

"I apologized to your mom that night," he says. "I told her I was sorry and that I didn't mean it. She, of course, knew that I hadn't. But I didn't know…*fuck*, Paige. All these years, you thought I didn't want you. It's why you moved away and never came home, isn't it? I should've known something was wrong. I should've forced you to talk to me. Debbie told me so many times to talk to you, to ask if I did something wrong, but I've never been the best at communicating. That's no excuse though. I'm your father, and I should've pushed…"

"It takes two," I tell him as tears drip down my cheeks. "I was hurt. And then you met Debbie and started this whole new life with her, and I didn't understand why you wanted Kristin and Ashleigh and not me. I should've talked to you. I shouldn't have let it go on this long."

"I swear I have always wanted you," Dad says. "When your mom first died, it was hard because you looked so much like her and had the same mannerisms, and I missed her like crazy. I knew you were upset with me for moving, but it felt like everywhere and everything was filled with your mom, and it was just so damn hard."

I release a soft sob because I get it. As much as I love London, it's not the same without her.

"I knew it was cowardly to move us away," he continues, "and I knew you were upset. But I didn't know what you had overheard. If I had, I would've done everything in my power to show you how much I love you. Damn it!" he barks. "Your mom left this world, thinking you would have me, and I failed you."

"No, Dad," I sob. "You didn't fail me. I should've asked, but I was too scared of hearing you admit it. Which was stupid because I went years without seeing you. Years we can never get back. I'm so sorry."

"It's okay," Dad says. "I'm just glad that you finally told me. I miss you, honey. Please tell me I can see you. I want a relationship with you, one with more than monthly phone calls."

"I want that too," I tell him. "I want to see you and get to know Debbie and my sisters."

"They're going to be so excited, Paige. They ask about you all the time. I know you're pregnant, so maybe we can come to you."

"I would love that."

"Good. Now, tell me everything. Tell me about your job and your life and how your pregnancy is going. I want to know everything you've left out all these years."

For the next couple of hours, I tell my dad everything, starting with my time in college and ending with Nate. We laugh and cry, and it isn't until my stomach starts to rumble in hunger that I tell him I'll call him soon.

When I hang up, I go in search of Nate since he left earlier to give me some privacy. I find him sitting on the bed, back against the headboard, typing on his phone.

When he hears me come in, he sets his phone on the nightstand and gives me his full attention. Something he always does when he's with me.

"That sounded like it went well," he says as I pad over to him.

"It did. But it never should've happened. I should've spoken to him fifteen years ago, when I overheard him. All those years wasted because of my pride and fear."

I climb into Nate's lap, situating myself so my knees are on either side of him, my soft belly lightly bumping against his. He wraps his arms around my waist and looks into my eyes, and my heart squeezes in my chest.

"I made a huge mistake with my dad," I tell him. "And I don't want to make that mistake with you." When he quirks a brow, I explain, "I don't know what the future holds, and everything with us has happened out of order."

I choke out a laugh, and he shrugs.

"But what I do know is that I fell for you in England, and I've only fallen harder since you found me. I was scared to let you in. First because I've been burned on more than one occasion when it comes to letting people in. And then because I felt guilty. I mean, why should you have to uproot your entire life because of me?"

"Because one of us has to," he murmurs, palming my cheek. "And I'm okay with it being me. Your home, your life, and your job are not any less important than mine. I love you, and I want a life with you and our little guy." He glides his hand down to my belly and presses his palm against it tenderly.

"I want that too," I tell him, hating that I can't tell him that I love him yet. I want to—I can feel it—but I'm still so scared. "I want to see where things go between us. We still have plenty of time before the baby comes, and I want to spend that time with you, getting to know you—and not just as the father of my baby, but as more than that. Is that okay?" I ask. "I know it's not what—"

"Stop," Nate says softly, refusing to let me finish. "That's more than okay. You need to take things slow, and I get it. I've been hurt too. But my wounds have since healed, and that's partly because of you. But yours are newer, fresher, and it's going to take time. And it just so happens I have plenty of time."

"Thank you," I mutter, sighing in relief that he understands.

I want to have it all with him. The family, the home, the love… but I need to take things one day at a time so I don't feel like we're rushing into things. The last thing I want is to go all in and Nate regret it and then be forced to break my heart.

"I'd do anything for you," he says, cupping my face with his strong hands.

His lips capture mine, and the kiss starts off gentle with the silent promise of a fresh start. But then his tongue slides into my mouth, and I'm overtaken with lust and want and need.

Without breaking the kiss, Nate lifts me off his lap and carefully lays me onto my back, then lifts my shirt over my head, exposing my simple black bra and boy shorts.

"Do you know how sexy you look like this?" he says as he kisses the swells of my breasts. "They were perfect before, but now…fuck," he now out. "I just want to lick and suck them for hours."

Pulling one cup down and then the other, he gives each nipple a gentle lick before he sucks one into his mouth, drawing a moan from me.

After he's given them both enough attention that I'm damn near coming from nipple stimulation alone, he moves on, kissing his way down my torso.

"Every time I see your stomach, it's grown a little more." He smiles warmly up at me and then gives my bump a soft kiss, making my thighs clench. "I think we should take a picture…for the scrapbook."

He sits up on his haunches and pulls his phone out, aiming it at me. With my body changing and my clothes no longer fitting, I've been feeling a bit self-conscious. But then Nate looks at me the way he does, and I can't help but feel sexy.

"You know this can't go into my scrapbook, right?" I say with a laugh when the click of his camera goes off.

"Oh, I know. But I think I'm going to start one of my own." He glances at me and waggles his brows. "It will be for our eyes only. A scrapbook of you growing my baby."

He takes a few more pictures of me and then pockets his phone.

"I love you like this," he says, gliding his hand over my belly. "As a matter of fact, I might have to keep you like this." His eyes twinkle with mirth and heat. "How many babies do you want?"

"I don't know," I breathe. "Maybe two or three."

My thoughts go to Nate reading our son a story, rocking him to sleep. They move to us having a little girl with his whiskey-colored eyes and playful smile. Nate playing dress-up with her. Taking them to soccer or dance. Birthday parties and holidays. Family vacations.

Five months ago, I couldn't even imagine having a family, but now, I can see it all with Nate.

"That sounds like a good number," he says, sliding his hand over my belly again as his gaze descends.

When he reaches the waistband of my panties, he tugs them down my legs and tosses them to the side so he can situate himself between my thighs.

"This is new," he says, tugging on my pubic hair.

I usually keep it neatly trimmed, but with my belly getting bigger…

"It's getting a little harder to see what's down there," I mutter, my face and neck warming in embarrassment.

"I like it," he says, spreading my lips and running the tip of his finger up and down my center. "But if you ever need help, I would be more than happy to volunteer my services."

"I'll think about it," I whisper, so turned on that I'm going to implode if Nate doesn't get me off soon. "But right now, I just really need you to make me come."

"Your wish is my command."

And with those words, he slides down the bed so he's eye level with my most intimate parts and gets straight to devouring me.

If the way he expertly licks and sucks on my clit weren't enough to bring me straight to the precipice, his moans of pleasure, as if he's the one being pleased instead of me, would have me dangling over the edge.

"I'm so close," I breathe, wanting the pleasure to continue forever and to come at the same time.

Nobody knows my body the way Nate does, and it's made me realize that it's not about how long you're with someone. It's about caring enough to actually get to know the person you're with. And Nate cares a lot.

"Fuck, you taste so good," he murmurs as he reaches up and tweaks my nipple.

When his tongue leaves my clit, the impending orgasm disappears, and I pout down at him, making him laugh.

"I was almost there."

"I know, Princess. But the second you come, you're going to push me away, and I haven't had my fill of you yet."

I laugh, knowing he's right. But in my defense, when I come, my body gets so sensitive.

Nate goes back to massaging my clit with his tongue, and

between his perfect strokes and pinching my nipples, it doesn't take long for the most intense orgasm to overtake me. I come so hard that my entire body shakes as blackness speckles my vision and the world around me becomes fuzzy.

When I come to, Nate is staring at me with a soft, smug smile on his face.

"What?" I mutter.

"I love watching you come," he says simply.

"Good. Now, get up here and fuck me so I can come again."

He barks out a laugh. "Anything for you," he says, leaning over and kissing me.

Tasting myself on his lips has me deepening the kiss. There's just something about knowing he was down there, licking and sucking my juices—and not because I asked him to, but because he wanted to—that's a turn-on in itself.

Without breaking our kiss, Nate guides himself into me. I'm wet, so he slides right in, filling me like my pussy was made just for him.

"So goddamn perfect," he murmurs against my lips.

I wrap my legs around him, and he takes that as his cue to start to move. He feels so good inside of me. It only takes a few strokes before I start to feel the stirrings of another orgasm.

"You feel that?" Nate asks as he languidly pushes in and out of me, stopping each time he bottoms out for several seconds before pulling back and then thrusting back in.

"Feel what?"

"Me inside of you…"

"It feels good," I moan.

"Of course it does." He licks the seam of my lips. "Because your body was made for me, and if I have it my way, I'm going to spend the rest of my life inside you."

His mouth captures mine, and while no more words are spoken, Nate shows me just how much he loves our bodies together as he makes love to me until we're both moaning each other's name when we find our orgasms.

When he pulls out, instead of lying next to me to catch his breath, he picks me up, bridal-style, and walks us into my bathroom, setting me on the counter so he can turn the water on. Then, he lifts me into the shower and sets me on my feet, where he insists on cleaning me head to toe while I stand there and enjoy the way he takes care of me.

"I want to go away with you," he says once we're both out of the shower and in towels. "Being away from you felt like hell. And then with the scare…I just want to spend some time with you."

I wrap my arms around his neck, my heart pounding in my chest because I've never felt as loved and cherished as I do with Nate. He has a million things going on, yet all he wants is to spend time with me.

"I would love that."

CHAPTER TWENTY-SEVEN

Nate

"OH MY GOD! LOOK AT HOW ADORABLE THIS IS!" PAIGE laughs as she lifts up a onesie that reads Plot Twist with an open book underneath it.

We've spent the weekend at my parents' vacation house in Southampton, just the two of us. Because I'm always so busy with work, I rarely take the time to fly to the East Coast to enjoy the house, but I figured it would be the perfect getaway for Paige and me.

It's nine thousand square feet, it has a pool and Jacuzzi in the backyard, and it backs up to a private beach. While Paige loves the amenities, her favorite part of the trip seems to be the shops. Now that we know the baby's gender, she's started to shop for clothes, and even though shopping is probably my least favorite thing to do, I love watching the way her face lights up every time she finds another adorable outfit.

"That's cute," I tell her, taking it and adding it to the basket of stuff she's already picked out.

She's browsing the rest of the baby clothes when her phone chirps with an incoming message. She stops to check it, and then she looks up at me with a glare.

"What?" I ask, my stomach dropping.

This weekend has been damn good, filled with delicious food, great conversation, and amazing sex, and the last thing I want is for it to be ruined.

"Why didn't you tell me your birthday is next weekend?"

"What?" I repeat.

She turns the phone around, and I read the text she just received…from my mother.

> **Joanne**: Hey, Paige! I don't know if Nathan told you, but his birthday is on Saturday, and we usually celebrate it here, taking him to his favorite steakhouse. I would love it if you came to Dallas with him. We miss you and would love to spend time with you.

I scroll up and see this isn't the first text my mom's sent her. There's actually several. Many of them asking how Paige is doing. There's one from Paige, sharing the ultrasound pics showing that we're having a boy. I, of course, already shared that info with my family as soon as we found out since Paige had said it was fine to do so, but I had no idea she'd been texting with my mom.

"You've been texting with my mom?"

"Umm…yeah," she says sheepishly. "She gave me her number when we visited, and after I texted her to thank her for a wonderful weekend, we continued to text. I hope that's okay."

"Of course it is," I say. "I love that you're comfortable with her enough to text with her."

"We talk on the phone too," she admits. "She's so sweet, and she reminds me a lot of my mom," she says, squeezing the fuck out of my heart. "I miss her so much, and with the baby coming, it's been nice, being able to talk to her. She's so excited about the baby."

"I'm glad you have her." I pull her into my arms and drop a quick kiss to her pillow-soft lips. "My family loves you almost as much as I do."

"Why didn't you tell me it's your birthday?" she asks again.

"It honestly slipped my mind. Between the shitstorm with the hotel and you being in the hospital and then us going away, I haven't thought about it."

"Are you going to Dallas for your birthday?"

"That depends." I hold her tighter, loving the way her bump presses against me. "Are you going with me?"

"I'd love to," she says, reaching up and pecking my lips. "We can make a long weekend out of it. I have tons of PTO, so we can leave Friday if you want and stay through Monday."

"That sounds perfect. Now, let's check out so we can go back to the house. I'm starved."

"You're hungry already?" Paige asks incredulously. "We just ate lunch."

"Yeah, but I didn't have any dessert."

I waggle my brows, and her eyes light up knowingly.

"Well, in that case, let's go."

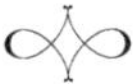

"Holy shit, I feel like I haven't seen you in forever!" Dustin pulls me in for a hug and slaps me on the back. "How does it feel to be an old man?"

"Thirty-five is hardly old," I scoff. "And you just saw me in our meeting yesterday."

I might be working remotely until we figure out what to do

about me leaving Bradford since I'll be moving to Rosemary perma-nently soon, but my brothers and I video-chat damn near every day.

"Yeah, but it's not the same as seeing your ugly mug in person."

Everyone laughs, but when I glance at Paige, I notice she's sport-ing a frown.

"You okay?" I ask.

"Yeah," she says, plastering a fake smile on her face.

If we weren't in front of my entire family, I would push her, knowing damn well something is wrong, but I let it go for now.

"Oh, Paige!" my mom coos. "Look at your bump. May I touch it?"

"Of course," Paige says, giving my mom a genuine smile. "And feel this."

She takes my mom's hand and places it on her belly. She holds it there for a few seconds while I grin, knowing what's about to happen.

"Oh my God!" Mom shrieks, tears filling her eyes. "Was that… did he just kick?"

"He did," Paige says with a grin.

We started feeling him kick a few days ago, and when Paige is asleep and my mind is running, I can lie there for hours with my hand on her belly, waiting for our little guy to make an appearance.

"Can I feel?" Penny asks.

"Sure." Paige guides her hand to her belly, and when the baby kicks, her face lights up again.

"I miss being pregnant." Penny pouts to Carmine.

"Oh no. No way." My brother laughs. "You can live vicariously through Paige. We agreed two and done."

"I know, but what's one more?" She flutters her lashes, and Carmine groans.

"We'll talk about this later," he says, making Penny grin.

There's very little Carmine wouldn't do for his wife, and I have no doubt that if she genuinely wants another baby, he'll happily give it to her.

"Come sit," Mom says, taking Paige's hand and guiding her into the living room. "Tell me everything. How was your trip? How are you feeling? Have you started to get the baby's room ready?"

We spend the day at my parents' place. My dad grills while the kids play in the pool, and everyone eats their weight in delicious food.

I haven't brought up to Dustin what Paige overheard, but when I find us alone in the kitchen while Paige is in the pool outside, I decide to mention it. It's not that I'm mad. I know he wouldn't say anything to hurt Paige, but he needs to be aware that she overheard so it doesn't happen again.

"Paige overheard you and Valerie talking when we were here for Dad's birthday."

Dustin's eyes go wide. "Oh shit."

"Yeah. She thinks you guys don't like her because you think she's taking me away from the family business."

"Fuck." He shakes his head. "I don't remember exactly what was said, but we'd never blame her, and we sure as hell didn't mean to upset her. Valerie and I are worried about what it will mean for the future of Bradford. Dad's been talking about maybe staying on as CEO a bit longer and training Valerie, but she's afraid of not being able to fill your shoes. Everyone knows you're the best at what you do. It's like you were made to run Bradford, you know?"

Damn it, I know how much my mom has been looking forward to my dad retiring at the end of next year. She's already started planning their vacations.

"I get it," I tell him. "But we'll figure it out. I can work remotely for the time being, and I can help train Valerie as well if she wants to take that leap."

"It would help, but there are too many meetings you need to be in Dallas for, and when your son is here, you're not going to want to be traveling back and forth."

"I know," I agree. "But we'll handle it. And just for the record, both you and Valerie are more than qualified to take my place. You guys don't give yourselves enough credit."

I hate that my family is stressing because of me, but I don't know how to fix it. After spending time with Paige, I know my home is where she is, and since that's in Rosemary, that means I'm going to have to eventually cut ties with Bradford and find a job locally because Dustin is right. Traveling is already a part of running a hotel chain, but if I try to work remotely after the baby comes, it will only add to the already-necessary travel, and the last thing I want is to leave Paige with the brunt of caring for our baby.

"We'll see." Dustin shrugs.

I open my mouth to say something else, but the sound of the French doors opening stops me, and it's a good thing since Paige walks in, glancing at my brother and me.

"Hey," she says carefully, her eyes darting between Dustin and me, obviously worried about what she walked in on. "I have to use the bathroom."

"I was thinking," Dustin says with a smirk on his face. "If you need help naming the baby, you could name him Dustin, after the smartest Bradford in the family."

Paige cracks a smile. "I'll definitely take that into consideration."

When she leaves us alone again, Dustin pats my shoulder. "Like I told Valerie, I can't imagine a life without her, and if she said tomorrow that she wanted to move to fucking Alaska, I'd buy the thickest jacket and follow her ass there. It sucks that Paige's life is four hours away, but no matter what, you have your family, and we support both of you completely."

"I love your family," Paige says as she slides her leg over my torso so she's straddling me. "They're so nice to me." She reaches back and strokes my cock through the material of my briefs, making me groan.

"Is that your way of flirting?" I say with a choked laugh. "Because I have to tell you, there are way sexier things you can say that don't involve my family." I grip the curve of her hips. "Like, *Oh, Nate, I love how your cock fills me.* Or *I love when you eat my—*"

"Okay," Paige says, slapping her hand over my mouth before I can finish my sentence. "Sorry, I was just thinking about how nice this weekend has been, and I hate that we have to go back home. These trips away are spoiling me."

"It was the perfect weekend," I agree.

It didn't matter whether we were at my parents' for the barbecue or my birthday dinner or at Sunday brunch at the country club with my entire family, Paige fit in effortlessly with my family.

She gets along with my brothers and sisters-in-law. She and my mom seem to have developed their own relationship, complete with Paige calling her Ma. Even my dad is smitten with her, offering to make the baby's bassinet—since woodwork is a hobby of his. He made one for Penny and Carmine, and they used it with both of their kids.

"But we can come back anytime we want," I remind her. "Now, enough about my family." I lift Paige's shirt over her head, exposing her luscious breasts that are spilling over her thin lace bra and her tiny matching underwear. "The only thing I want to think about is being inside you."

I reach around and undo her bra, watching as her breasts drop and her nipples harden. Then, I take one into my hand and bring her nipple to my lips, swirling my tongue around the hardened tip while I pinch the other nipple.

Paige throws her head back with a loud moan, her body so damn sensitive since she's become pregnant.

I pull my briefs down, my hard cock bouncing up and hitting the back of her ass since she's wearing a tiny thong. Before I can peel the material to the side and plunge into her warmth, she leans over, her perfect raindrop tits hanging in front of my face, and reaches behind her, grabbing my shaft and rubbing it along her ass crack, pushing the material to the side so we're skin to skin.

"Fuck," I breathe. "You know what your ass does to me. Don't tease me unless you're gonna let me have it."

She smirks and then leans in so our mouths are almost touching. "You can have it."

"What?" I question in shock at her response. "Are you sure?"

"Uh-huh." She nods. "I want you to fuck my ass tonight. But you'd better make it good because the last time a guy—" She cuts herself off, her eyes going wide.

"The last time what?" I ask, wanting her to finish her thought. "Tell me."

"You want me to talk about another guy in bed?"

"I want you to always tell me exactly what you're thinking. Nothing is off-limits."

"Okay," she says. "Well, the last guy who tried to..." Her face tinges pink, and I have to stifle my laugh at how adorable she is. "You know..." she continues. "It wasn't good. It hurt. So, if you don't make this good, I'll probably never let you do it again."

"Oh, baby," I say, one hundred percent up for the challenge. "I'm going to make it so good that you'll be *begging* me to fuck it again."

I lift her off me and set her on all fours so she's facing the side of the bed with her ass facing the other side, and then I pad to my bathroom to grab the lube.

She waits exactly how I left her—with her tits and belly hanging and her ass in the air. She looks like a fucking wet dream, and I can't believe she's mine.

Before I focus on her ass, I come up next to her and palm her tits, rolling her nipples between my fingers. She moans in pleasure and then shocks me when she reaches down and fists my cock, bringing it straight to her mouth and swallowing my entire length.

I let her go to town on my cock, bobbing her head up and down, for a few minutes while I get lost in the pleasure. But when my balls start to harden, I force her mouth off me.

When she pouts, licking the saliva from the corners of her mouth, I shake my head.

"The only place I'm going to be coming is in your tight ass."

As I walk around the bed, I glide my hand under her, palming her heavy breast and feeling her protruding belly that continues to grow my baby in it. When I get to her pussy, I hook my finger around the waistband of her underwear and tug them down her legs, tossing them to the side. Then, I slide a single finger down her pussy, starting at her clit and working my way through her wetness and up to her ass.

"You talk about me teasing you?" She glares back at me. "I'm going to explode if you don't fuck me soon."

"You want it to be good?" I ask, raising a brow. "Then, don't rush me. I bet whatever dumbass fucked you back here didn't take his time. He was too damn selfish to think about your pleasure above his, and that's why it sucked. Now, let me make us both feel good."

Without waiting for her to respond, I spread her cheeks and lift her ass. Then, I dip my face down and lick my way through her wet center and up to her hole. Paige drops her head and moans, and I have no doubt she's going to love this.

I spend some time tonguing her tight hole, getting it nice and wet, while I massage her clit. It doesn't take long for her orgasm to rip through her, her pussy dripping with her juices.

"My God, that feels so good," she groans when I gather her juices, spread them all over her asshole, and push a single digit inside.

"You haven't felt anything yet. Play with your tits while I get you ready for me."

She does as I said while I finger her tight ass, adding another digit and then another. I work her up higher and higher until I feel her clenching around my fingers.

"That's it, baby. Come for me again," I tell her.

The more satiated she is, the easier my cock will slide into her tight ass.

A few seconds later, Paige calls out my name, coming for a second time.

Before she can come down from her high, I pull my fingers out, squirt some lube onto my cock, stroke it a couple of times to make sure it will slide in easily, and then guide myself into her.

She's so blissed out from her two orgasms that she doesn't resist, letting me slowly slide right in.

When my entire cock is in her ass, I stop and wait for her to get used to it, but my little minx once again shocks me when she wiggles her ass and says, "Please, Nate. I need you to fuck me," as her hand disappears under her, no doubt to stroke her needy fucking clit.

Gripping the curves of her hips, I start to fuck her. I start off slow to make sure it feels good, and when she moans, I pick up my pace. She's too warm and tight, and it feels too good. And when Paige begins to meet me thrust for thrust, I know I'm never going to last.

And then her third climax hits, her body shaking from the

overstimulation, and her ass tightens, choking my cock like a fucking vise. And I come so damn hard that I swear I almost black out.

She doesn't stop thrusting against me until her ass has milked my cock dry, and then she moves forward and drops onto her side, her eyes closed. She looks completely wrung out from her three orgasms and ass-fucking.

"Was it good?" I ask, lifting her into my arms to carry her to the bathroom.

"So good," she says, her words coming out slurred, like she's drunk off her orgasms. "But that doesn't surprise me," she murmurs. "Everything you do to me is good."

I chuckle as I set her down in the shower and wash us both off. Once we're clean, I dry her off, towel-dry her hair, and then help her get her pajamas on, all while Paige works to simply keep her eyes open. She might be horny, but she's still pregnant, and she tires easily.

I lay her in bed, wrapping myself around her from behind, and she turns over so her head is nestled in the crook of my arm and her belly is pushing against my side.

"Thank you for taking such good care of me," she murmurs once she's situated. "I was so scared to let you in, but you always put me first."

"And I always will," I tell her, watching as her eyelashes flutter against the apples of her cheeks.

Her breathing evens out, and her body goes lax with sleep.

I lean down and kiss her forehead, inhaling her scent that I've grown addicted to. "I'll always put you and our baby first. Always."

CHAPTER TWENTY-EIGHT

Ana: Where are you?

Before I can respond, my phone rings with an incoming call from her.

"You didn't even give me a chance to respond," I say with a laugh.

"Sorry, you know I lack patience."

"I do. What's up?"

"We're going to brunch."

"And by we…"

"Me, you, and Kira."

"And do I have a say in this?" I ask, giving her a hard time even though I'll be going.

Nate and I were supposed to spend the day together, but at the last minute, he told me he had a bunch of work to get done, including some meetings, so he was going to be at the hotel. It's the first time he's chosen to work from the hotel instead of at my house in months—and on a Saturday, no less, when we usually don't do any work on Saturdays. So, I was a bit taken aback, but since it's his home away from home and I haven't asked him to move in with me yet—and he was already set on leaving the moment he woke up—I didn't argue.

"No," Ana says through the line. "I'm on my way to you, and Kira is meeting us at the restaurant, so be ready in twenty minutes."

"Jeez, a little warning would've been nice," I mutter as I stand from my desk and head to my bedroom to get ready.

"See you soon," Ana says before hanging up.

I send a text to Nate to let him know my plans, and he responds with:

> **Nate:** Sounds good! I'm buried in work, so I probably won't be able to come over until dinnertime anyway.

After throwing on a cute maternity shirt and jeans, paired with my ballet flats since I'm still on a no-heel kick, I take my prenatal vitamin and then head out to sit on my front porch while I wait for Ana to arrive. And while I wait, I scroll through the *baby names* app I downloaded. It's been two months since we found out we're having a boy, but we can't decide on a name. Joanne said she and Cary didn't name any of her kids until she saw them, and then the name came to her.

When Ana pulls up, I lock the front door and then hop into her SUV. Okay, maybe I don't quite hop…more like I slide in slowly since I'm twenty-nine weeks pregnant, but tomayto, tomahto.

"Look at you," Ana says, glancing at me. "You're glowing."

"I am not." I roll my eyes. "I'm sweating because I'm nearly the size of a small house and hot from the walk down the sidewalk since we're in the dead of summer in Texas, but we can pretend I'm glowing if you'd like."

"You're not the size of a small house." She laughs. "You're pregnant and glowing."

"Well, thanks. And thanks for the brunch invite. I feel like I never see either of you anymore."

Sure, I see Ana at work, and we've gotten together for the occasional barbecue and book club meeting, but it feels like we're all busy doing our own thing.

"I agree," Ana says. "We're going to need to schedule a weekly or biweekly girls' lunch, so we don't go too long without seeing each other. It's like time just gets away from us."

"Doesn't it sometimes feel surreal? Not that long ago, we were living in London, our only worries being how to deal with our grump of a boss…"

"And now, I'm a wife and a mother of two, and you've got a baby on the way," she finishes. "Life doesn't stop—that's for sure."

"No, it doesn't," I agree, getting a bit emotional at the thought of how much has changed and all that will be changing in the near future.

When we arrive at the restaurant, Kira is already seated at a table.

"Hey!" She gives Ana a hug and then attempts to give me one, but with both of us pregnant, it ends up being more like a side hug that makes us both laugh.

Ana has a seat next to Kira, and I sit across from her, all of us piling our purses on the empty chair next to me.

"How have you been feeling?" I ask Kira once we've ordered drinks.

"Good! Ryder and I had a 3D scan done since we couldn't find out the gender at our twenty-week appointment, and it was so cool!"

"Well, don't keep us in suspense," Ana chides playfully. "Are you having a boy or a girl?"

"A boy!" Kira shrieks.

"Oh my God! Congrats!" Ana says, hugging her.

"I'm so happy for you," I tell her. "Is Ryder excited?"

With them already having two girls, they were hoping for a boy, but Ryder is such a girl dad that he said he honestly didn't care as long as the baby was healthy.

"He is," Kira says. "I think he's hoping it will even out the gender field, but I reminded him that three girls versus two guys means we still win, and we've decided after this little guy comes, we're done. We're good with three."

"Three is good," I agree, remembering the conversation Nate and I had regarding how many kids we want.

The thought of little Nates running around fills my heart with happiness…which is something I shouldn't even be thinking about since we're not even living together yet. He's been spending the night at my place every night, but he still has the hotel room in Houston.

Because you asked him to take things slow, my subconscious reminds me.

Which has me wondering, at what point do we take the next step? And how will I know when I'm ready? The last time I moved in with a guy, I thought he was the one, and it ended horribly—with him choosing his job over us and then choosing my friend over me.

But Nate isn't John, and it's unfair to compare the two.

Unlike John, Nate is all in.

Then, why are you so scared to fully commit to Nate? To move to Dallas?

The second question hits me like a ton of bricks, forcing me to suck in a harsh breath. Move to Dallas? That's not even an option… right? My house is here, my life is here…I told Nate I couldn't move.

Then, why are you thinking about it like it's a possibility?

"Have you told the girls they're going to have a little brother?" Ana asks Kira, shaking me out of my thoughts.

"Yeah, they're excited," Kira says. "Though Violet is a little concerned he might not be up for having tea parties." She rolls her eyes playfully, and we all laugh.

"I'm sure she'll bribe him into doing them," Ana says. "That little girl could convince an Eskimo to buy ice by simply batting her lashes."

Kira snorts out a laugh. "That is true."

The waitress sets down our drinks, then takes our food order. Once she's gone, Ana turns her attention to me.

"I know you've been busy with Nate, but how are things going?"

"Good," I say, taking a sip of my orange juice.

"Umm, you're going to have to give us more than that," Kira says with a laugh.

"Things are good." I shrug. "As you know, we went to Dallas for Nate's birthday last month, and his family is amazing. His mom is sweet and excited to have another grandchild. His mom and sisters-in-law have added me to their group chat, and they're all so kind, always asking how I'm doing and when we can get together again. They have a close family, and even though I'm not used to that, it's really nice."

Ana and Kira both nod in understanding.

"Julian's parents are the same way," Ana says. "I miss my mom like crazy, but it's nice to be close to my dad and in-laws, and as you know, my stepmom is as sweet as it gets. She treats my kids like they're her blood. It's nice, always having someone around in case we need anything."

"When they say it takes a village, they aren't kidding," Kira adds. "We only have Ryder's grandpa and my mom here, but I'm so thankful for them both."

"And you have us," Ana points out. "But I get it. We're all so busy with our own lives."

"I feel bad we haven't made it back to Dallas yet, but I've been so busy with rolling out the Kingston-Bradford partnership. I haven't even gotten a chance to see my dad yet since we cleared the air."

"Don't put work above family," Ana says, using that CEO tone she only uses when she's dead serious. "Family is important. I'm glad I moved back to be close with my dad. Life is too short to not spend it with the ones we love."

My heart drops because unlike Ana and Kira, my dad's and Nate's families are all long-distance. There won't be any calling someone if we need anything, and if anyone wants to visit, they'll have to fly to us. It will just be me and Nate and our baby…

"Everything okay?" Kira asks, noticing that I've gone quiet.

"Yeah," I choke out. "Just have a lot on my mind."

"Baby brain is the worst," Kira agrees with a dramatic shiver as I pull my phone out to text Joanne and my dad to see if either of them is up for a visit.

Maybe we can visit Nate's family this weekend or next and then my dad. Soon, I'll be too far along to go anywhere, so I want to get the visits in while I can. Ana's right. Life is too short, and I don't want to waste a moment.

> **Me:** Hey, Joanne! I was thinking about asking Nate if he wants to make a trip to Dallas to visit you guys. Let me know if/when you're up for company.

Before I click out of the thread to send my dad a text, Joanne responds.

> We are always up for company! But we're actually out of town this weekend.

Immediately following her text is a picture of her holding the most adorable onesie that reads **Please pass me to grandma** with a huge smile on her face.

The thought that my mom will never meet her grandson nearly takes the breath out of me, and before I know what's happening, tears are spilling down my cheeks.

I'm pregnant, and my mom is gone. She'll never hold her grandson, and he'll never know who she is. No matter how much I tell him about her, show him our scrapbooks, he'll never know her. He won't get to experience her comforting hugs and listen to her words of wisdom.

"Paige, what's wrong?" Ana asks, getting up and coming around to me.

"I just…I really miss my mom," I whisper, grabbing a napkin to dab my eyes. "She's never going to meet my son. And Joanne is so sweet, and we're going to be living four hours away. What if I made the wrong decision?" I blurt out through a sob, looking up at Ana and then Kira. "What if living here is the wrong choice?"

I was so stuck on putting myself first that I didn't consider how my decision would affect my son. Sure, I have my home and job and friends, who I love like family, but we have no actual family here.

"Only you can decide that," Ana says gently. "I loved London, but I knew the moment I stepped into Julian's house that I was home. Only you know where home feels like for you."

"It's here," I say. "It has to be. This is where my job is and where you guys are, and I bought a house here. And what if Nate and I don't work out? I don't know anything about Dallas."

With every word spoken, my heart pumps faster as a panic attack quickly surfaces. It's hard to catch my breath, and as I try to suck in air, my vision starts to get fuzzy.

"Hey," Ana says, wrapping her arms around me. "Breathe, Paige. Breathe."

I do as she said, focusing on one breath at a time.

"That's it. Just breathe," she repeats until I've gotten my breathing under control and my vision is clear.

"You don't have to figure anything out now," Ana says. "And you aren't required to live anywhere."

"This is where my job and house are," I point out.

"So?" Ana shakes her head. "You can always find a new job—or hell, be a stay-at-home mom like Kira. And if you want to live in Dallas, you can easily sell your house here or keep it. And if you think moving four hours away would keep Kira and me away, you're crazy." She laughs. "I mean, what's the point of having a private jet if I can't use it, right? An hour, tops, and I'm to you, or vice versa."

I laugh, loving how positive my best friend is.

"And do you really think Nate is going anywhere?" Kira chimes in. "I've only met him a few times, but even I could see how in love with you he is."

"Oh, for sure," Ana agrees. "Just take it one day at a time. You'll know what the right move is when you know. It might be days from now or weeks or months. But no matter what you decide or when, you have so many people in your corner even if it means they're a plane ride away."

I sniffle back my sobs and wipe under my eyes, hoping I put on waterproof mascara today.

"Thank you," I tell them both. "It all just feels like a lot right now."

"I get it," Kira says. "Moving to another state was the hardest thing I'd ever done. But I'll never regret it because it meant meeting and falling in love with Ryder and Addie. But that doesn't mean the journey was easy." She reaches across the table and squeezes my hand. "We're all here for you though."

The waitress delivers our food, and the rest of brunch goes a lot smoother—with less tears—the three of us keeping the subjects surface level so there's no more crying.

Ana tells us about potty training Kingston and how the only reason he's agreed to wear underwear is because he wants to go to school and she told him he can't wear diapers to school, and Kira shows us where Ryder is taking her for their kid-free babymoon vacation. It's on the beach, and it reminds me of Nate's and my time in Southampton.

After we finish brunch, I assume Ana's going to bring me back to my house, so I'm shocked when Kira jumps in the back and says, "We're going shopping!"

CHAPTER TWENTY-NINE

SHOPPING TURNS INTO BUYING OURSELVES NEW OUTFITS, getting manis and pedis, and getting our hair done. When I text Nate to see if he wants to go to dinner tonight since I'm all dressed up with nowhere to go, he doesn't respond, but I chalk it up to him being busy with work.

I tell myself I'll give him until I get home to answer me, and then I'll try to call him, but instead of going to my house, Ana insists that we go to hers to continue our girls' day. When we pull into her driveway, there's a bunch of cars there, but she tells me it's because Julian has friends over to watch a basketball game.

"Isn't it the offseason?" I ask, remembering Nate telling me that basketball doesn't start until the end of October. He and his brothers always go to at least one Dallas home game together.

"Umm, I don't know," Ana says, waving me off. "Maybe it was football or golf. I can't even keep up."

Kira snorts out a laugh, and Ana playfully smacks her ass.

I'm so busy laughing at the two of them that I'm not paying attention when Ana opens the front door, and everyone shouts, "Surprise!"

"What the heck?" I gasp, my hands going to my chest.

"It's your baby shower," Ana says with a big grin.

"What?" I look around, shocked by everyone I see.

Nate's entire family is here, including his niece and nephew. I give his mom a smile, now understanding why she told me she was out of town.

Ana's family is here, including her dad and stepmom.

Kira's husband, Ryder, is also here with their two little girls.

A few other colleagues from work who I'm friends with are standing there with smiles on their faces.

And then I look to the left of Nate and see…

"Dad!" I breathe, tears filling my eyes.

I've seen pictures of him on social media, but it's been years since I've seen him in person.

"Paige," he says, walking over to me and enveloping me in a hug that has me breaking down in sobs.

"I can't believe you're here."

"You look so beautiful," Dad says as he hugs me. "You remind me so much of your mother when she was pregnant with you."

"I miss her so much," I whisper. "Thank you for being here."

"I wouldn't have missed it for the world," he says, kissing my temple and then stepping back.

I glance over and see his wife, Debbie, and their daughters.

"Thank you for coming," I tell them, giving each of them a hug before I look around at the blue, white, tan, and green decorations filling the living room.

There's a beautiful cake with jungle animals all over it—the same theme I showed Nate I was considering for the baby's nurs-ery—and tons of other goodies spread out along the tables.

"This is amazing," I say to Ana.

"Don't look at me," she says. "This was all Nate's doing. I just offered my home and to take you to breakfast so you wouldn't be suspicious."

I look at Nate, who's grinning softly. "You said you were working."

He chuckles and shakes his head. "Putting together a baby shower is hard work."

"Thank you. This is perfect." I lean on my tiptoes to give him a kiss and then address the room. "Thank you, everyone, for coming. This means so much to have all of you here to celebrate with us."

The baby shower is beautiful. Everyone talks and laughs and has a good time. There's enough food to feed an army, and after we play a few games that I'm shocked Nate found online—like pin the tail on the pregnant belly, guessing the baby's weight, and find-ing who can drink the baby bottle the fastest—we cut the cake and then open presents. The day is beyond perfect, and what makes it even better is when Nate tells me that our families are in town for the rest of the weekend and we'll be going to brunch with them tomorrow.

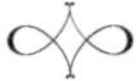

"I don't know why, but seeing all this stuff makes it feel that much more real," I tell Nate later, once we're home and he's unloaded the baby gifts into the guest room that I haven't yet started to make into a nursery.

"It is real," he says. "In a few months, you'll be giving birth to our little boy."

"Thank you for flying our families out," I tell him, wrapping my arms around him. "Today was perfect. More than perfect."

"I wish you could stay longer," I say to Joanne as we say goodbye to them after brunch.

Since they flew over on their private jet and the guys and Valerie all need to get back to work tomorrow, they can't stay any longer.

My dad and his family left after brunch to catch their flight with the promise to visit soon. At the very least, they'll come to see us once the baby is born.

"I do too," Joanne says. "But we'll text and video, and we'll see you soon." She wraps her arms around me in a motherly hug and kisses my temple. "I love you, Paige. Thank you for making my son so happy."

Once everyone has said goodbye, Nate slides his arm around me. "Ready to go home?"

"I already miss everyone."

Nate chuckles. "I get it, but we'll see them soon."

"Yeah, I know," I say with a sigh. I don't know if it's because I felt so high with everyone here, and now that they're gone, it's like I've crashed, but I'm suddenly feeling extremely exhausted. "I think I'm going to take a nap when we get home."

"Everything okay?" Nate asks, concern etched in his features.

"Yeah, I think I just need to catch up on my sleep. I didn't sleep well last night."

When we get home, Nate insists on taking a nap with me, so after we both change out of the outfits we wore to brunch, we climb into bed, and I lay my head against his chest while he runs his fingers up and down my spine.

"Thank you for this weekend," I tell him as my eyes start to close. "I hate that we go so long without seeing everyone."

You wouldn't have to go that long if you stopped being stubborn, my subconscious thinks. *If you lived in Dallas, you'd only be away from one family instead of both.*

"We'll figure it out," Nate says, leaning over and kissing the top of my head. "We have plenty of time to figure it all out."

I wake from my nap, alone, Nate's side of the bed empty. I don't know how long I slept for, but when I glance out the window, it's already dark.

Jeez, I must've slept all afternoon.

The time on my phone confirms it, along with the missed calls and messages since my phone was on silent. After checking and replying to everyone—Nate's family and mine both made it home safely—I go in search of Nate, finding him in my guest room with the furniture and floor covered and a few different splotches of paint on the walls. I immediately recognize the colors as the ones I showed him I wanted to paint the nursery.

"Hey," I say, making myself known. "Whatcha up to?"

Nate turns around and grins. "I couldn't sleep, so I figured I'd get started on the nursery. I ran to the store and picked up samples of the colors you'd mentioned and put them on the walls so you can see which ones you like the best. One of these would be for the main walls." He points to the samples on the left. "And one of these would be the accent wall you said you wanted. What do you think?"

I walk inside the room to give them a better look, trying to imagine the nursery in each of the colors he painted on the wall, but for some reason, none of them feel right. They're the exact colors I showed him, but they all feel wrong now. Which makes no sense because when I looked at the bedding sets online with these colors, I could visualize the crib and the changing table on the back wall…the rocking chair in the corner.

But now, nothing feels right. And that scares the hell out of me.

"Paige," Nate prompts, his brows pinched together in concern, "any color pop out at you?"

He looks at me, patiently waiting for an answer, but the words are stuck in my throat because nothing about this room or the colors feels right, and I don't know what's wrong with me. This isn't the first time I've felt like this, and it only seems to be getting worse.

"I…I don't think I'm ready to do the nursery yet," I stammer, having no clue how to explain what's going through my head when I don't even know. I thought I had it all figured out, but now, it feels like my head and heart are having conflicting emotions, and everything is all garbled up.

"Is everything okay?" Nate asks, worry etched in his features.

"I don't know," I breathe. "I thought I wanted those colors, but now…it just…" Tears prick my eyes. "I don't know," I repeat, feeling like I'm about to have a panic attack, similar to the one I had yesterday while at brunch with Ana and Kira.

"Hey," he says, pulling me into his arms. "It's okay. We don't have to do the nursery yet."

He guides us out of the room and shuts the door behind him, and it's only then I feel like I can somewhat breathe again. I don't know what the hell is wrong with me, but I think I need to do some serious soul-searching to figure it out. One thing I know for sure is that everything I thought I knew...I don't know.

"I'm sorry," I whisper. "I appreciate you trying to help."

"Stop," he says gently, sitting on the couch and pulling me down next to him. "It's all good. Nothing has to be done now."

Nate wraps his arms around me, and I settle into his side, resting my head on his chest and exhaling a relieved breath. When I'm in Nate's arms, everything else seems to fade away.

"I just found out I have to go to San Diego tomorrow to handle a few issues with a hotel expansion," he says after a few minutes. "I was going to send Valerie, but she's heading to Vegas."

"How long will you be gone for?" I ask, trying not to sound disappointed at the fact that Nate is leaving.

"I'm hoping for only a few days." He kisses my temple. "I was thinking we could have a quiet night in. How about I run you a bath to help you relax, and then I'll order us some food?"

"That sounds perfect."

While Nate runs the bath, I grab a drink of water, take my vitamins, and then meet him in the bathroom.

The tub is filled with bubbles, he's lit a couple of candles, and the book I'm currently reading is sitting on the edge, waiting for me.

"I used your lavender bubbles since you said it's the one that helps calm you," he says while I strip out of my clothes.

"Thank you," I tell him, overwhelmed by the patience Nate shows me.

He doesn't get annoyed with me—ever. He simply loves me the way I am and wants me to be happy. It's not something I've experienced in my previous relationships, which makes it hard to accept.

With Nate's help, so I don't risk slipping and falling, I step into the tub and slide down. Once I'm settled in the warm water, he gives me a quick kiss and disappears so I can relax.

I pick up my book and turn to the page I left off on, reading the first sentence, but several minutes later, I find I still haven't gotten past that same sentence, stuck in my own thoughts, trying to figure out why I've felt so off lately.

I started the year feeling alone, unsure of what the future held. I was in a toxic relationship with a selfish man I should've broken up with months before I did.

But eight months later, I'm in a healthy relationship with someone who loves me and makes me a priority. I have an actual relationship with my dad that I didn't think would ever happen, and I've gained so many friends and family—including Nate's mom, who I absolutely adore.

Rather than spending fifty hours a week at work, I find myself wanting to be at home with Nate. I look forward to our time together, whether it's cuddling on the couch, watching a movie, or going away for the weekend.

Spending time with our families and friends this weekend was absolute perfection. Everyone got along and the baby shower was more than I could've hoped or dreamed for.

For the first time, I feel like my life is full of so much good, yet I still feel off, and I can't quite pinpoint why that is.

"You look like you're doing the opposite of relaxing," Nate says, snapping me out of my thoughts.

I glance up at him leaning against the doorjamb with his arms crossed casually over his chest and his brown eyes filled with love and concern, and my heart squeezes in my chest. Nate is such a good man. He's smart and selfless. He cares about those around him, and he's going to make such a wonderful husband and father.

"I'm just thinking," I say, closing my book and setting it down.

Nate comes over and kneels next to me, reaching for the loofah and squirting some soap onto it. He dips it into the water and then, lifting my legs slightly, runs the loofah along my leg, starting at my shin and working his way up my thigh. He stops when he gets to the apex of my legs and starts all over again with the other leg.

As he runs the loofah up my leg, I close my eyes and lean my head back, enjoying the way he takes care of me. My body is tired, my brain is exhausted, but my heart feels so full, and I know that's because of Nate.

"I don't want you to go," I admit softly as he runs the loofah over my belly. "I know you have to, but I'm going to miss you."

Nate continues washing me, focusing on my breasts and then my neck and arms.

"I don't want to leave either," he admits. "I never minded traveling before, but now, I dread it."

His movements stop, and when I open my eyes, I find him staring at me.

"I love you," I tell him. "And I'll be here when you get back."

His eyes turn glassy, and he reaches up, palming the side of my face. "I love you too, Princess."

He leans over and kisses me tenderly, his tongue licking across the seam of my lips, and I part them, giving him access. The kiss quickly becomes heated, both of us trying to show one another how much we love and want each other through our actions.

When kissing isn't enough, Nate lifts me out of the tub and carries me over to the bed, where he makes love to me several times throughout the night, like we're both trying to make up for the fact that he's leaving tomorrow—only stopping long enough to eat the dinner he ordered. And it isn't until we're both satiated and we can barely move that he pulls me into him, and we fall asleep, skin to skin.

When I wake up in the morning, Nate's side of the bed is empty, and I already miss him. There's a note in his spot, and even though it doesn't make up for him being gone, my heart hurts a little less because I know he's going to miss me as much as I'll miss him.

> Princess,
>
> I didn't want to wake you since I know I wore you out last night. It was hard to leave this morning, but knowing that the quicker I get this done, the sooner I get to come home to you motivated me out of bed. Behave while I'm gone.
>
> Love you.
>
> Your Prince

CHAPTER THIRTY

Nate

EIGHT DAYS.

That's how long I've been gone.

Without Paige.

Without kissing her, making love to her, feeling our baby kick inside her.

It was only supposed to be a quick visit, but then one thing turned into another, and the next thing I knew, I was on a plane to New York, and now, I'm in fucking Portofino, Italy.

"Fuck, where the hell is that tie?"

My phone rings, so I stop my search to answer it and smile when Paige's face lights up the screen.

"Hey, is everything okay?" she asks, immediately noticing my anxiety.

"Yeah." I scrub my hand over my face. "I have that dinner tonight, and I can't find my blue tie."

It's my lucky tie. I made my first deal wearing it, so I wore it to another deal and then another. I've never *not* made a deal while wearing that tie, but now, I'm going to have to because it's not fucking here.

"This one?" Paige asks, holding up the tie.

"Yeah, that's it."

"It was in your other suitcase, nestled under your gray tie."

"Thanks," I say, "At least now, I can stop looking for it."

Between living in the hotel and spending most nights—well, really all of them—at Paige's, and still having a house in Dallas, it's making it difficult to keep track of what I have and where.

I sigh heavily, and Paige's brows narrow in concern.

"Sorry," I say, forcing a smile. "Just a lot going on."

She nods in understanding. "Traveling is part of your job. I get it. I miss you, but I get it."

My phone dings with a reminder that I need to leave for dinner. "I have to go. I'll call you when I get back to my hotel."

"Okay, I love you."

"I love you too."

We hang up, and I grab another tie and then change my mind, choosing to go without one, hoping it won't fuck up my track record. *No tie is better than the wrong tie, right?*

I'm in the car, on the way to dinner, when I get a text from Paige that reads

Incoming…NSFW.

And then, a moment later, the sexiest fucking photo I've ever seen pops up. It's of her, completely naked, wearing only my lucky tie around her neck, leaning back in her chair in her home office with a caption that reads

I'm wearing your tie for good luck.

New fantasy unlocked. When I get home, I'm going to fuck you just like that.

Come home soon, and you can fuck me however you want.

Soon.

I can't wait.

Since I have a good thirty-minute drive to the restaurant, thanks to traffic, I give my dad a call.

"Hey, son. How's it going?"

"Good. Hoping to close the deal in Portofino and then get back to Rosemary."

"Your mom mentioned you've been gone for over a week. I'm sorry." He sighs. "I know this isn't what you want to be doing…"

"It's not. But I'm not going to leave my family hanging. Speaking of which…I know we talked about me working remotely, but I think it's too much."

"I know," Dad agrees. "I've spoken to Valerie, and she's going to take over for you. You'll have to spend some time getting her caught up to speed, but she's a hard worker and motivated."

"But that doesn't help with your situation," I point out.

Dad was supposed to retire at the end of the year. If he can't find someone to fill his shoes…

"I've made the decision to push my retirement back," Dad says. "Dustin offered to step up as CEO, but I know he doesn't really want to, and the last thing I want is my son in a position that makes him unhappy. Valerie is willing to learn, but she has a long way to go."

"Fuck, Dad," I mutter, hating that I'm putting him in this position.

"Nate, it's okay. I'm going to interview some candidates and see what we're working with. You need to focus on Paige and my grandbaby. Have you thought about where you'd like to work there?"

"I don't know. Nothing feels right. I was thinking about maybe taking a year off. I have enough saved from investments. I can cash in some stocks if I need to. It'll give me time to figure out where I want to go from here."

"You'll figure it out, son. It feels hard right now, but your mom and I are proud of you. You're putting your family first. As you should."

I know I'm doing the right thing, and I'm content with my decision. I meant what I told Paige—she and our son come first. They always will. But Bradford Hotels has been a huge part of me since I was born. I'd be more concerned if walking away from it didn't hurt as much as it does.

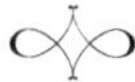

It's late, a little after ten, and when I texted Paige that I landed, she didn't respond. So, using the key she gave me, I open the door quietly, not wanting to wake her.

As she gets further along in her pregnancy, it's harder for her to sleep, so the last thing I want is for her to wake up and be unable to go back to sleep.

Only, when I get to her room, the bed is empty.

What the fuck?

I check her bathroom, but she's not in there.

Her car was in the driveway, so she has to be home. The house only has three bedrooms, so I check the in-progress nursery first, but it's exactly how we left it after she said she's not ready to work on it yet.

And then I head to the last room, her home office. When I open the door, it's dark, save for the desk light that's illuminating the area where Paige is sitting, exactly how she was sitting when she sent me that picture.

With her feet propped up on the desk and her ankles crossed, she's leaning back. She has her hair up in a messy bun, her reading glasses on, giving her the look of a sexy businesswoman, and she's completely naked, except for my blue tie that's hanging down the middle of her cleavage, the bottom landing on her swollen belly.

"I thought you'd be asleep by now."

"I was, but when you texted that you had landed, I woke up and wanted to surprise you." She drops her creamy legs from the desk, her feet hitting the floor, and stands, then saunters over to me. "I figured we could start a new tradition, aside from you wearing this tie." She lifts it up and grins. "Every time you close a deal, you get a blow job."

She tugs me by my shirt, guiding me over to her desk, and then turns me around and pushes me into the seat, unbuckling and unzipping my pants.

"I missed this," she says, pulling my cock out of its confines and pressing an open-mouthed kiss to the crown.

I can't help the moan that escapes my lips when she swirls her tongue around the tip and then takes me all the way down her throat.

As if my woman couldn't get any more perfect, I learned during our time together in London that Paige loves to suck cock—like really fucking loves it—and doesn't have a gag reflex.

I reach around her and fist her hair so I can watch as her head bobs up and down on my shaft, wetting and sucking it like it's the best thing she's ever tasted.

I haven't had sex in over a week, so it doesn't take long before my balls are tightening up and I'm close to blowing my load. But after a week of not being inside my woman, there's no way I'm going to let that happen.

Gently, I tug on her hair, and her mouth pops off my cock, a bit of saliva dripping from her lips as she looks up at me like I'm stopping her from indulging in her dessert.

"Princess, I need to be inside you," I tell her as I help her onto her feet and then lift her onto her desk. "It's been too long, and the only thing I want is to sink into your warmth."

"Fine," she sighs playfully, as if I were putting her out. "I guess you can fuck me."

She spreads her legs, exposing her glistening cunt, and my cock drips pre-cum, knowing it's about to slide home.

"I don't *fuck you* ever," I say, gripping her thighs and pulling her to the edge. I guide my cock to her opening and run the head up and down her wet slit. "I make love to you—always."

"Well then, what are you waiting for?" she groans, hating when I tease her. "Make fucking love to me!"

With a chuckle, I push into her, reveling in how warm and wet she is, and once I'm all the way in, we both moan in unison. It's been too long, and as I make love to Paige, I tell myself I'm done traveling, I'm done being away from her this long. There was a time when I thought I'd never have a future with her, but now, I not only have her, but she's also pregnant with my baby, and I'll be damned if I'm going to spend my life away from her when I can be right here, buried deep inside her, loving her.

A smart man learns from his mistakes, and there's no way I'm going to lose Paige because of my job. She means too much to me, and I'm going to put her first. Always.

We find our releases quickly, and once we come down from our high, I pull out of her, already counting down to when I can be inside her again.

"Shower?" I ask, grabbing a few tissues from atop her desk to wipe the cum dripping out of her.

"Sounds—"

Her phone rings, and when she glances at it, she says, "Can I meet you in there? It's Ana. I texted her earlier, asking her to call me when she got home because I needed to talk to her about something."

"Of course." I lean down and kiss her and then unbutton my shirt and hand it to her so she can put it on. "Don't be too long," I murmur against her lips. "I have a week to make up for."

CHAPTER THIRTY-ONE

"I'M GOING TO ASK NATE TO MOVE IN WITH ME."

"Well, it's about time," Ana says with a laugh.

"What is that supposed to mean?"

I glance back to make sure Nate can't hear while I pad to the guest bathroom to clean up since I have his cum dripping out of me.

"It means just as I said. It's about time. We all knew this would happen eventually. We were just waiting for you to catch up."

I roll my eyes and huff. "I was taking things slowly. Being cautious."

"I get it," she says. "But Nate isn't your dumbass ex. He's the real freaking deal. But you needed to see that for yourself. So, when are you going to ask him? And really"—she laughs—"are you going to actually ask him? Because we both know he's going to say yes."

"That's why I'm talking to you."

"Why does it sound like you're echoing? Are you in a bathroom?"

"Yes, Ana!" I whisper. "Nate just got home, and he's in the

shower, and I'm supposed to be in there, too, but instead, I'm hiding in the guest bathroom because I don't know how to do it."

"Take a shower?" she asks in confusion, and it takes everything in me not to bang my head against the wall.

"Oh my God, no! Ask him to move in."

"Oh! Just ask him while you're giving him head," she says with a laugh. "Julian always says yes to whatever I want while I'm giving him head."

"I heard that!" Julian yells.

"Too late for that," I mutter, making Ana crack up.

"Wait! Did you answer my call while you were—"

"No!" I hiss. "We already…*did it*. Then, you called, and I was freaking out in my head about how to ask him to move in so I told him I needed to talk to you and that I would meet him in the shower in a minute."

"Paige, I love you, but you overthink everything." Ana sighs. "The guy is in love with you. Simply tell him you're ready for him to move in."

"But what if he's changed his mind?" I whisper.

"Not happening, and we both know that. You're just nervous. But deep down, you know he's not going anywhere. So, get off the phone with me and go make that man's night by telling him you want him to move in with you."

She's right. I know she is. I know Nate loves me. It's just so hard, being vulnerable. But this is what I want. This past week without him has solidified how much I want Nate in my life—and not just him spending the night. I want to live with him, create a life with him. I love him and want a future with him.

"Okay, I'm going to tell him."

"Good girl. Let me know how it goes tomorrow at work."

We hang up, and I head to the bedroom, my body vibrating with excitement at taking the next step in our relationship.

"Finally," Nate says. "I was about to get out and drag you in here."

"Sorry! I'm coming in now."

I set my phone next to Nate's, but before I pull my hand away, his phone lights up with an incoming call from his mom. It ends before I can accept, and his screen shows several missed calls and texts.

"Hey, Nate, your mom just called."

"Paige," Nate says, popping his head out from behind the glass. "I've been without you for over a damn week. My mom can wait. Get your ass in here."

"I know but—"

I swipe at the screen, something in my stomach churning. His mom wouldn't call and text this many times and this late unless something was wrong.

"Let me just check the text she sent."

Nate grumbles under his breath, and I roll my eyes, secretly loving how much he missed me. When I unlock his phone, there isn't just a text from his mom. There are also texts from his brothers and Valerie. I click on the most recent one from his mom, and my heart sinks.

> **Mom**: Please call me back. We're at the hospital, and your dad is in surgery.

"Babe!" Nate yells over the sound of the water.

"Nate, I need you to get out of the shower," I say as I scroll up before reading the very first text sent from his mom.

> **Mom**: Your dad has had a stroke. We're on our way to the hospital. Please call me.

"What?" Nate asks, but my words are stuck in my throat.

My heart is pounding behind my rib cage, and it's hard to breathe.

Is his dad going to die? Will Nate lose him like I lost my mom?

No.

My mom was sick and weak, and the stroke was the end. But Nate's dad is strong, and he'll get through this. He has to get through this.

Nate turns off the water and gets out. "Paige, what's going on?"

I take a deep breath, reminding myself that this isn't about me. I need to be strong for Nate. It's his dad who had the stroke, and me freaking out isn't going to help him.

"Your dad had a stroke," I tell him, keeping my voice level. "They're at the hospital now."

Nate's face pales, and he rushes to grab his phone out of my hand.

He's dripping wet, getting water all over the floor, so I get him a towel and wrap it around his waist while he reads through the texts and then calls his mom back while he quickly gets dressed.

While he talks to her, I get dressed as well and pack a bag because we need to get to Dallas.

Damn it! We're going to have to fly because we don't live close by. Or maybe we'll have to drive? I don't know where his plane is.

I hear Nate talking to his mom, or maybe it's one of his brothers—I don't know. But I can't hear what's being said. I grab Nate's luggage from the doorway where he left it when he got home and dump it out so I can pack it with new clothes.

When he comes into the room, he looks at me with glassy eyes, and my heart clenches in my chest as I pray that his dad is okay.

"There was brain bleeding, and he's in surgery," he says, his voice filled with raw emotion. "I…I need to get to…"

"I packed our bags," I tell him. "Do you want to fly or drive?"

"Fly," he says. "Dustin said the jet is waiting for me."

"For us," I tell him, walking over and wrapping my arms around him. "I'm going with you. It's going to be okay."

My thoughts go back to Nate showing up in the hospital when I fell. He said those same words to me. Now, I have to hope mine ring true the same way his did.

I drive us to the airport since Nate is in no condition to drive, and the flight is quiet. Nate texts with his family, but there's no news yet. Either that or they don't want to give him bad news through a text message.

The car I ordered takes us to the hospital, and once we're there, we find his family in the waiting room. I hug his mom, telling her I love her while she sobs in my arms, and then Nate and I give each family member a hug. I've been missing them since they left from visiting for the baby shower, and I was hoping to see them soon, but not under these circumstances.

Once the greetings are over, Nate asks for an update.

"They haven't given us any news yet," Carmine says, his eyes bloodshot. "They took him back to handle the brain bleed, but that's all we know."

"They said he was stable," Dustin adds. "So, that's a good thing."

I nod, trying to push away my negative thoughts, not daring to mention that when my mom had her stroke, she slipped into a coma and never woke up.

Nate pulls me into his arms, and we sit in silence, waiting for the doctor to update us. The entire time, I pray that Cary's outcome is different from my mom's. That they'll fix him up and he'll be okay. And I don't stop praying until the doctor comes out and gives us the good and bad news: They got the brain bleed under control. But he had clogged arteries, so it required a surgery to unclog his arteries—which is why it took them longer.

"What now?" Joanne asks.

"We've moved him into recovery," the doctor says. "He'll slowly wake up. We'll keep him here for a few days to monitor him, and then he's going to need to rest for at least eight to twelve weeks. No stress. Healthy eating. He'll meet with his doctor to go over what they want him to take prescription-wise."

"Thank you," Joanne says. "I'll make sure he does all of that."

The doctor leaves, and everyone sighs, thankful that Cary is okay.

And then Joanne starts freaking out.

"He's going to need a nurse," she says, "and a dietician. I've told him for years that he needs to cut back on the high cholesterol foods. He's going to need to exercise. He sits at that darn desk too much." She pulls out her phone to, I assume, make a list. "I need to see about a gym membership, or maybe we can turn one of the guest rooms into a home gym. And he needs to retire."

She glances up, and her eyes meet Nate's. "He needs to retire," she chokes out, fresh tears filling her eyes. "The stress of the job isn't good for him."

Nate nods in understanding, but doesn't offer what we all know his mom needs. Instead, he says, "I can help Valerie learn the ropes, and Dad mentioned having some potential candidates."

"You know how stubborn he is," she cries. "He's going to go right back to work." She glances from Nate to his brothers. "We all know it. He's going to refuse to retire, and the stress is going to kill him, and I can't lose my husband. We're supposed to travel. Go on cruises. He promised."

Nate pulls me tighter into his side, not saying anything because he's trying to put me first. But I can't let him do that. His family needs him. They've been so good to me, so understanding and loving. They've accepted me into their life without thought.

"Nate," I say softly, looking up at him, "I think you should step up…as CEO."

Nate's eyes widen. "I can't," he says. "I can't do the job remotely and—"

"Your dad needs you." I palm the sides of his face. "It will only be temporary. When your dad wakes up, the last thing we want is for him to stress out. And your mom is right. Unless you step up, he's not going to walk away."

"Thank you," Joanne cries, pulling me into her arms. "Thank you, Paige. You don't know how much this means to me. To my family."

"Mom," Nate says, his voice devoid of all emotion, "I need to talk to Paige…alone."

He takes my hand in his and guides us down the hallway and out of earshot from his family. Then, he turns and faces me, his features etched with a mixture of pain and concern and—he smiles softly at me—love.

"Baby, if I step up as CEO, it will mean being the face of the company. I'll have to stay in Dallas. It will look bad if—"

"Stop," I say, pressing my hand to his heart. "It's okay. It'll only be until you get it all sorted. Besides, it will be easier to handle everything in person versus remotely."

"I don't want to be away from you," he murmurs, his bright brown eyes filled with fear.

"I can call Ana. I'm sure she'll let me work remotely. At least until I have to fly back to Rosemary for my checkup. Besides, we still have a couple months until the baby comes. That gives you time to figure out what to do."

Nate shakes his head and then wraps his arms around me. "I love you so much. I promise I'm going to work around the clock to get this all sorted so my dad can retire and I can be back in Rosemary before the baby comes."

"I know," I tell him, already missing him even though he's still right here in my arms.

But this is what his family needs, and it would be selfish of me to keep him in Rosemary when they need him here.

"I love you too," I tell him. "We'll get through this together. And once you get everything sorted and are able to come back to Rosemary, I don't want you in that hotel anymore." I look up at him, and his brows furrow in confusion. "I want you to move in with me. I'm ready, Nate. I'm ready to take the next step with you. I want to live with you. And when we bring our little guy home, I want us all under one roof…as a family."

Nate pulls me back into his arms and nuzzles his face into my hair. "Thank you, Paige. You've just taken the worst day and made it better."

CHAPTER THIRTY-TWO

"I THINK I LIKE YOUR TUB BETTER THAN MINE," I TELL NATE while we lounge in his humongous spa tub, complete with jets that massage you while you relax.

"Enough to stay?" he asks, tightly wrapping his arms around me from behind.

"I wish," I moan as Nate trails kisses along my neck and shoulder.

It's been several weeks since we arrived in Dallas, and I have to fly back tomorrow for my doctor's appointment. I already rescheduled it once, so I can't do it again. Nate offered to come with me, but I told him to stay. It's only a quick checkup, and we won't even see our little guy.

I'm going to be starting my maternity leave soon, so I have a lot of loose ends I need to tie up at Kingston, which will mean staying in Rosemary instead of coming back to Dallas. The hope is that once the baby comes, Nate will work remotely with the help of Valerie while they continue to interview candidates for the CEO position.

When Nate reaches around and plucks my nipple, I moan in pleasure and then carefully turn around, with the help of Nate, so I can face him. Getting around with my pregnant belly isn't easy, and as I get closer to my due date, it only gets harder, but I want to be close to Nate, kiss him and memorize his features before I have to leave.

"It's going to suck without you here," he mutters before he captures my mouth with his, kissing me like it's the last time he's going to see me for a long time. And I guess, in a way, it is.

For the past several weeks, we've been inseparable. Nate even set up a desk in the corner of his office so we could work near each other. We have breakfast, lunch, and dinner together. And while one would think we'd get sick of each other, I can't seem to get enough of him. Sometimes—okay, most of the time—our lunches even end in office sex.

"We'll text and FaceTime," I tell him as I wrap my hand around his shaft and guide him inside me, trying to convince us both that everything's going to be okay. We've done this before—been away from each other for weeks—and we'll get through this just like we did in the past.

After we make love and move to the shower to rinse off, we get dressed, and then I finish packing up my stuff since I won't be returning anytime soon.

"Can we go by and see your parents?" I ask when I'm all packed.

We've been visiting with them almost every day since his dad got discharged and went home.

Cary is so excited to have another grandson, and he loves to tell me stories about Nate when he was little. He was like a mini version of his adult self—big heart and driven. His dad said he used to go to his office when he was younger and pretend to be in charge, telling everyone what to do. I can totally see it. Nate was made to be CEO.

"I was just about to ask if you wanted to go," he says. "Penny made her famous lasagna as a goodbye meal for you because she knows you love it."

"Oh, yay!" I cheer. "Penny's lasagna is the best. I'm going to miss it," I say with a frown, as it hits me that I'm not only leaving Nate, but also his entire family.

A family I've gotten close to the last several months. Penny has been talking to me about all things baby, about breastfeeding or bottle-feeding, what diapers she recommends, and her birthing plan that she had with her babies. Since Nate and I haven't been home, we haven't done the tour of the hospital or registered yet, but we did discuss the birthing plan.

"Why didn't she text me?" I ask.

"She didn't want to put you on the spot. Make you feel obligated since it's your last night here."

I nod in understanding as tears fill my eyes. "I hate that I have to leave," I choke out.

We've spent these past several weeks with Nate's entire family as Cary recovers, and I've grown close to everyone. It's been nice, being surrounded by family, and I'm going to miss them all.

"We'll be back," Nate says, leaning in and giving me a kiss. "And I'm sure they're going to come visit when the baby is born." He wipes the tears from under my eyes. "Let's get ready to go."

Dinner with his family is bittersweet. Everyone hugs me, telling me to be safe and that they'll see me soon. I thought I'd be excited to go home since I haven't been there in weeks, but the truth is, I'm not looking forward to it at all. I'm actually kind of dreading it.

And the next morning, as Nate drives me to the airport, my

heart clenches in my chest. I feel as though I'm *leaving* home instead of going back to it.

When we arrive at the airport, I'm shocked to see Joanne waiting for me with a carry-on bag next to her.

"What are you doing here?" I ask, giving her a hug.

"I'm coming with you."

"What?" I glance from her to Nate in confusion.

"I love my husband, but he's driving me nuts at home," she says with a wink that tells me she's not being serious. "The nurses are taking care of him, and Nate is taking care of Bradford Hotels. So, I want to take care of you."

Her words cause me to sniffle back a sob.

"You don't have to—"

"I know," she says, not letting me finish. "But I want to. You're family." She places a loving hand on my belly. "I don't want you to be alone, so if it's okay with you, I thought I'd come along to keep you company. I know you have to go to work, but I figured I can help get the baby stuff and nursery ready. Nate mentioned you haven't started on any of it yet since you've been in Dallas."

A sob I was holding in releases, and I throw my arms around her.

"Thank you," I cry. "That would be wonderful." I've been stressing about the house not being ready for the baby, dreading going back and having to face it alone.

After I give Nate several kisses goodbye, promising to call as soon as we land, Joanne and I take off to Houston. Since I left my car at the airport when we flew to Dallas, it's still there—along with a hefty parking bill.

I call Nate to let him know we've arrived and then order dinner for Joanne and me.

As she bustles around the nursery, gathering the baby's clothes to wash them, I try to picture the nursery again, but I still can't.

I thought being away would help me see my home with fresh eyes, but it's only made me realize something: It's not the house that makes it a home. It's the people inside it, and Nate is my home. Whether we're here in Rosemary or with his family in Dallas, as long as we're together, that's what's important.

"You've been standing here for a while," Joanne says with a soft smile. "Are you envisioning the nursery?"

"Actually, no," I admit. "I was thinking about how I can't picture the nursery, and I finally know why. The baby doesn't belong here, and neither do I."

Joanne's eyes go wide. "Paige, what are you saying?"

"I thought by being independent, I was saving myself from being heartbroken again. But what I didn't realize is that my heart has been safe all along because it's in Nate's hands and he loves me too much to ever break it. This is just a house, a dwelling with four walls. But it's no longer my home, and my heart doesn't belong here."

"And where does your heart belong?" Joanne asks, hopefulness laced in her words.

"In Dallas…with our family."

CHAPTER THIRTY-THREE

"I KNOW THIS ISN'T IDEAL, BUT I CAN'T BE HERE," I say, scrubbing my hands over my face. "I missed her doctor's appointment, and I get that she said it was fine, but it's not. The baby can come anytime in the next several weeks, and I can't be here when it happens."

"I get it," Dustin says with a smirk. "But how about we focus on these numbers, and we can discuss this later?"

Carmine chuckles, and I glare at my brothers, who don't seem to give a shit that I'm being pulled in a million different directions and the only one I want to be pulled in is where Paige is. I appreciate her supporting me taking over as temporary CEO, but this isn't where I should be. I should be with her, in Rosemary—

My thoughts are cut off when there's a knock on the door, followed by Paige walking into the office. Since she's supposed to be in Rosemary, I shake my head, wondering if I'm seeing shit, but, nope, she's here, dressed in a beautiful maroon wraparound dress that shows off her belly.

"Hey," I say, pulling her into my arms.

I don't know why the hell she's here, but I'm so glad she is.

"We were just talking about you," Dustin says. "Nate was about two seconds away from getting on a plane and going to you."

Paige laughs, and the melodic sound hits me straight in my chest. I love this woman so much, and I can't go another month without seeing her. FaceTime and texting aren't enough.

"You're not going anywhere," she says, taking my hand and threading our fingers together. "This is your home, and it's where you belong."

"No." I shake my head, confused as fuck. "My home is with you."

"Then, you're going to have to stay," she says, her eyes filled with love. "Because this is my home now too."

"Wh-what?" I stammer because she can't possibly mean...

"I love you." She lifts her other hand to the side of my face. "And I love your family."

"I know," I tell her. "But they understand that you want to live in Rosemary."

"But I don't." She shakes her head. "While I was fighting to keep my house, to remain in Rosemary, to hold on to my job, I didn't re-alize that I was fighting for all the wrong things. When, the entire time, what I was craving was the magic that I'd felt when my mom was alive. It had disappeared when she passed away, and I couldn't seem to find it again until I met you.

"I thought you'd helped me find it again, but what I didn't un-derstand at the time was that the magic wasn't London. It's not the house or the job or the location. It's the person. It was my mom... and now, it's you.

"And that magic, it's not actually magic. It's the feeling of love...

of *being* loved. It's in the way you care about me and take care of me. The way you always put my wants and needs first. And now, it's my turn to do the same for you."

Fuck, this woman. She's everything I've ever wanted and more, but I can't let her do this.

"Paige, I appreciate you putting me first, but I don't want you to do that. I want to live where you want to live."

"And I want to live here with you and your family."

Dustin clears his throat, reminding us that him and Carmine are still here. "Not *his* family," he says. "We're your family too."

Paige smiles a watery smile. "Thank you."

"What about the house?" I ask, trying to wrap my head around all of this.

"I've contacted a realtor to put it up for sale. The movers have been hired to get my stuff and bring it here so we can sort through it all, and since you left your key card to your hotel room at the house, we stopped by there and got all your stuff."

"And the baby?" I ask.

"I spoke to my doctor, and she's transferring my file to Penny's OB."

"Her doctor is awesome," Carmine adds.

"People move all the time," she says. "The important thing is that we have the baby somewhere safe, and Dallas Regional is a good hospital with an amazing birthing center and pediatric unit."

"Holy shit, you looked into everything." And then I remember one thing she didn't mention. "What about your job?"

"I planned to take time off to be home with the baby anyway. I spoke to Ana and I'm going to finish everything remotely, and then Jill, one of the marketing team leads, will be taking over. Eventually, I'd like to work again, but I'll cross that bridge when the time comes."

"You could always work for the family business," Carmine says with a smile. "You'd be a damn good asset to our marketing team."

Paige's eyes glisten as she looks at my brother, and she sniffles back a sob. "Thank you. That's definitely something I'll consider. That is, if the CEO would be willing to hire me." Paige winks at me playfully, and I bark out a laugh.

"You're serious?" I ask because I can't fucking believe it. "You really want to live here in Dallas?"

She nods.

"You have no idea how much this means to me."

"Actually, I do," she says softly. "Because this is all I've ever wanted since the day my mom died…to be part of a family. And thanks to you and your family, I finally have one. Rosemary is just a place. But my heart is with you. This whole time, I thought the magic was gone, but it was only because I was waiting on you."

EPILOGUE

Paige

Five Months Later

"I CAN'T BELIEVE WE'RE BACK," I SAY TO NATE AS I LOOK AROUND at the people below us from the top of the Tower Bridge. "Do you see that?" I ask Finn, our three-month-old son, who's strapped to his daddy's front. "That's London."

We named him Finn in honor of my mom, Finley. She would've absolutely adored her grandson, and I hate that she's not here when he gets to see London for the first time, but thankfully, Finn and I have an entire family of people who love us.

"And this is where I knew your mom was the one," Nate says to Finn, causing me to tear up.

We aren't naive enough to believe that Finn has any idea what we're talking about, let alone know where he is. But when Nate suggested we take a trip to London, I couldn't say no. I have every intention of coming back often. After all, it's the place where I met

Nate, the love of my life. London and Bath will always be special to us. And it's also where I feel close to my mom.

"I love it here," I say, turning to look at my boys.

Only instead of Nate standing next to me like he was a second ago, he's on one knee with our little guy still strapped to his chest.

"Nate…" I breathe as I take him in, looking up at me with love shining in those beautiful whiskey eyes—the same color our son has—with a small black box in his hands.

"Princess," he says softly. "One year ago today, you stumbled into my life…"

I snort out a laugh. "You make it sound so graceful. More like I tripped and fell and almost died."

"I never would've let anything happen to you," he says with a smile. "My point is, one year ago today, I wasn't looking for love, but the moment you stumbled into my life, I knew you were the one. You were crying, and all I thought was that I wanted to make your tears go away."

I suck in a harsh breath, remembering that day. It sucked. But Nate made it better. The way he's made every day better since then.

"During our time together, we created the most precious gift"—he nods down at Finn, who's wiggling his legs and grinning in contentment—"proving that our love was meant to be more than just a fling in London. It was meant to last forever, and that's exactly what I want…forever with you."

He pops the top of the box open, and nestled inside is the most beautiful engagement ring. It's a simple platinum band with a single princess cut diamond atop. Perfection.

"Paige Abrams, will you do me the honor of becoming my wife and spending forever with me?"

"Yes!" I whisper as I blink back the tears blurring my vision. "Yes, I want forever with you."

I reach my hand out, and Nate slides the ring onto my second-to-last finger. Then, we both stand, and with our beautiful little miracle between us, we kiss.

"I'm glad you said yes," Nate says once we break apart, "because I have another surprise for you."

It's then I notice Joanne standing near us with a camera in her hand.

"What are you doing here?" I ask, rushing over to give her a hug.

"Did you think Nate would propose without getting any pictures for your scrapbook?" she says, her eyes puffy from crying. "Congratulations." She pulls me into her warm, motherly embrace that I've grown used to and look forward to. "I can't wait for you to officially be my daughter."

I choke up, noticing she left off the in-law. Because she's too close to her son's daughters for that. She's like a mom to all of us, and she wouldn't have it any other way.

"I can't wait either," I tell her.

"Well, you aren't going to have to wait long," Nate says, threading his fingers through mine.

We take the elevator back down to the bottom, and when we step out, I find all our family and friends standing there, waiting for us.

"She said yes," Nate announces, lifting my hand up to show them my ring.

Everyone cheers and then come over to congratulate us. I give my dad and Debbie a hug first, and then move on to Ana and Julian, and then Kira and Ryder, while Nate gets hugs from his brothers and their wives.

"I can't believe you guys all came and didn't come up for the proposal," I say once I've hugged everyone.

"I wanted it to be just us," Nate says. "The same way it was the first time you took me up there. Well," he adds with a smile, "plus this little guy." He rubs the top of our son's head. "And my mom since she was playing photographer."

"I love that, but that was seriously a long flight just for everyone to come here and congratulate us," I say with a laugh.

"We took our plane," Ana says with a shrug.

"And the engagement isn't the reason they're here," Nate says with a smirk.

"What did you do?" I ask, recognizing that smirk. It's the one he gives when he's up to something.

"I planned our wedding."

"What?" I shriek.

"We're getting married on Saturday at the top of Tower Bridge. And everything is done. Your *dream wedding* Pinterest board came in handy," Nate says with a laugh. "And with the help of these ladies"— he nods toward Ana and Kira—"we handled everything, including having your dream dress made."

"The one that looks like my mom's?" I ask, fresh tears pricking my eyes.

Nate and I talked about getting married before Finn was born, but I told him that I wanted to wait because my dream was to get married in a dress similar to my mom's and it wouldn't look the same if I was nine months pregnant.

Nate brought it up after Finn was born, but we were so busy with him running Bradford Hotels and us being new parents and then add the holidays to the mix that I felt too overwhelmed to even think about getting married, let alone plan a wedding.

"Yep," Ana says. "We had it custom-designed by Alexander McQueen."

Some women might be upset that they didn't have a hand in

planning their own wedding, but I'm beyond excited. I might want a dream wedding, but the thought of planning it gives me anxiety.

"I can't believe you did all this," I say to Nate, giving him a kiss. "Thank you. I can't wait to marry you."

"Good," Nate murmurs against my lips. "Because I've been waiting way too damn long for you to be mine in every way."

ABOUT THE AUTHOR

Nikki Ash is a *USA Today* Bestselling author of contemporary romance, focusing on single parent, secret baby, and surprise pregnancy romances. She spends her days and nights getting lost in words. When she's not writing, she's reading. From the Boxcar Children, to Wuthering Heights, to the latest single parent romance, she has lived and breathed every type of book.

Nikki resides in South Florida with her husband, two children, and dog that she considers to be one of her kids. When she's not reading or writing, she's traveling the world with her family—in search of inspiration.

www.ingramcontent.com/pod-product-compliance
Lightning Source LLC
Chambersburg PA
CBHW071412300726

48976CB00006B/2070